THE
TWELVE DAYS
OF SNOWBALL

Books by Kristen McKanagh

SNOWBALL'S CHRISTMAS

THE TWELVE DAYS OF SNOWBALL

Published by Kensington Publishing Corp.

THE
TWELVE DAYS
OF SNOWBALL

Kristen McKanagh

KENSINGTON
PUBLISHING CORP.

www.kensingtonbooks.com

KENSINGTON BOOKS are published by

Kensington Publishing Corp.
119 West 40th Street
New York, NY 10018

ISBN-13: 978-1-4967-2993-4 (ebook)
ISBN-10: 1-4967-2993-5 (ebook)

ISBN-13: 978-1-4967-2992-7
ISBN-10: 1-4967-2992-7
First Kensington Trade Paperback Printing: October 2021

10 9 8 7 6 5 4 3 2 1

Printed in the United States of America

To John

Thank you for giving me a chance with Snowball
and loving this kitten as much as I do!

Acknowledgments

I get to do what I love surrounded by the people I love—a blessing that I thank God for every single day. Writing and publishing a book doesn't happen without the support and help from a host of incredible people.

To my fantastic romance readers: Thank you for going on these journeys with me, for your kindness, your support, and generally being awesome. Sophie and Daniel's story was one written in the middle of a pandemic. Being able to escape into a world where people are truly lovely to each other—even when they disagree—was both a blessing and a challenge in those circumstances. But one I welcomed and I love the result. I hope you fell in love with these characters and their story as much as I did. If you have a free second, please think about leaving a review. Also, I love to connect with my readers, so I hope you'll drop a line and say "howdy" on any of my social media!

To my editor, John Scognamiglio: I love writing this kitten and her humans with their foibles and need for HEAs with you. Thank you for your support, feedback, and yay for more Snowball books to come!

To my agent, Evan Marshall: Thank you for your belief in me and constant, steady guidance. You are my rock.

To the team at Kensington: I know how much work goes

viii   *Acknowledgments*

into each and every book, a ton of which authors never see. I thank you so much for making this book the best it can be!

To Nicole, Anna, and Courtney, who really helped me pull out the angst of the pandemic that snuck into the first draft and keep this story true to itself.

To my support team of writing buddies, readers, reviewers, friends, and family (you know who you are): I know I say this every time, but I mean it . . . my stories wouldn't come alive the way they do if I didn't have the wonderful experiences and support that I do. And that's all because of you.

Finally, to my husband, I love you so much. You are why I know what a good man is and how he acts in this world, which means I found my hero. To our amazing kids, you are my light, my laughter, and my love.

Chapter 1

My job as "official kitty" at Weber Haus is the *most* important one. At least in my opinion. Helping to greet and keep tabs on all the guests who visit the Victorian inn near the mountain town of Braunfels can be taxing. My forever family—Emily and Lukas, and Lukas's great aunt Miss Tilly—own and run the inn, as well as the new shops recently added. I love it here. So much to see and do. Plus, everyone wants to pet the "pretty white cat" and, other than the one specific exception of Daniel Aarons, I let them.

Now I finally get a free second to myself to stalk a bird, only to be interrupted by one of the many humans who stay at the inn calling my name. Downright rude. Can't she see I'm clearly in the middle of a hunt? She might scare away my prey.

"Snowball. Get back here!" The female voice doing all the interrupting is new around here.

Sophie Heidt.

That's what Miss Tilly called her when she introduced us. When we met, Sophie—I don't know human ages, but in cat years I'd place her around three or four—had flashed even white teeth in a kind smile and given me a lovely pet, tickling that spot under my chin that tells me she's a cat person. I guess I'll give her the benefit of the doubt in this case that she's not trying to ruin my day. She just doesn't know better than to disturb a predator mid-pounce.

The good news is the idiotic bird hasn't noticed. *That's right, rat with wings, stay right there.* . . .

I ignore Sophie, in full stalking mode where I hide under one of the bushes that remains green even in winter. After a year of practice, I'm getting better. One of these days, I'm going to actually catch one of those pesky birds or squirrels who think they can come into *my* territory.

My fluffy white tail whips behind me, snagging a bit on the leaves of the bush, as I hunch low to the ground. The timing must be perfect. I give my butt a preparatory wiggle, the kitty version of revving my engine. This bird is going to be a pile of feathers.

One more wiggle, fully focused on my adversary. I'm downwind, so Tweetle-Dumb doesn't know I'm this close.

All it's going to take is—

"Snowball!" Poor Sophie sounds frantic. I'd help her, but this bird is going down.

With a symphony of finely honed feline instinct, I burst from my hiding place under the bush and sprint for the offender. The horror on her beaky face is everything I love to see before she flies away, not far, up into the branches of a tree. Without breaking stride, I follow, finding easy purchase, allowing me to scale the trunk quickly, my claws sinking deep with each shuffling jump. I get to the branch she's on, but she smirks and hops higher. Is she toying with me? With a warning growl, I follow. The darn bird does it again. I follow again.

But then I make the huge mistake of looking down.

A frightened squeak escapes me before I can hold it in, and the bird gives a twittery little laugh, mocking me from her safety perched on the branches above. She doesn't say anything. Birds don't like to talk to cats, but she cocks her head.

If she had human eyebrows, I'm sure she'd raise them at me in mocking question.

I don't know which is worse—the need to wipe that fowl grin from her beak, or the fear freezing my muscles in place like that statue owl Miss Tilly sets out on the wraparound porch in the spring to scare away . . . ironically . . . the birds.

I try to move, but I've gone too high. Yes, I know I'm a cat—all of a year old and full grown now and super awesome in trees. But when I was little, I jumped from too high up and misjudged the landing. That scared me enough that I try to stay lower in trees these days.

"Meow," I call out.

After all, that Sophie woman is nearby. She can help me down. I can feel beady bird eyes boring into the back of my head. This humiliation will not be forgotten. Better to live to fight another day, though. Ignoring her, I send out another few cries for help and, sure enough, I look down into a pair of eyes so gray they're more silver. Pretty. I've always loved shiny things. Yesterday they twinkled at me like stars, but right now they're narrowed, and her hands are on her hips.

Emily, one of my forever humans, does that sometimes. Usually when she informs me that I've done a bad thing.

What did I do now, though?

I was doing my humans a favor and running the vermin off this property. That's what the old cat next door tells me is my special job.

Below me, Sophie bites her lip and glances around her. She won't find much. This tree is located in the back of the house between it and the barn, which, along with the old carriage house, has recently been converted to shops.

"Miss Tilly will fire me if I lose you," she said, more to herself than me. "On my first official day, too. I left that door open for two seconds at most."

She shakes her head.

Probably at herself, because everyone else in Weber Haus

knows that keeping me inside is impossible. It took me nearly a year, but I've mapped that house from attic to cellar, places big old humans can't get, forgotten windows still unlocked, spaces between the walls in the old house, and a very handy pipe that runs underneath. Miss Tilly and Lukas and Emily— the people I love most in this world—have mostly given up keeping me indoors, trusting me to safely return on my own. I know the grounds now as well as I know the house, including all the people in the shops and many of the regular visitors. I'm famous around here.

Everyone loves me. Sophie just doesn't know. Yet.

"Well, come down," she prompts.

Silly. Obviously, I wouldn't have called for help if I could do that. The bird, meanwhile, perches above me, watching the whole thing, no doubt laughing behind my back.

"Meow," I respond. A clear cry for help in my most adorably pathetic voice that usually gets humans to do what I want.

She wrinkles her tip-tilted nose. She did that yesterday, too, when Miss Tilly was giving her a tour of the house. She said something about delayed construction and possibly having to reschedule guests soon, and Sophie'd made that face.

"I'm not coming up there," Sophie calls at me. Then mutters vaguely about broken necks and not having time for that, or some such thing.

"Um, hello?" A male voice has both of us turning our heads. "What are you doing here?"

Out of the corner of my eye, I see how Sophie straightens, dropping her hands to her sides. Forget the future feather duster who got me into this situation. I'm too busy glaring at my most fiendish foe.

Daniel Aarons.

The man who tried to break up my Emily and Lukas. He wanted Emily for himself, and I've never forgiven him for almost ruining their happiness and my family.

Fear replaced by purpose, I manage to scoot to a slightly lower branch, getting ready to scare him off.

Why hadn't anyone given Sophie a heads-up about the inn's small family cat sneaking out? Mischief would be a better name than Snowball. Though her lovely, pure-white fur and big blue eyes made her own name more than appropriate. Just not enough of a warning to the unsuspecting.

Especially the brand-new manager for the inn on her first day of work.

For a woman who mapped out every path her life would take, Sophie was still trying to figure out where she'd taken a wrong turn.

Actually, she knew.

Malcom Sommerholder. Dating that genetically blessed, nepotism-wielding, job-stealing excuse for a boyfriend, even if he had perfect teeth, had been one of the worst mistakes of her life. With his aww-shucks attitude, big blue eyes, and floppy little-boy-lost hair, Malcom had flattered his way into her life, picked her brain for all her best ideas for the hotel chain she'd worked her way up through the last ten years, then kleptoed the position that *she* had earned right out from under her unsuspecting nose. Someday he'd marry a model and their perfect-teethed children would probably also inherit the job that was supposed to be Sophie's.

Which was why she was here now. New location. New role. New start. New . . . everything.

And it will be great.

Already she had ideas. . . . That was, if she kept her job after this.

Coaxing her new boss's precocious cat out of a tree was not exactly how Sophie had pictured her first day going. She stood with her hands on her hips, staring at Snowball, trying to decide how to handle getting her down.

This was definitely *not* on her list of things to do today.

Familiarize herself with the computer systems and get an idea of bookings coming up, go through inventory, meet with the staff—currently two maids, a cook, and a part-time high school kid for the front desk—and a hundred and three other items graced the neatly typed checklist she could pull up in her leatherbound tablet that she'd left on the kitchen table when she'd run outside after Snowball.

"Um, hello?" A male voice interrupted her battle of wills with the cat. "What are you doing here?"

Sophie's first instinct was to cringe inwardly. Heat was already flaming up her cheeks at being caught out, reminding her oddly enough of the day her fourth-grade teacher found her sneaking her favorite-colored crayon out of Madeline Brecht's box. Surely, she could figure out how to get Snowball down without help . . . or witnesses.

Luckily, common sense prevailed as he walked closer and it struck her that he looked the handy type. Tall, with broad shoulders, he wore his sandy-brown hair a bit on the shaggy side and had the growth of a beard that was neatly trimmed but managed to put her in mind of a rugged mountain man. Pretty accurate for these parts, not far from skiing. The jeans and plaid button-down under a thick black coat only added to her impression. Not to mention his heavy-duty, steel-toed boots.

She almost asked where he was hiding his ax, except she'd learned a while ago that many people often didn't appreciate her brand of teasing. He was probably with the construction crew currently on-site adding a new wing of rooms to the property.

Tempting to ask him how that was coming—given the impact to guests already booked for after Christmas—but she'd talk to this man's boss soon enough. A friend of Miss Tilly's, it seemed. Maybe the owner of Weber Haus had gone too easy on him, which meant Sophie was going to have to be firmer to be sure the project was completed on time.

Cat. Fix the cat situation, she reminded herself. She sized up the man in front of her. Definitely handy. At this point she'd take any help she could get. "Hi."

"The shops are around that way," he said as he got closer, expression turning slightly pompous, as if he owned the place. Obviously under the mistaken impression that she was lost. "Or if you're here for the inn, you should go back that way." He pointed.

Sophie offered a smile, one that worked with most wayward guests, that she hoped put him at ease. "Thanks, but I'm not lost," she said.

She opened her mouth to tell him she was the new manager for the inn and to point out the dilemma she had with Snowball. Only he beat her to it.

"This area is off-limits to guests and shoppers," he said. "You might have missed the sign."

The vertebrae in her spine stacked up neatly and stiffly in response to his words, and especially his tone. Not another all-knowing male. She'd had enough of those lately.

Malcom used to do that.

Still, she was a stranger around here, and maybe they'd had trouble with shoppers getting lost on the grounds? Mental note to ask Miss Tilly about that.

She took a breath to tell him who she was, but he beat her to it again. "So . . ." He drew the word out. "Let's get you where you're *supposed* to be."

Sophie swallowed a growl of frustration. Maybe this man was in a hurry? Clearly, he wasn't interested in the who or what or why of her being here. He just wanted her gone. Better to get straight to the point. "Actually, I could use a little assistance with *her*." She pointed straight up.

He tipped a frowning gaze into the branches of the tree Sophie stood under, then sort of jerked back a half step before he pulled himself up short and huffed what she guessed was a laugh. "Well, look at that. You've found a partridge in a pear tree."

Maybe he'd been hit in the head with a falling hammer a few too many times. "I'm pretty sure she's a cat."

"Definitely a city girl." She caught the murmured comment and, having grown up on a dairy farm, almost laughed at the wrong assumption.

He pointed. "She was chasing *that bird* up the tree."

Sophie stepped back and angled her head a bit. Sure enough, a gray and brown bird with striking black and white markings around its face and wings and a red beak peered down at her. Squatted there a little smugly, in fact.

"And . . ." Her impatient helper continued in a voice gone lazily amused. "That happens to be a pear tree, believe it or not."

"What are the odds?" He *had* to be putting her on.

Her lumberjack simply shrugged, uncaring if she believed him or not.

Right. Maybe he was impatient because he was so busy. "Either way, I let her out of the house by accident, and I don't want something to happen to her."

He eyed the tree, and Sophie swore a flash of dread crossed his features. Hard to tell with the beard. "She'll come down on her own when she's ready," he said.

He'd just walk away from that poor, pathetic mewling? What kind of heartless person did that? Sophie's ability to give the benefit of the doubt stretched a little thinner.

"Unfortunately, *I* don't have the time to wait. I have a lot to do today." She glanced over her shoulder at the Victorian house with its white painted siding, wraparound porch, bay windows, dormers, and decorative wood and iron work.

Despite her colossal disappointment and the collapse of her childhood dream, she'd found herself surprisingly ready to start this new one. At the very least she'd landed herself in an idyllic location and a chance at a different kind of experience to put on her résumé.

But every minute under this tree was a minute less doing what she was supposed to be doing, and she hated the idea that this situation was starting her off on a very wrong foot.

"Plus," she tacked on, "I'd worry until I knew she was safe." Then she tried batting her eyelashes at him, a move that felt as unnatural as it probably looked.

His expression didn't change by so much as a blink, but she got the sudden, uncomfortable feeling that he was laughing at her behind that beard.

"Please?" she tried.

He heaved a heavy sigh. "Fine. If it means that much to you, I know a way to get her down."

"Great." One less worry, coming right up. To show her appreciation, she tossed her stranger a grateful smile.

But in return received a grimace. "Yeah."

She expected him to turn away and leave her to go get a ladder or something. Instead, he watched the cat warily and took another breath, as though preparing for horror. Then he started walking under the tree. One cautious step after another.

"What are you—"

Suddenly, the cat gave a cry a banshee would envy and sprinted down the trunk of the tree to attack his legs, clawing her way up his jeans.

Sophie couldn't help it. The tiny white fluffball attack on this mountain of a man was too incongruous not to strike her as funny. Laughter bubbled up and spilled over. Only he *had* got the cat down, albeit in an unusual way, so she slapped her hand over her mouth when he tossed a glare her way.

"Could you get her off me, please?" the man asked through clamped lips.

"I'm not sure I should risk my city-girl hands," she teased, though she moved closer as she spoke.

"She won't do anything to you. Just me." He squinted one eye as the cat held on with her front claws and proceeded to scratch at him with the back ones.

"That looks painful," she offered. Either that or laugh again.

"It is." His voice came out strained.

Sophie knelt down beside him and gingerly disconnected Snowball's sharp claws from his clothes. Sure enough, the little cat didn't turn her maniacal attentions on Sophie. Standing, she cuddled the small body close. Miss Tilly said Snowball, a rescue abandoned in the nearby woods, was a year old, but she'd obviously been the runt of the litter, because she was still tiny.

The cat nestled into her, thankfully, giving a rumble of a purr, which cut off when the mountain man spoke up.

"Better take her back to the house. If you put her down, she'll come after me again."

As if to emphasize his point, Snowball gave a little warning growl that reverberated against Sophie's hands, almost like holding on to a toy car, blue eyes trained on him in full kitty menace.

"Just try it," the man muttered back at her.

"What did you do to get on her wrong side?" Because as far as she could tell, Snowball was a people cat the way Sophie was a people person. She doubted his brand of communication, which was a little rough around the edges, would bother a cat. Then again, she'd been wrong about a lot of things lately.

"Nothing." He screwed his face up, clearly offended that she'd implied *he* was to blame in the relationship.

She swallowed back yet another urge to chuckle. Maybe first-day jitters were getting to her. It had been a long time since she'd started a new job. "Well . . . I'd better get back to work. Thank you for all your . . . err . . . help." Her mama raised her with manners.

"Work?" he asked as she started to turn away.

Sophie didn't pause. "I started today."

"Doing what?" His voice, farther away now, told her he hadn't followed.

"Managing the inn." She tossed a glance over her shoulder and lifted a hand in a wave, strangely eager to put a little distance between them.

Probably because being both grateful and annoyed with him was an uncomfortable place to be. Besides, after this, at most she'd probably see him only in passing until the construction was over.

"I'd really like to know what *you* have against him, though," she murmured to the cat nestled in her arms. She truly was more fur than body, her petite frame more obvious when holding her by the belly, the ridges of her ribs delicate but obvious through her skin and fur.

Snowball gave Sophie's finger a dainty lick, as though saying she'd never attack her that way.

"No more sneaking out. Deal?"

The cat blinked, the angelic picture of total innocence.

Sophie wasn't buying it. "Promise me now?"

Snowball sneezed so delicately, if Sophie didn't know better, she might have thought the cat had just snorted a laugh.

Sophie mentally rolled her eyes at herself. Running away from an impatient, brusque lumberjack and reduced to bargaining with a piece of fluff.

Not the most auspicious beginning to her fresh start.

Chapter 2

Definitely a city girl. Daniel watched as the new manager walked away from him.

He vaguely remembered now. Miss Tilly and Emily had been more than thrilled with her level of experience. She'd been the assistant manager at some prestigious city hotel for the last few years, apparently. Daniel couldn't remember which one.

Starlight-colored eyes...

Almost silver. Striking enough that at least twice he'd had to remind himself to respond to something she'd said. A confounding reaction he puzzled over now.

Women had taken a back seat to his career lately. Getting his construction business off the ground took his entire focus. If he did this project right, several other big jobs would fall into place. In particular, he had his eye on the secret project George Becker was rumored to be contemplating. Becker worked with several contractors—including Jannik Koch, who wasn't the nicest player on the board—so the competition for the job would be fierce. Finally... finally Daniel might get his foot in that door. Everything depended on getting this one right.

Definitely not the time to be distracted by a woman.

She hadn't given him her name. They got enough city folk

around here, searching for an escape at the idyllic inn, that he was used to their abrupt attitude by now. She'd learn to loosen up soon enough.

The woman, inappropriately dressed for the weather in thin city clothes and without a coat, disappeared into the house through the back door that led to the kitchen.

At least Miss Tilly finally got someone else to take on the heavier duties of managing the inn. The older woman—who'd inherited the house from a long line of her family and turned it into a small bed and breakfast almost thirty years before, which over time had grown—was as spry as they came. However, old age was creeping up on her and she was starting to slow down. Maybe now she could finally sit back and enjoy all she had built here.

Weber Haus really was a beautiful building, and now the shops, which included Lukas's photo gallery and Emily's bakery, enhanced the property and brought more business to the grounds.

All the renovation work to retrofit the barn and carriage house had been done by him and his crew. Work that, as a friend of the family, the Webers had been happy to send his way. That had led to a few more smaller renovation jobs, but still not the full build-from-scratch work he was looking for.

But thanks to the shops, the small number of rooms at the house itself booked up too fast, so they were now turning the inn into a full hotel with a separate new wing of rooms, though still relatively small to keep the homey feel. His project. The one that would land him more clients. He just needed to bring this one in on time and under budget.

He tossed a glare at the gray skies overhead, turning darker with each passing moment, threatening more rain. Not snow, which was more normal this time of year, but rain. Turning everything to mud. He didn't need more setbacks. He had only until Christmas to wrap up. Nothing else could go wrong.

He turned to walk back to the construction site but got

only two steps before he remembered why he'd been heading in this direction in the first place.

He'd promised Miss Tilly he'd check a leaky spot in the roof on his lunch break. His now much shortened lunch break. With plodding steps, he turned back toward the house, following the new manager's path inside. Hopefully, the devil cat would already have gone somewhere far away by the time he got there.

Silly to be wary, but Snowball, who was an angel of feline sweetness to everyone else, had had it out for him long enough now that he was becoming a running joke, and those claws were sharp, even through his thick jeans. He cracked open the door to the kitchen, assured himself Snowball was nowhere in sight, suddenly glad the new manager wasn't around to see him acting like a scared child checking for ghosts, then stepped fully inside.

Jenna Bailey, the cook who'd taken over for Emily after she'd started her own bakery, stood at the sink with her pleasantly plump back to him. She glanced over her shoulder from where she was peeling carrots into a bowl. Then chuckled. "Snowball's not around."

Pathetic that everyone knew about it. Darn cat.

Daniel paused to take off his mud-crusted boots. Years of his mother yelling at him about dirty floors had made that a hardened habit. Muscle memory by now. He found himself doing the same when he got home, even if he wasn't in his work boots. He sniffed appreciatively. No one could top Emily's cooking, but Mrs. Bailey came close. "Any way a guy can get one of the best hot lunches in town before he heads back out into the cold and damp?"

His begging earned him another chuckle. "Charmer," she said. "Yes, of course you can."

Daniel grinned. "You're a treasure, Mrs. Bailey. Truly."

"Said every hungry man in the history of the world," she scoffed.

"Doesn't make it any less true. I'll be back in a bit." Picking the boots up by the laces, in case he needed to climb outside, he trudged off through the levels of the house to the hidden staircase that led to the attic.

He'd just opened the narrow door that concealed those stairs when a now-familiar voice sounded behind him. "Can I help you?"

He turned to find the new manager standing in the dim hallway, arms crossed and expression oddly wary. Of course, she didn't know him, or his relationship with the Weber family. She seemed to have pegged him as an errant construction worker wandering where he shouldn't be.

It occurred to him that he'd made a similar assumption about her, though he really didn't have time, after helping with the cat, to deal with her now.

Hiding his bemusement behind what he hoped was a suitably neutral expression, Daniel shook his head. "Nope."

Irritation swept across her face, darkening those fascinating eyes. Why? He didn't need any help. With a nod to let her know she could leave now, he headed up into the attic.

He'd been up here before, so didn't pay much attention to the surroundings. Like most attics, the space was full of cobwebs and dust-covered boxes and furniture no one needed now but didn't want to get rid of, either. Light came in from several small dormer windows, but he tugged the string attached to a naked hanging lightbulb for more, then pulled a flashlight from the belt strapped around his waist.

The pitter-patter of smaller feet on the stairs was his only warning she'd decided to follow. Was she making sure he didn't steal something?

"So . . . what are you doing in the attic, exactly?" the new manager said from behind him.

He opened his mouth to explain, as well as introduce himself and find out her name, because he couldn't keep calling her "the new manager" in his head.

"Daniel?" A shaky voice drifted up the stairs. "Is that you up there?"

Well, that took care of that. He moved carefully to the head of the stairs to peer down at Miss Tilly. A stubborn, pointed chin and fading blue eyes that still managed to sparkle told you she was still up for a bit of sport as she peered up at him.

"I just got started," he said. Then, mischief creeping up on him that he couldn't resist, he tilted his head. "Have you had a problem with pests lately, Miss Tilly?"

"Pests?" The old face creased in concern. "Not that I know of. Oh, Emily will be—"

Contrition balled up in his stomach. "I'm teasing," he hurried to assure her. "Your new manager is up here with me."

"Oh?" Now Miss Tilly's face reflected total bewilderment.

"Hilarious," the woman behind him drawled softly, voice dry as the layer of dust coating things scattered around the attic. She also stepped closer to poke her head over the stairs. "I was checking on why he was up here," she called down. "I was thinking of calling the police."

Daniel choked at that admission, then turned his head to take a closer look. She wasn't joking. Total honesty. A rare trait these days, even in a small town where everyone was into everyone else's business.

And she smelled of springtime. A soft scent that put him in mind of wildflowers and green fields.

Miss Tilly chortled. "Give him hell, Sophie."

"What did I do to deserve such treatment?" he complained, softening it with a wink for Tilly.

The older woman waved a hand at him. "Pooh."

Sophie. So that was her name. It fit. Delicate but spunky with a dash of snooty.

As Miss Tilly left, they both straightened, eyeing each other. In an exaggeratedly slow move, he held out a hand. "Daniel Aarons. I *own* the construction company working on the expansion and also happen to be a *close* friend of the Webers."

Granted, in a roundabout way. Emily's brother, Peter, had been his best friend growing up. No doubt Sophie didn't care about details. Though she frowned slightly at the way he emphasized the word "close," she reached out to grasp his hand, hers small and soft against his work-toughened calluses. He hid a grimace and immediately had to wrestle with a sting of impatience with himself. He'd never apologized for his roughness, both in person and personality, to anyone. Never felt the need to. He was proud of what he did and who he was.

So why, all of a sudden, was he worried what the heck she thought?

"Sophie Heidt," she said. "Pesky new hotel manager for Weber Haus."

Who would probably expect to have input on his construction job. Another helpful opinion he could do without at this point. *I'd better play nice.* "Welcome."

"Thank you." She considered him for a second, expression turning subtly but distinctively all business. "I'd love to talk to you about progress with the new wing."

That hadn't taken her long.

"I'd be happy to." Not really. What could she possibly contribute at this point that would be of any help? More than that, if she started changing anything this late into the process, no way would he meet his deadlines.

"Lukas is supposed to give me a tour of the grounds, including the construction site," she said. "Maybe after that?"

"Sophie?" Another voice called up the stairs. Speak of the devil.

Her eyebrows popped up as if to say exactly what he was thinking. How did Lukas know she was up here?

She leaned over the stairwell again. "Yes?"

"Do you mind coming downstairs? We've got a situation and it will most likely end up affecting you."

Daniel paused over the tone in Lukas's voice. Tight. Worried maybe.

Because of that, he followed Sophie down the stairs. She flicked him a glance that clearly wondered at his feeling the need to join her but didn't say anything otherwise.

Good. Because these were *his* friends. If something was wrong, he wanted to be there to help.

"I didn't see you up there, Daniel," Lukas said as soon as he came into view. "You'll want to hear this, too."

They followed an unsmiling Lukas downstairs to the front parlor, where Emily stood with Miss Tilly. Snowball sat on the velvet-covered antique sofa, her tail curled daintily around her. The second she laid eyes on him, she issued her usual, nothing-dainty-about-it warning growl, but didn't make a move. He also didn't come farther into the room than the doorway.

Nor did he miss the small tug of amusement on Sophie's lips as she flicked a telling glance between him and the cat before she met his gaze, then tucked away her silent laughter and disappeared behind a wall of friendly but firm professionalism.

But the way Lukas crossed to Emily's side and the way she slipped her hand into his snagged Daniel's attention.

Once upon a time, Daniel hadn't liked Lukas all that much. That was last year when he'd realized how much Emily, his best friend's little sister, had grown up, his own interest in her growing. But he'd backed down from pursuing her himself when it became obvious that her interest in Lukas was serious. Wary at first of the other man's intentions, now he had no doubts the couple was meant to be together. Though, these days, their romance was a little hard to stomach. Not that he wasn't happy for them, but still, a guy could handle only so many glowing looks and passionate kisses a day.

"I had a call from my mom," Emily started. Then swallowed. "Peter's been . . ." She stopped, screwing up her face, clearly fighting back tears.

Daniel took a step forward, caught a twitch of movement from Snowball, and stopped, balling his hands at his sides.

If this was bad news about Peter, it could be horrible. Best friends since grade school, he owed the guy who'd been by his side during the whole thing with his brother. The guy who'd been his defender against bullies when Daniel's growth spurt had been late coming, leaving him scrawny and defenseless.

Pete had joined the navy out of school, making his way onto a Special Forces team. Most of the time, they had no idea where he'd been or what he had to do. Daniel once asked Pete if any movies came close to reality. He'd named a few that had made Daniel blink. And stop asking questions.

Emily glanced at Sophie. "Peter's my brother," she explained, still sounding watery.

"Is he alive?" Daniel asked. *Please, God, not—*

"Yes." Emily nodded.

He let loose a silent breath of relief. Peter's family would be devastated if they lost him. "What happened?"

She managed to speak around the tears clearly clogging her throat. "They can't tell us much." She rolled her eyes, at the military's reticence no doubt. "But he's in a coma."

Daniel tried to picture his friend—uber serious, get-things-done, no-time-for-bull personality—unconscious in a coma. At the mental image he tried damn hard not to think of his own brother, Drew, but hospitals always did that to him. He focused instead on the moment. "Pete won't put up with a coma for long."

Emily gave a watery chuckle. "No, he won't."

Lukas, seeming to sense that she needed him to step in, took over. "He's been sent home from wherever he was and is being treated in a hospital where we can visit."

"You should go then." This from Sophie, who'd remained quiet so far.

Emily brightened slightly, then bit her lip. "The thing is, we'd really like Tilly to come with us. She's family as far as we're concerned, so the hospital might let her in, though they're pretty strict, according to Mom. But Peter would want—"

She had to break off the words to swallow again.

"Of course," Sophie said. "I know I've only been here a day, but I'm confident I can take charge of Weber Haus." By her calm, assured air, shoulders back, expression firmly pleasant, she clearly believed that.

Even so, Daniel slid her a dubious look. She'd been here less time than that. Didn't she say today was her first day? In that moment, he realized with a sinking heart that as much as he wanted to go see Peter, too, he couldn't. Family only, it sounded like, though the Diemers would probably sneak him in. But too much needed to be done here.

She glanced his way, gave him a small warning frown, then turned back to Emily. "What do you need?"

"There are a few other things we might need you to take on in addition to the inn," Miss Tilly warned.

Sophie's expression didn't even flutter at the news. "Walk me through the immediate things that need doing while you're gone. I assume I'll work with Daniel on the construction side of things."

What now?

She continued blithely on. "I can always call if I have questions."

"I can handle the construction and report to Miss Tilly when she calls," he said. "No need to get involved—"

Sophie turned that polite, but determined, expression his way. "I was already planning to step in there, as it impacts timing for bookings already in place. I've worked with renovations and additions before, so—"

"Really. I've got this."

Sophie flicked a glance in the direction of the other three listening closely, then clasped her hands in front of her. "Of course."

Now why didn't he believe that she'd backed down?

"There are lots of other things," Tilly said, apparently assuming the construction side was all dealt with. "Holidays are always extra busy."

She continued on, but this time Daniel was the one who wanted to step in. An hour was not going to prepare Sophie to cover everything going on around here. Maybe her overabundance of confidence was why she no longer worked for the big, fancy hotel where she'd been prior to this. A small country inn—even with the expansion and shops—certainly sounded like a step down to him.

I'd better keep an eye on her, just in case.

The last thing his friends needed was to return home to a catastrophe, especially at the holidays. Daniel cleared his throat. "I can help, too. I'll be on-site every day anyway. That way Sophie won't be alone."

The way Emily's shoulders dropped as she glanced between the two of them made it easy to ignore the resentful waves radiating from the woman at his side. Why should she resent an offer of help? She'd have to get over that attitude quickly in a town like Braunfels. Everyone offered a helping hand when someone needed it.

"That would be wonderful," Emily said. "Are you sure?"

"Of course," both he and Sophie said in stereo.

If they hadn't been standing in front of her bosses, he had a feeling he would've learned the feel of her sharp elbow in his side.

"You can leave it with me," Sophie added, clearly wanting to have the last word.

*   *   *

What were Emily, and Lukas, and even Miss Tilly thinking, putting that man in charge with sweet Sophie? She gave me a lovely snuggle all the way back to the house and told Mrs. Bailey she's a cat person.

Much better than Daniel.

I glare at his stupid bearded face. The only reason I haven't run him out of this room is because Emily is so upset. Kitties know when their humans are upset. We can sense these things. It's why we cuddle up when humans cry, or when they are lonely, or when they need to feel better.

Sometimes.

We only do that for the special humans, and all three of these people are *my* special humans.

But Daniel . . .

It's a very good thing I was around to show Emily how big of a mistake she'd be making choosing Daniel over Lukas. In the end it worked out, but I'll never forgive Daniel for almost messing that up.

Still . . . if he can be helpful in this time of trouble, which I have my doubts about, then so can I. So I let him stay in the room while they discuss the boring parts of how Emily, Lukas, and Miss Tilly will be leaving Sophie and Daniel in charge.

At least Sophie will be around.

She has a few silly notions about my not being let outside, but she is a terrific cat snuggler. Plus, I overheard Emily saying to Lukas that she came "highly recommended." Whatever that means. It sounds good.

"Oh!" Emily cries. "What about Snowball?"

What?!? I blink a few times, sure I didn't hear that right. Only I did. I give a little *pfttt* of sound. They forgot about me? They never forget about me. I am the most important part of this family. I tie us all together with love.

Emily smooths a soothing hand over my fur, and I lean

into her touch, but then bat at her hand so she knows that I don't consider a quick pat enough of an apology.

"Don't look at me," Daniel says, holding his hands up. Like I'm a disease or something he doesn't want to touch.

I give him a solid, unblinking stare long enough that he goes stiff. Then lift my leg and give myself a bath.

"I can watch Snowball," Sophie offers.

Oh, that's much better. I lightly drop to the floor to go wind around her feet and rub against her ankles and Emily beams, which makes my sacrifice of letting them go off without me worth it.

"Good luck," Daniel mutters.

I give a little growl, and he snaps his mouth shut. He doesn't leave, though. I will give him this much . . . he's loyal to his friends.

Chapter 3

Sophie was used to getting up before the crack of anything even resembling dawn. A light sleeper already, morning person was too cheerful a term for what she was, but she rarely slept past six. However, three in the morning was ridiculous. Especially if she wanted to make it through her packed schedule today without collapsing.

She rolled over to her stomach and slammed her pillow down over her head, not that there was any light or sound to block out at this time. Just her thoughts.

Daniel Aarons was going to be a problem. That much had been clear yesterday.

He clearly didn't want her to have anything to do with his construction, despite the fact that she needed to be directly involved. Bringing her expertise with hotel management on the new wing that needed to blend seamlessly with the rest of the property was part of it. The other part was keeping in lockstep with him on the progress. Otherwise, she'd need to start changing bookings soon.

On top of that, he seemed determined to keep an eye on her own work. After helping run the Crown Liberty, she was more than capable of taking on this smaller property. Granted, all the extras they'd piled on would be a lot. Like a ridiculous amount of a lot. Not that she would go back and do anything differently. She may have only just met them, but the people she worked for were good people, and this was an emergency. This wouldn't be for long. Hopefully.

So Daniel could just back off.

Her shifting around disturbed something that moved next to her with a rustle of sheets. Her eyes popped wide open as she jerked up to her elbows and searched to her right, but in the pitch-black room she couldn't see anything. What was in here with her? Darn Daniel for talking about pests yesterday. That had put her in mind of rats. She hated rats, with their creepy tails and the skittering sound of their claws. Especially since they seemed to be all over the city.

He'd been joking about pests, though. That had been a poke at her. Right?

Oh God, oh God, oh God!

A small chirp sounded a second later. Loud, close to her ear, and followed by an even louder rumble of purring.

Snowball.

Sophie dropped her forehead to the bed and sucked in a breath of relief. Of course. The little cat usually slept with Emily or Lukas, but they were gone, so Sophie had taken her in. Still, Snowball was a way better option than the myriad of options flying through Sophie's head. Rats with sharp, gnawing teeth being uppermost in her list of concerns. Thank goodness she hadn't flung something at the source of the sound, or, heaven forbid, grabbed the "rat" and flung it from her bed. She was pretty sure feline-icide, if that was a word, would definitely get her fired. Not to mention the guilt.

That was twice in two days Snowball had come close to tipping Sophie into the realm of unemployment. Maybe this was punishment for abandoning her hotel in a snit. Maybe she should've stayed and continued to pursue that dream.

Malcom's flashing smile appeared in her mind and she managed to set aside her guilt. No. Leaving was the right thing to do.

Now . . . about sleep. Sophie screwed her eyes shut. Then lay there counting her breaths, counting Snowball's breaths, counting creaks the old house made with surprising regularity. Only the adrenaline shot from her scare didn't seem to be dissipating. That on top of already having trouble staying asleep, and basically . . . yeah.

She was awake.

Because now she was walking through the to-do list that awaited her as soon as she started her day.

In addition to the inn, and the construction—which she had every intention of being involved in—she'd be helping to get Weber Haus ready for Christmas, working through the various holiday events the grounds would be hosting, staying on top of the standard events that came to such an idyllic location, including a wedding ceremony just before the Christmas Market opened, of course.

But that wasn't all. Like a rusted star on top of the Christmas tree, she also got the dubious joy of helping to organize the *first* annual Christmas Market.

That one might have been the straw that broke the proverbial camel's back. She'd managed to hide her growing panic from the Webers. Maybe not from Daniel, though. A microscope had less focus than he did.

Still, determined to prove herself, even in these unusual circumstances, she'd managed to cross her fingers behind her back and hoped like heck that Emily would be back in time to deal with the majority of the Christmas Market situation. Even with some woman named Giselle Becker, whom she hadn't met yet, leading a committee who was mostly in charge, there remained a ton to do on the Weber Haus side of things.

Event planner, Sophie was not.

What had to be at least thirty minutes later, she gave up on sleep and rolled out from under her pillow, glanced at the clock, and ground her teeth. Nope, not thirty minutes. Not even ten. Terrific.

But lying here wide awake wasn't accomplishing anything, either. Might as well get a jump on what she was well aware was going to be a run-off-her-feet kind of day anyway.

Snowball gave a protesting squawk as Sophie threw back the covers, and she wagged a finger at the cat. "No protesting, little miss. The early wake-up call is your fault."

Mostly. Feeling a little guilty since the sleepless state started before that silly scare, she gave the cat a friendly pat, then headed to her en suite bathroom.

For now, she was living in one of the smaller rooms in the house. After the new wing was finished, she'd been promised the next step was to renovate and update the small cottage on the grounds that had once been the caretaker's. Unlivable right now, though if she got a second to herself, she might pop by to have a look around.

An hour later, she was showered and dressed. Strange to not be in a uniform or even, when she'd risen up the ranks, the formal, tailored suits she'd been wearing for years. But Miss Tilly had insisted that suits wouldn't fit the "vibes" of the inn. After arriving here, Sophie had to agree, because Weber Haus was so cozy, staying here felt more like being in a lovely, inviting home. Instead, she'd changed things up to wear stylish but more casual slacks, and luckily most of her suit blouses were fine. She'd pinned her blond hair out of her way in a neat coil at the base of her neck.

Now, to face the day.

At least rising this early meant she wouldn't have to deal with Daniel straightaway. She might be able to be reasonably productive without his interference. The rest of yesterday had been an exercise in self-restraint, as Daniel had not only insisted she not be involved on his side of things, but meanwhile tried to take over her side.

He'd followed along as the Webers walked her through what needed to be done, asking questions she'd already asked or had answers to before now, and regularly implying she wasn't up to the task. Or insisting that he could help with things she had under control. At one point he'd even said the words, "I don't think Sophie can handle all this. Why don't you split things up between her and me?"

She got that these were his friends, but seriously? Interfering so and so. Besides, who was he to be doubting her? *His* construction was behind schedule.

She didn't want to paint him in the same light as Malcom, but he didn't make it easy, trying to take over everything. By the end of the day she'd been tempted to break into a rousing chorus of "Anything You Can Do (I Can Do Better)." Irving Berlin might as well have seen into the future and written that song about her and Daniel Aarons.

Just try to keep up with me, she silently challenged the absent man. Because she was brilliant at what she did. She put her heart and soul into it.

On that mental pump up, she quietly left her room, locking it behind her. Trying to walk quietly, hard to do with old wood floors, despite the runner down the long hall, she snuck through the house, her trusty tablet in one hand, cell phone in the other, and Snowball right behind her.

Lovely scents wafted toward her, and she followed her nose down the steep, dimly lit back stairs that led to the kitchen to find that Mrs. Bailey, who lived off-site, had already arrived and was working hard on breakfast. The woman, who could do a passable Mrs. Claus impersonation if she wore a red coat trimmed in white fur, gave a little jump at Sophie's sudden appearance, putting a hand over her heart.

"Sorry," Sophie murmured, aware of the sleeping guests she didn't want to disturb. "I didn't mean to startle you."

Mrs. Bailey waved her off with a smile and went back to stirring something or other in a big silver bowl. A quick glance at her tablet told Sophie that today's breakfast was supposed to be a sausage and egg casserole served with a fruit salad and toast from homemade bread served with an assortment of honeys and marmalades.

Despite the early hour, Sophie's stomach growled in anticipation.

One of the perks of living and working on-site was that Sophie's own meals were included as part of her compensation. Sniffing appreciatively, she grinned. "I'm going to have to watch my figure around you, Mrs. Bailey. I can tell already."

That lovely lady patted her own generous curves and grinned. "Gives a man more to hold on to, love."

I wouldn't know. She kept that thought to herself. Malcom hadn't done much appreciating or holding, in hindsight. Why hadn't she seen his motives? They'd dated for months.

She shoved the bitter thought down deep. Beyond learning her lesson and moving on to greener pastures—okay, white and brown pastures right now thanks to the season—she couldn't do anything more about it. No use shouting into the wind.

Sophie never did anything halfway and usually had the type of optimism that bounced back, even after a good knocking. Though, even at the idyllic new inn where she'd landed, it was hard to see those silver linings through the dust still settling from that final blowout with Malcom before she'd thrown the fact that she'd quit the hotel in his face and walked out.

She'd make the absolute most of her stint at Weber Haus for a year at most, before reevaluating her options. Find a new dream, maybe. The Crown Liberty wasn't the only hotel of its caliber where she could pursue her ambitions.

And stop thinking about Malcom.

"Would it disturb your rhythm too much to tell me about how the kitchen works while you cook?" she asked.

"I'd enjoy the company, actually," Mrs. Bailey said affably. "Usually I'm the only one up at this hour."

Sophie hitched out a stool at the wide butcher-block table that took up the large center area of the kitchen space. With a high-pitched sound somewhere between a squeak and a purr, Snowball leapt nimbly onto the chair beside her, then curled up in a contented ball of fluff.

With a quick pat for the cat, Sophie glanced around, checking the notes on her tablet as she took stock of her surroundings. Apparently, Weber Haus had originally been built with a large kitchen area with several entrances. A door to the formal dining room. A more casual swinging door led out to the hallway, the door to the back stairs she'd come down, and finally the back door leading outside.

Over the years the Weber family had updated the space, bringing it more into the modern era with its copper farmhouse sink and built-in cabinetry. They'd kept the large butcher-block table in the center and the free-standing antique cabinet along one side, as well as the original wood flooring, recently refinished.

In the last year, the Webers had partnered with a hotel chain—coincidentally a competing one to the chain Sophie had just quit—enabling them to update everything else, including replacing the fridge, stove, ovens, and dishwasher, update the countertops to a lovely white and gray swirled granite, and add a new white subway tile backsplash. In combination with the original dark wood trim and flooring, the space was both modern and cozily antique.

A perfect balance. No need to change anything more that she could see.

"Right . . ." she murmured more to herself, tapping the screen to bring up the questions she'd already vetted to discuss with Mrs. Bailey. "Let's start with your daily routine. As I understand it, breakfast is complimentary for guests, but lunch and dinner are now additional fees."

"Aye." A slight brogue slipped from Mrs. Bailey's lips.

"And we now serve meals to anyone not a guest provided they make reservations at least forty-eight hours in advance."

Nodding, Sophie took note of that and moved on to the next question.

After an hour or so, feeling well-versed in everything that had to do with the kitchen and meals, Sophie left Mrs. Bailey to finish setting up the buffet-style breakfast in the dining room, where guests could serve themselves as they wandered in and out, and headed to the small room tucked in the back of the house that had recently been converted into an office.

Her office. A far cry from her sleek and modern office at the Crown Liberty, but, somehow, she sort of adored it anyway. The space was cozy, and private, but still accessible if she was needed. However, her long to-do list included reorganizing and maybe even redecorating this room to her liking, but that would have to wait. Instead, she sat down at the desk and pulled up her checklist. Luckily, they had only one guest checking in today and no other events, which gave her a small buffer of time to familiarize herself with the house and routine.

Tomorrow afternoon would be her first meeting with the Christmas Market committee chair, a woman Emily had delicately referred to as "particular." Not that Sophie was worried. Most guests who could afford the Crown Liberty for events fell in that category. As long as this lady took on most of the responsibilities of the Market, Sophie could deal with particular.

With a satisfied hum, she started a detailed inspection of the house and grounds, making notes as she went through the day of ideas, most of them small, for improvements, eventually ending up back in her office, where she lost herself in spreadsheets and data.

The ring of the bell that accompanied the front door opening, as it had multiple times throughout the day as guests came and went, barely pinged on her radar until a gruff male voice called out.

"Oy. Anyone here?"

Her first guest at Weber Haus. Sophie's heart quickened. Maybe she was silly to be this excited about something that was a regular part of her job, but still . . .

Then the high-pitched *ting* of the smaller bell at the check-in desk in the foyer floated back to her over and over. The man must've mashed it down several times. All of which had her hurrying to slip her feet into her sensible but stylish flats and hurrying down the long hall to the foyer, where an older gentleman with a face that reminded her of a salty sea captain but with the clothing of Dr. Doolittle stood waiting none too patiently.

Pinning her best customer-friendly expression in place with practiced ease, she moved behind the small check-in desk, more a podium with a small flat-screen computer—which Emily had told her was new and had replaced an old-fashioned guest book—and resisted the urge to put her hand out and quiet the lingering of the bell's tinny ringing.

"You must be Mr. Muir," she said instead, at her cheerful best.

Greeting guests was one of her favorite things to do. Learning where they were from and why they were visiting, helping them get settled into their trip.

"Must I?" he asked with a curled lip.

Oh my. Sophie's enthusiasm dimmed slightly, matching the watery sun trying valiantly to break through the early-morning fog outside. "You are Mr. Muir, correct?"

He sucked on his teeth for a moment before giving a twitch of a shoulder that said he was indeed the new guest.

At least she hadn't got her first guest wrong. Sophie tried her friendliest smile again only to meet with the great wall of grumpy in return. "Welcome to Weber Haus," she offered, determined.

That only earned her a harrumph.

Gently ignoring his crabgrass attitude, she turned to the computer, bringing up the details of his stay. "I see you'll be here through the twenty-third?"

"Yes."

"I believe someone was in touch about there being no first-floor accommodations available in the house, as you requested, but we have an elevator if you'd rather not take the stairs." She waved a hand toward the back of the hallway.

"I said it was fine." Impatience sat on his shoulders like the old, well-worn coat he wore, and he was probably equally as comfortable with both.

Sophie let herself wonder if maybe he wasn't a little lonely traveling on his own at this time of year. Even with everything going on with the house and grounds, she made a mental note to check in on Mr. Muir a few extra times.

When he raised his eyebrows in impatience, she gave herself a mental shake and continued with the check-in process. "Excellent. We already have a credit card on file." She read off the last four digits. "Is that the card you wish us to use, or do you want to use a different card?"

"How many cards do you think I have?" He eyed her as though he thought she might rifle through his wallet and take off with said cards at any second.

She raised her eyebrows at that. "I'm sure I have no idea, sir." Then held his stare with an easy patience waiting for him to back down.

"That card is fine," he said after a battle of locked gazes, glancing away.

With a nod, she finished checking him in and provided him with a key and a map. "Breakfast is complimentary. Served buffet-style between six and nine in the morning. Lunch and dinner are also served daily for an extra fee each, or there are a few places to eat in the shops behind the house, and of course the town nearby. Can I help you with your luggage?"

"Not if you expect a tip."

"Not at all," she said with cheerful good grace.

Mr. Muir was practically a carbon copy of her own grandfather, whom she had loved to bits, finding his gruffness hilarious. Grumpy old men were some of her favorite people.

"Need help?"

She did her best to hide the way Daniel's sudden appearance made her jump, trying to put it down to surprise. What was the guy? A magician hiding in the shadows waiting to appear from a puff of smoke? But the way her stomach fluttered along with her increased heart rate fell in the realm of disconcerting.

"No need, thank you," she said, turning her back on him to follow Mr. Muir out.

Only the older gentleman was frowning at Daniel. "Who are you?"

"Daniel Aarons, sir. I'm a friend of the owners."

"Might as well come along," Mr. Muir said. He turned to eye Sophie's form dubiously, hopefully not noticing her sudden crossness. "She could blow away on a puff of wind any second."

"I'm scrappier than I look," she assured him, her smile more forced than a minute ago. Then she turned to Daniel. "Don't you have a building to finish?"

The second the words were out of her mouth she regretted them. She'd sounded judgmental, when really she was just trying to get him to leave her to get on with what was *her* job.

After a quick frown, hands stuffed in his pockets, he shrugged. "I came to check on you. Make sure you didn't need my help."

Which put her in her place with kindness while still stepping on her toes, presuming she couldn't get through even the morning without him.

"I'm fine," she assured him. And tacked on a begrudging, "Thanks."

"Great. I'll just help with the luggage and be on my way then." With that, he indicated the door with a wave of his hand.

Beyond arguing in front of a guest, there wasn't much else she could do to prevent Daniel from following them out the door. She'd even glanced at his feet, sort of hoping having to put his shoes back on would slow him down, only to find he hadn't taken them off as he had yesterday.

Mr. Muir had parked in the circular drive that brought visitors right to the front of the house to check in before parking in the back lot reserved for guests only. He popped his trunk and Daniel immediately started pulling out more luggage than a diva with a full concert's worth of costumes needed. Every case was stuffed to overflowing.

For some odd reason, her gaze dropped to Daniel's arms, where the sleeves were rolled up to the elbow exposing tanned skin over leanly muscled forearms with a dusting of hair. A shiver chased goose bumps down her arms as she stood beside the car. She'd forgotten her jacket. Again. That had to be the reason for the shiver, because she needed her head examined if a strong forearm generated that kind of reaction. Granted, it wasn't uncomfortably cold outside, which was unusual for this time of year. Christmas would be upon them before they knew it.

But still, definitely a cold shiver, not anything to do with awareness. She was sticking to that story like gum under bleachers.

"Uh-oh," Daniel suddenly murmured at her side.

"What?" she whispered. If he'd thrown out his back lifting luggage when she needed him healthy to finish that darn construction she might just—

"You might want to do something about *that*," he said, and tipped his chin at where Mr. Muir was struggling with something at the passenger side door.

What? Sophie straightened to find that gentleman pulling, of all things, a bird cage out of the front seat.

She blinked, then, abandoning the luggage to Daniel's capable hands, hurried over to Mr. Muir. "Sir. You didn't warn us that you'd have pets with you."

"These aren't pets," he scoffed. "They're family."

Then he proceeded to lift the cage to coo at them. "Aren't you? You're my babies. Sweet pets."

Sophie ignored a choked sound from behind her that might've been Daniel laughing and gave the two birds silently staring back at her from behind gilded cage bars a quick frown. "I'm afraid we have a strict policy about animals."

And birds were *not* on the allowed list.

"Your website said pets allowed."

"True, but it also stated that cats kept in the rooms or small dogs under thirty pounds, on a leash outside the rooms, were all we accepted . . . and therapy animals, of course," she tacked on.

His bony chest puffed out. "That's what *these* are. Therapy birds."

Trying to hide amusement behind a firm look, she clasped her hands in front of her and waited.

Sure enough, after a second Mr. Muir dropped his gaze with a mumbled, "They could be therapy birds."

She didn't comment on that, wondering how close to the truth that might be and reiterating her silent plan to check on him during his stay here. "I'm afraid we have a cat in the house who wanders freely about. She also seems to have a particular beef with . . . birds."

As Sophie could personally attest to.

Mr. Muir shrugged. "I'll make sure I keep her out of my room. Don't truck with cats anyhow. Snooty animals."

But birds are warm and fuzzy cuddlers?

As if to prove her wrong, he put his hand against the cage

and the closest bird to him gave a purring little coo, scooting down her perch to lean up against his touch through the bars.

I stand corrected.

"They were a gift from my late wife, God bless her soul. I don't go anywhere without Westley and Buttercup."

The man running for Sourpuss of the Decade did *not* just tell her the birds were named after *The Princess Bride* characters. Except another choked sound from Daniel told her she'd heard right. Sophie buttoned her lips over her own amusement, not wanting to hurt the older man's feelings.

"Well . . ." She thought through her options. "You'll need to pay a deposit, which you'll get back if there's no damage or cleaning needed, a daily pet fee in addition to your hotel charges, and sign a waiver saying it's your responsibility to keep them safe from the cat."

Mr. Muir cast her a dark look, muttering about how everyone only cared about covering their own butts these days—which Sophie silently agreed with—and how people in his day used to be able to take birds anywhere they wanted.

Probably not true. But she let it go.

She also caught the twinkle in his eye as he turned away. That sneaky old man knew he'd just gotten away with something and was relishing it. Hiding a chuckle of her own, she moved to the back of the car and picked up the two smallest cases, leaving the two largest for Daniel. He'd offered, after all.

"You just broke the rules, you know," he murmured quietly as they made to follow Mr. Muir inside.

She was well aware. "I'm the manager," she said. "It's within my purview."

"The words you use." He shook his head, then, before she could say anything, suddenly smiled. A smile that made her realize darker flecks floated in the hazel golds and greens of his eyes, and how that smile softened his features with sincerity, giving him a boyishness behind his beard that tried to sneak past the defenses she'd erected around herself after . . .

I really need to stop thinking about Malcom. He wasn't worth it.

"Good choice," he said.

She'd been ready to argue just that with the man who seemed to have designated himself her personal babysitter. Which should only raise the level of her irritation with him several more degrees to a hard boil. Only he'd meant what he said.

He was being . . . kind. Again. She wasn't quite sure what to do with that.

When she didn't respond, the lines at the corners of his eyes deepened with his grin. "He obviously loves those birds."

Turning away from his teasing hazel gaze, she eyed the cage Mr. Muir carefully kept from swinging as he walked.

"What kind of birds are those, Mr. Muir?" she called after him as she followed. The mostly gray birds had some brown on their wings and a little white around their necks.

"Turtledoves, of course," the older man shot over his shoulder.

Sophie stopped in her tracks. Two . . . turtledoves? Seriously? What kind of warped version of the twelve days of Christmas had she landed herself in?

"Now what would be the odds?" Daniel murmured, laughter rippling in the words, before he nudged her with one of his cases to keep going.

Those traitors.

I always greet our new arrivals so that they have a chance to admire my beautiful white fur and so that I can make sure they are worthy of Weber Haus. When that annoying bell rang, I made my way down from the attic, where I'd been checking for the pests I heard Daniel mention yesterday— there weren't any, by the way.

But Sophie had already gone outside with our newest arrival, so I slip into the large sitting room at the front of the house, the one with the big bay window that faces the wraparound porch. With an easy leap I pop up onto the windowsill, then search around bushes and porch posts to get a glimpse of them. I balance on my hind feet, my front paws using the screen to stay steady, very handy for my claws, so that I could see them.

Sophie is out there, along with an older gentleman. We get a lot of older people visiting here. Miss Tilly once said something about school holidays, which made no sense since only children go to school. Then I catch another movement and realize another human is out there, so I scoot over on the sill to see better. What the heck is *Daniel* doing helping a guest? That is *not* his job.

A small growl escapes me.

But then that old man pulls a cage out of his car. One with birds in it. Then Sophie actually let him in the house with them. Let those creatures into *my* house.

She knows after yesterday that my mission in life is to rid Weber Haus of all birds, squirrels, and other vermin. I thought we had that clear between us. What is she thinking?

In my rush to jump down, the sheer curtains Emily had added beneath the heavier curtains in here—why humans need two sets of curtains is a question I haven't got answered yet—tangle around me and I wiggle and shake until I finally get free of them.

Then I chase upstairs after them, deciding along the way if I should go for Daniel first, or for those trespassing feathered flying rats. Following the sounds of their voices, I turn the corner and sprint for the bedroom door, only to have to pull up at the last minute as they close it in my face.

A taunting coo sounds from the other side of the door.

Chapter 4

For a woman who, every time Daniel opened his mouth, looked as though she were valiantly trying not to bop him on the head, Sophie sure had a lot of patience with the new guest.

Rather than going directly to the construction site, he had stopped by the house to see if she'd be more open to his taking some of the workload. Why she'd been so annoyed by his offers yesterday, he had no idea. Coming in the back door through the kitchen, he'd snagged a crescent roll warm out of the oven, then paused in the shadows of the stairs to munch on his treat and listen in on how Sophie was handling a guest.

He had to give her credit—she was handling the irascible old man with a professional courtesy, and a lot more tolerance than even Miss Tilly, who could hold her own in the feisty stakes, would've shown. Sophie stood, perfectly composed and unruffled—matching the image he assumed she deliberately projected with the conservative black slacks and classy white blouse she wore and the way she'd coiled her honey-colored hair at the nape of her neck.

Impressive actually, her restraint.

Given his interactions with her so far, he wasn't sure what he would have expected. Granted, Sophie was an experienced hotel manager, and Tilly Weber was no dummy. She wouldn't have hired someone not good with people to run the family inn that meant so much to her. Except she'd come from a posh-sounding hotel. A different feel, a different clientele.

"This'll do," Mr. Muir said as they set down his things inside his room.

Daniel wasn't sure what he had in those bags, but they weighed probably more than Mr. Muir. He raised his eyebrows at the comment. This would do? Sophie had put him in the King's Suite. Other than the honeymoon suite and Tilly's room, which was originally the master bedroom, this was by far the nicest in the house.

One of the birds cooed as if to agree with her master. Daniel was still laughing over the coincidence and Sophie's face when she realized what kind of birds they were. She might . . . just maybe . . . even have hidden an answering twinkle of amusement before following their guest up here.

"I'm glad you like it," Sophie murmured. Then went into a quick speech reminding him about the times meals were served and where he could find information about the shops and grounds, as well as the town nearby.

"You already told me all that," she was informed gruffly.

"Of course. We'll leave you to it," she said. Then she sort of hip-checked Daniel out the door.

In the hall she paused, staring at him as though debating exactly how she wanted to go about getting rid of him, brows drawn down in a tiny frown.

"Thanks for the help," she finally said, sounding like a reluctant but well-parented child.

"Those bags were pretty heavy." He refrained from adding that there had been so many of them, it would have taken her three trips.

She flashed him an indecipherable look in a sideways glance. One he was pretty sure took in his arms and chest. "I would have used the elevator," she said. "But nice not to have to just the same."

"You just checked out my muscles, didn't you?" For extra fun, he added a cocky grin and flexed a bicep.

"Wow," she huffed under her breath.

Which only had him wanting to tease her more, though he had no idea why. She was as much a thorn in his side as she apparently thought he was in hers. His mother, if she'd been standing here, would not be impressed—she'd taught him better manners than that.

At the bottom of the stairs she swung to face him abruptly, and he raised his eyebrows in question. She crossed her arms, and he tried really, really hard to keep his gaze eye level. Probably not the time to be noticing her slender curves.

"Did you need me?" she asked pointedly.

Loaded question. "Actually, yeah. I thought you might like to do a walk-through of the construction site, since Lukas skipped that on the tour yesterday, and to look over the plans, get an idea of where we are."

He had no trouble interpreting the wary interest that flitted over her expression. And no wonder, as adamant as he'd been yesterday about not needing her involvement. And he didn't, not beyond her needing to know the timeline of progress so she'd know when they could open up more rooms to guests. He had everything under control. However, sitting at home thinking through the situation last night he'd come to a realization: the appearance of cooperation might get her to back off him and might also get her to accept his help on her side of things. An exchange, so to speak.

Nothing to do with an odd unwillingness to leave her struggling alone with so much to handle. They hadn't just thrown her into the deep end of the pool, they'd tossed her into shark-infested waters with no paddle.

He'd simply be extremely clear that no more changes could be made to the plans, and that she had little to no say on the progress. Just sharing of information was all he'd offer. That should work for both of them.

"Is now not a good time?" he asked. "I know how busy you are."

Deliberately he put a combination of concern and doubt she could handle one more thing into the implication of his tone.

Earning a small growl. "Now is fine."

He turned on his heel to hide a satisfaction he couldn't quite bite back, but which he was fairly confident would only make her stubborn streak break out. One day and he already knew that much about her. That and how her starlight eyes changed colors with her emotions.

The soft tread of her feet behind him told him she'd followed him out. This time he didn't need to stop to put on his boots. The ground had been dry and hard this morning, so he hadn't had to worry about tracking mud across those newly refinished floors.

They made their way around the back side of the carriage house, essentially the back of the shops now, past the barn and crossing in front of the shops, then through a field of ankle-high brown grass, crispy with frozen dew under his boots, to the two-story framed building his men were working on. Sounds of a wet saw being run reached them, along with hammering and the low murmur of men's voices.

Daniel paused at a temporary table made of rough two-by-fours and a plywood top laid out with the plans, and grabbed his safety helmet from the shelf underneath, plus an extra, handing it to Sophie.

"Um," she said after a second. "This can't be right." He turned from securing his to find her head half-buried under the white brim of the helmet, eyes and nose completely hidden, her lips twisted in what might even be mistaken for amusement.

"Here." He slipped the helmet off her head to adjust the

inside bands to fit a smaller girth than his men's meaty melons. "This should do it."

Rather than hand it back, he popped the thing on her head and fiddled with the under-chin clasp for her.

"I could have done that myself," she murmured. Less petulant or irritated than resigned, unless he was misinterpreting again.

"I know." He lifted his gaze only to pause at the mercury-colored hue of her eyes. Not blue, not gray, and his ribs decided to squeeze his lungs into a smaller space. What would she do if he kissed her?

Punch him in the nose, probably.

What was wrong with him, even entertaining a thought like that? His job was his focus right now. No distractions.

Needing to do something to ease that sudden, strange tension, he tipped his head. "Why don't you like to accept help?"

The question was a deliberate distance-inducing attempt, one he expected to result in her snapping back to being irritated with him. Instead, a flash of vulnerability had him feeling like he'd knocked a small bird out of its nest with a rock.

"I don't mind help, if that's all it is." He raised his eyebrows and she glanced away. "Let's say the last guy I let help me wasn't into helping so much as . . . taking." On that combination of cryptic and revealing, she stepped back.

So some guy had done a number on her. Must've been a fool. Only Sophie's closed expression clearly indicated she didn't want to talk about it.

Despite his curiosity, now struggling with pictures of what kind of guy she would be with, Daniel turned to the table, flattening out the latest iteration of the plans they were working toward. He pointed out the key features—how they were designing the two-story wing to match the house itself with the same white siding, black shutters, and red tiled roof.

The entire time he was picturing a slick city guy in a perfect suit, with perfect teeth and a square jaw, hands that weren't rough with calluses, and a smoothly shaven face.

"So no connecting point between the new wing and the house?" she asked, pointing over the space in the schematic.

Daniel had to hold back a groan. This had already been discussed a dozen different ways. "Tilly decided to go with sidewalks only."

"Open to the elements?" Sophie persisted.

"Yes, like the rest of the grounds and shops." No more additions. One more issue and he'd miss the deadline, and then there went all his potential clients.

"Except the shoppers aren't necessarily staying at the house, or eating breakfast or other meals there," she pointed out.

"This was *Tilly's* decision." He might as well be a bear the way he was growling. "She didn't want to have to cut into the house to add a door, or have a long corridor cutting up access ways between buildings or covering the windows along the back side of the house to reach the kitchen door."

There. That should end the conversation.

"Of course. I'm just asking to get an idea. Do you know if she considered covered walkways?"

Actually, he didn't remember that coming up, but he also wasn't the architect. He was the builder. "I'm sure she did."

"I'll check with her next time she calls." Sophie nodded as if that was the end of that.

Daniel made a mental note to get to Tilly first. They could always add covers to the walkways later if they determined it was an issue. This project couldn't afford any more creep.

Shaking off the thoughts, he led her to an unfinished doorway, through the open interior—which was further along than the exterior, only the detail trimming needing to be done—and out another door to the back side of the structure.

As they stepped into the space where most of his men were hard at work, she didn't seem to notice that they all paused to look first at her and then at him with raised eyebrows. Even the married ones. Andreas even pursed his lips in a silent whistle, only to wipe all expression from his face at Daniel's warning stare.

"As you can see," Daniel said to Sophie, "we're finishing up the roofing and starting the exterior siding. We're hoping to complete the roof today." He cast an evil-eyed stare at the clouds overhead.

This had been the project from hell. Anything that could go wrong, had. From delays in weather, which had been anticipated, just not to this extent, to a flu that ran through every guy in his crew in October, to a completely wrong pallet of roofing tiles. On and on.

Now Pete was in the hospital fighting for his life.

Which put Daniel's troubles into a rather harsh perspective. The least he could do was quit his grumbling, even if only in his head, and do everything he could to finish the project on time. For Emily, for Miss Tilly, so they could be there for Pete when he couldn't.

"You have a Christmas deadline, correct?" Sophie asked, almost as though she'd been reading his mind. At least she hadn't sounded skeptical.

"That's right."

"From what I understand, weather has been an issue. Any concerns there?"

"Of course, though we budgeted for a certain amount of delays." Just not this many. Still, he put all the confidence he could muster behind the words, ignoring his foreman's grimace and the glance every man shot the skies.

Wide silver eyes turned his way. "Is there anything *I* can do to help make sure this is finished on time?"

Yeah, don't convince Tilly to add covered walkways or anything else. "Not that I can think of."

He must not have hidden his thoughts well because his foreman snorted and turned it into a cough at Daniel's look.

Sophie glanced at Levi with his massive shoulders, beefy hands, and round, bald head that didn't seem to need a neck to attach to his body. A man who looked like he spent a lot of time in bar fights, which he had, once upon a time.

Daniel had given him work when no one else would.

Sophie smiled, a real one that lit up her eyes, and she walked over, holding out her hand unflinchingly. "Sorry. I'm butting in all over the place, and I haven't even introduced myself, either. I'm Sophie, the new hotel manager."

Levi shot a blinking gaze over her head at Daniel before taking her hand. Most *men* didn't feel comfortable approaching Levi, let alone women. "Levi Meyer, foreman," he said with his usual judicious lack of words.

"Pleasure to meet you." Words she had distinctly *not* said to Daniel. He crossed his arms, watching with interest and trying his darndest not to be offended on his own behalf.

She tipped her head, smile still in place as she addressed Levi. "So the earlier delays . . . I take it they were out of the ordinary?"

Levi shot him another look, this one tinged in interest, and Sophie waited. The entire crew had stopped working at this point, listening in.

She glanced around and color rose up her neck into her cheeks. "Sorry. Again. I'm asking because I need as accurate a picture as I can get. The rooms are already booked starting at the new year." Her glance included Daniel in the discussion.

He crossed his arms. "As long as nothing new comes along, and no one adds anything new to the plans"—he paused and gave her a pointed look—"we should be done right in time."

"Fair enough."

From her definitive nod, he could tell she'd taken his word for it, and a smidge of the tension eased from his shoulders. Maybe she wouldn't interfere.

"All I ask is that you keep me up to date." She slipped in the reasonable-sounding request. Only Daniel was pretty sure that if she'd been a lawyer writing a contract, she'd just fine-printed her way into keeping her nose in his business.

"Of course."

She suddenly turned to stand shoulder-to-shoulder with Levi, looking at Daniel. She tipped her head to the side, a decided twinkle in her eyes that he didn't quite trust. "He's a stand-up guy, right?" she asked Levi. "He looks like a stand-up guy, but one never knows with construction managers."

She delivered the words with a bewitching grin that had all his men, himself included, chuckling, until the words sank in.

"Hey," he protested, earning an innocent stare from her.

"Sorry," she said, holding up both hands. "The last construction manager I dealt with had a bad habit."

"What was that?" Levi asked before Daniel could.

"He'd pretend there were more squares on the calendar than there actually were." She winked. The woman actually winked. Aimed right at him, and even as he was offended on behalf of his fellow construction managers, he wanted to laugh.

To Daniel's shock, Levi did. Threw his head back and gave a big, out-of-character guffaw. "There are days when I wonder that myself," the big foreman said.

"Traitor," Daniel said, but gave a reluctant grin to show no hard feelings.

She just shook her head. "No. No, I can already tell that Daniel is more trustworthy than that character."

She could? Because so far, their interactions had been . . . a mixed bag.

"Actually, ma'am," his foreman said. "Daniel's the most honest man I know."

Again, she cast an assessing gaze his way, warming him from the inside out. "I'm glad to hear it."

What just happened?

He wasn't sure if he'd been insulted, challenged, or complimented. Based on the sappy smiles aimed her way from every man on his crew, he was pretty sure she'd managed to wrap them all around her pretty little finger.

"I'll stop interrupting and let you get back to it," she said. She included all the men in a friendly wave. "Nice to meet you, fellas. Keep up the good work. Just let me know if you need anything."

He escorted her back through the building and on the other side, she paused to take off her helmet, patting at her hair with a wince as she handed it back to him. "Thank you," she said. "That was informative. Would it be possible to get daily updates on your progress?"

There it was.

He'd wondered when she'd toss a request like that his way. Only, reporting to her in person would give him an opportunity to check up on her work, too. Which fell right in with his plans to make sure nothing fell through on her side, too. For his friends' sakes. "I'll stop by in the mornings before I come to the site."

"I'd appreciate that."

Daniel pulled a small black walkie-talkie from his back pocket and held it out to her.

Only she didn't reach for it. She glanced at the device, then back at him. "What am I supposed to do with that?"

"Take it." He gave it a shake.

"For what?" She inspected the walkie-talkie as if he was the evil queen hawking poison apples.

"To get in touch with me easily."

Sophie's back went so straight she could give the steel beams holding up the new wing a run for their money. "What? So you can check up on me?"

"That's not what I'm doing." A twinge at the lie didn't sit well in his stomach, but this was for Tilly and Emily and Lukas.

"Uh-huh." Sophie wasn't buying it anyway. She scrunched up her nose. "Wouldn't a cell phone be more convenient?"

"We can trade numbers, but I don't carry one with me onsite." After he'd broken the third one in a year, despite the heavy-duty cases they were in, he'd given up. "Also, cell service out here is still spotty, and I frequently need all the crew to hear what's going on. If you can't get in touch with me, one of them can."

Her spine lost a bit of its stiffness at his explanation. "I hope I won't need you, as you've got this end of things covered." She waved at the building behind him. "If anything, it's the other way around, and you'll need to contact me."

Why did the choice of words—not need *you*—itch at him like a wool sweater? He pushed the odd reaction aside. "Maybe not, but I'm a handy guy to have around in a pinch."

"I'm sure you are when it comes to construction—"

"And lifting luggage, and getting devil cats out of trees . . ." He almost chuckled as those expressive eyes of hers turned almost molten silver with her indecision.

"Despite what you seem to think, I really *can* take care of everything else," she continued as though he hadn't spoken.

"I have no doubt," he agreed, and patted her placatingly on the shoulder.

Apparently the wrong thing to do. She stepped around him, saying, "Look. I have a lot to do today. I'm sure you do, too—"

"Peter is my best friend," Daniel reminded her softly. "I'm not trying to step on your toes. This is just the only way I know how to help him." He hadn't been able to help Drew, and maybe Peter wouldn't make it—Daniel cut that thought off like chopping a head off a snake.

Sophie stopped, her back to him; her shoulders rose and fell in a silent sigh, and she spun around, hand held out, but her gaze softer than a second ago. "I understand. I'll take it."

"And promise to call if there's anything you need?"

She hesitated, reluctance vividly sparking in her eyes. "This is my job," she said softly. "They hired me because I'm really good at it."

"This is more than what you were hired for," he countered. "I know this place, and I know most everyone in the shops and around town. I'm a good guy to have in your corner."

Reluctance turned to resignation, her lips pressing together firmly, and finally a short laugh. A huffy one, but still . . . "I do appreciate the offer."

No, she didn't. Not really. And he had no idea why.

Then her eyes tilted in a way that reminded him of Snowball when she was about to pounce. "I'll promise to call if I need anything, if you promise not to use it to check up on me."

Dang. He *had* been planning exactly that. "It's not a crime to ask for help every once in a while, Soph," he pointed out, the shortened version of her name slipping out. "Or take the offer of it."

Which earned him a smile he didn't entirely trust. "Then anytime you need me, I'm happy to help," she said.

Should've seen that coming.

Her expression shifted suddenly, as though she was letting down a small sliver of the invisible walls she'd erected around herself. "It's not that I mind asking. I mind being *told* I need help."

That's not what he'd done. Had he? He thought back over their interactions. Maybe he had. Though not because of her necessarily. More the circumstances.

He searched her gaze and gave in a little. "I tell you what . . . I promise not to call you on it *if* . . . you admit you were checking out my muscles earlier in the house." Deliberately he flexed his pecs—something he hadn't done for a girl since high school.

The series of emotions that chased across her face—

incredulity, exasperation, followed by a hard eye roll and a groan—had him laughing.

"I'll see you around." Still chuckling, he waved and turned away before she could hand the walkie-talkie back. Sophie Heidt wasn't boring. That was for sure.

"She's not so bad, boss," Levi said when he appeared through the door.

"She questioned my ability to count squares," Daniel said dryly. Indirectly, at least.

"Well, someone has to help you with that every once in a while." Levi chortled.

Daniel ignored him and got to work. Ten minutes later, the walkie-talkie at his hip crackled. "I forgot to mention," Sophie said, "we're meeting with the holiday festival planner at four tomorrow afternoon. Over."

Daniel shook his head. Nope. Not boring. A clearly compulsive need to get the last word, but not boring. It also hadn't escaped him that she was already using two-way lingo. Had they used these in her hotel, too? He unhooked his own radio from his belt loop. Pressing the button on the side, he spoke into the device.

"Ten-four. Over."

"And Emily said the woman meeting us is . . . particular. So we shouldn't be late. Over."

He'd grown up with Giselle. Emily was being kind. "Punctuality is my middle name. Over."

He ignored a series of derisive snorts from his guys.

"Awww. Did your parents not like you?"

Snorts turned into full-on laughs. He would've shot them a glare, but now he was grinning like a fool. Except he couldn't come up with a snappy retort to that one. So he changed it up.

"You didn't say over. Over."

Silence.

He tried again. "I'll be there. With bells on. Over."

"Are you sure you want to do that with Snowball around? It'd be like cowbells. An easy way for her to track you down. Over."

"She's got you there," Levi mumbled.

Someday, that cat and he were going to have a reckoning.

"Speaking of which," he shot back at Sophie, "I didn't see her anywhere in the house when we left. Have you already lost her again? Over."

A long silence greeted his answer. Long enough that guilt started pulling his feet away from work and back out of the building to head to the house and help her search. He shouldn't have teased.

"She's right here. Over and out." Smug didn't begin to describe Sophie's tone of voice, loud and clear even through the crackling of the two-way.

He should have known she'd be the one to use "over and out" first. Maybe he should have just exchanged cell phone numbers instead. The problem was, he'd discovered with his own crew that cell phones were easier to ignore than a walkie-talkie. Why, he wasn't sure. Something about the immediacy of it and the fact that anyone standing nearby could hear, maybe.

Mental note not to underestimate Sophie Heidt.

Although that didn't mean he wasn't going to keep an eye on her, all the same. With her aversion to asking for help, he had a feeling he'd need to make sure he was frequently in the right place at the right time.

Hopefully, she forgot about the covered walkway thing and didn't have anything else to add to his side of their unspoken bargain to keep Weber Haus moving forward while the Webers were away.

I stare at the door to the room those caged vermin with wings had gone in. I'd been sitting in the hallway on and off since yesterday, when they arrived, pausing only to eat and sleep in Sophie's room, waiting for the man to come out so that I could slip inside.

It hadn't helped that Sophie had found me here yesterday afternoon, scooped me up to knock on the door and warn the man—a Mr. Muir who'd given me a cockeyed glare. She'd put me down in the kitchen, but I snuck my way back up here just the same, hiding anytime I heard Sophie's feet on the stairs.

Those creatures in my house are an insult.

A taunting coo sounds from the other side of the door. Those birdbrains know I'm out here. My fluffy tail flicks from side to side in annoyance. This plan is not working. Suddenly a light vibration of sound rattles in the room beyond. Human snoring. I know that sound well. Apparently, the man is taking his afternoon nap, which means he won't be coming out anytime soon.

With a snit, I get up and pad my way downstairs to Sophie's office. The woman in question lifts her head. "I hope you left those birds alone."

Not a chance.

I go wind myself around her feet, the base of the chair in the way, but I work between her legs anyway. "What do you want, you silly cat? I need to get this done."

She doesn't pet me, though. So I leap to the desktop and walk across the keyboard where she's typing.

"Snowball!" Sophie makes a clicking sound with her tongue, then puts me back on the floor.

Unacceptable.

All humans should be well aware that if a cat bothers to show them attention, they must reward her with petting.

I jump back up on her desktop, batting at her hand with my paw, my claws sheathed so I don't hurt her.

"Shoo." She waves me away. Then gasps. "Oh my gosh, my meeting. I'm going to be late. After I warned Daniel to be on time. I'll never hear the end of it."

In a rush of papers and snapping up an odd device that reminds me of a cell phone only bigger, she rushes out of the room. I try to follow her out the kitchen door, but she turns and pushes me back inside.

"Not this time," she says, and shuts the door in my face.

I sit there staring, tail swishing, and trying to decide what to do next.

Chapter 5

Sophie pulled up sharply at the corner of the shops and took a few precious seconds to collect herself and try to stop breathing so hard. Not to mention make a mental note to work out more, because jogging such a short distance should not have winded her this way. Not having to walk city blocks daily was making her soft.

This Christmas Market business was probably the most complicated cog in her wheel, and that included Daniel's construction. At least the town of Braunfels had a committee in charge of the event who had been working at it for months, apparently.

A quick glance at the time on her tablet and she crossed her eyes. She was late already, but regardless, it wouldn't do to appear harried and unprofessional, too.

Five bucks says Daniel mentions being on time, an unhelpful part of her brain piped up. Because that was something he would absolutely delight in doing.

A confident smile pasted to her lips while still trying not to suck wind so hard—maybe a small gym would be a good addition to the next round of renovations to the Weber Haus property—she rounded the corner at a more serene pace and made her way to the large gazebo. White with red roofing and ornate iron details around each post, intended to match the rest of the buildings, the Webers had planted it in the center of the main thoroughfare between the barn and carriage house. A lovely focal point for shoppers and also a makeshift stage when needed.

Like for the upcoming Christmas Market.

She'd seen pictures of the before and after. They really had done a remarkable job retrofitting the spaces while still keeping that original Victorian ambiance. She could just picture it through the year with different seasons and holidays, different events, and how that would draw more people to stay at the inn.

Daniel stood in the gazebo with a cool blonde dressed in red slacks and a clinging white sweater that highlighted her admittedly charming assets. Maybe a new friend? Sophie could use a few friends after the holidays were over. Emily was a solid prospect, but she wasn't here, so, at the moment, beyond Mrs. Bailey, and Daniel, if you counted him, Sophie hadn't made any around here yet. As she neared, the blonde tucked her hand into the crook of Daniel's arm, laughing up at something he'd said.

Sophie's steps slowed at the cozy little scene. She had the sudden mental image of hissing like Snowball did at Daniel every time the cat caught sight of him. Not hissing at him, though, but at the blonde. Which was beyond ridiculous. Besides, maybe this was Daniel's girlfriend, in which case, best of luck to her.

Luckily, she'd regained her equilibrium about the time Daniel lifted his gaze and spotted her.

"Here she is," he boomed in an over-jovial way, letting go of the blonde to cross the stairs to Sophie. "You're late," he murmured, hazel eyes laughing.

Ha! Five bucks to me, thought Sophie. She peered around his shoulders to address the blonde. "I apologize for making you wait."

The blonde's answering smile could've cut glass, it was so diamond hard.

"Giselle Becker . . . Sophie Heidt." Daniel introduced them as he, oh so casually, slipped an arm around Sophie's waist.

Her body went stiff in reaction, mostly because instead of wanting to smack him with her tablet, she had the oddest urge to lean into him. Maybe she needed more sleep. More to the point, what did he think he was doing? Trying to throw her off her game before she got started? Because they were definitely not at the touching, let alone proprietary hand around waist, point in their relationship.

They didn't have a relationship to speak of.

Before she could call Daniel on his odd behavior, he gave her a small push toward Giselle. Horribly aware of their audience, she decided to let it go and shot the other woman another apologetic smile, offering a hand to shake while trying to gain some space.

"So you're the little helper they put in charge while they're gone," Giselle said, with one of those limp, society princess–style shakes.

That puts me in my place, Sophie thought wryly.

A glance at Daniel's easy expression told her he hadn't caught the undercurrent, like a typical male, but she hadn't missed it. He stood there, hands stuffed in the back pockets of his jeans, watching the interchange with vague interest. Meanwhile, the other woman had effectively dismissed her as an underling, not worthy of this project.

Still, odds were that Giselle would probably be a lovely spring breeze compared with the high-society mamas planning elaborate and incredibly expensive wedding spectaculars. "I'm here to do what I can to help from a Weber Haus perspective," she said.

The other woman merely hummed, but her doubts in Sophie's abilities couldn't be plainer. "Well, it's a good thing we have Daniel," she said, and moved so that she could pet his arm with her perfectly manicured fingers. "He's always so . . . helpful."

"Yes, he is," Sophie agreed, and enjoyed watching them both blink, especially since she was being honest. He might have his doubts about her abilities—and she'd absolutely prove herself worthy—but he *had* also been helpful. She could give credit where it was due.

"It's unfortunate Emily felt the need to take Miss Tilly with her, as well." Giselle made a small moue that did bring attention to her lovely mouth, but even Daniel frowned over that ill-worded bit of selfishness.

"Yes," Sophie murmured in sympathetic tones. "Poor Peter's situation is distressing for everyone." She found herself on the receiving end of a sharp look, which she returned with a sweet smile that could've given the Sugar Plum Fairy a cavity.

Time to take charge and turn this conversation to business. "Now, why don't you walk me through what still has to be done and what support you were expecting from the property?"

Daniel lifted a single eyebrow, probably at her use of "me" instead of "us," excluding him from the need to be there, but said nothing. Except, suddenly she felt a little mean. Lollipop thieves might experience this kind of regret.

His friends, she reminded herself. *Let him help.*

"The first thing we need to do is put up all the decorations," Giselle said after a pause. "Miss Tilly told me they already have decorations covered as they'd planned for them with the renovations."

Sophie pulled out her tablet and brought up her notes. "Yes, she has them all in storage above the barn shops."

Then she glanced around the area. What Tilly hadn't said was who, exactly, was going to be in charge of hanging all these decorations. Much more complicated than simply putting up lights on the house, which, as tall as it was, wouldn't be easy, either. "Are there any services in town who will put up lights and decorations?" she asked, not lifting her head.

The hole of silence that greeted that question had her lifting her head to find Giselle staring at her with pursed lips. "I assumed Miss Tilly had a plan already in place. Decorations are for the shops, not for the Christmas Market."

In other words, I'm a total idiot for not knowing, Sophie translated silently.

"Actually," Daniel said, "she hired me."

They both turned to face him, Giselle beaming suddenly, Sophie not so much. "In the middle of construction?" she asked. "When is this happening?"

No way did he and his team have the time. Not now. Why hadn't Tilly hired someone else?

He flicked a glance between the two women. "We have equipment already on-site to easily get to those high spots," he said.

Which sounded simple enough but wasn't. It would still be hours of work. Maybe even days. "When did you agree to this?" she asked.

"This summer."

And he still planned to do it, anyway, even with the hours he and his crew would have to put in on the hotel? Gosh, when would he have time to sleep?

The concern must've shown in her eyes, because he shifted on his feet, expression turning as stubborn as the baby goat she'd reared as a kid. "I promised Miss Tilly," he said.

One of the most honest men, Levi had said—who struck her as the type of man who didn't easily trust. Daniel Aarons might be a well-intentioned, interfering barnacle she couldn't get rid of. He was also, apparently, a total softie under that construction lumberjack exterior.

She filed that tidbit away for later scrutiny.

"You're sure it's not too much?" she asked. "Given the delays, I'm happy to check around for another crew to come in and save you the trouble—"

"We'll take care of it this weekend. I had it on the schedule leading into December."

Sophie gave a short nod. "So that's decorations," she said, and turned to Giselle. "What else?"

I should consider myself lucky that I didn't get slapped for that arm around Sophie's waist.

Daniel listened to both women discussing everything to be done for the Market with half an ear and a few sidesteps, subtly keeping Sophie between himself and Giselle when he could. If she touched his arm flirtatiously one more time, he might have to chew his arm off. He'd known her since grade school and she'd never—not ever—shown any interest in him whatsoever. In Peter, captain of the baseball and basketball teams, then the impressive navy man, yes. But not in Daniel.

Not that he'd been a slouch in high school. He'd also been on those teams and pretty darn good, if he said so himself . . . but he'd also been short, not hitting the bulk of his growth spurt until the tail end of his senior year. Even then, she'd shown little notice of him. Until this year, when things started going so well for him.

Amazing what a few extra inches and an up-and-coming business could do to make a man more interesting to the opposite sex.

The problem was, he needed Giselle's father—George Becker—on his side. Daniel was determined to win that secret project, whatever it was. Maybe even right out from under Jannik Koch's nose.

His gaze drifted to Sophie, who kept shooting him small frowns, and he bit back amusement and amended the thought. More interesting to *some* of the opposite sex. Others, on the other hand, were harder to impress.

Why that made him want to poke a proverbial stick at her in response was, no doubt his mother would tell him, a juvenile response. He just couldn't seem to help himself. Besides, if Giselle's flirting meant she'd set her sights on him now, he needed a buffer, and Sophie could obviously hold her own. If he had to put money on the two, he'd put it on Sophie every time. Giselle didn't stand a chance. Win-win.

". . . we're going to need fencing around the construction site . . ." she was saying.

The words suddenly registered. What was this about?

Before he could ask, a crackle sounded a heartbeat before Levi's voice came over the walkie-talkie at Daniel's hip and echoed from Sophie's, which she held. "We got a . . . situation, boss. Over."

Both women stopped mid-discussion to glance up. Sophie with concern, Giselle with ill-concealed impatience, as well as a curious glance at the two devices.

He pulled the thing off his belt and pressed the button. "What situation? Over."

"Chickens. Over."

Sophie started walking closer, a small frown pulling at her brows.

"Sorry?" Daniel said over the mic. "But did you say chickens?"

"Yeah, three of them. Three fat hens sitting on our wet saw and refusing to move."

Three hens for Christmas? Seriously?

His gaze met wide starlight-colored eyes and Daniel grinned as she lifted them heavenward, then closed them in resignation with a shake of her head. Not able to entirely keep the laughter from his voice, he pressed the button again. "It's beginning to look a lot like Christmas," he said. "We'll be right there. Over and out."

"I hope you have a license for those animals," Giselle said as soon as he hooked the walkie-talkie back in his belt.

Daniel jerked his head up at the intolerable comment to find she'd directed the words to Sophie. "That was—"

Sophie cut him off. "Of course. I'm guessing these might be the petting zoo chickens." Which made sense. The new chicken coop was relatively close to their site. "Why don't we meet again in three days after the decorations are all up. I'll email you about the other items we've discussed."

After a second, Giselle nodded. "I'll wait for your communication." Then she sashayed closer to where he stood. "I'll see you around, Daniel."

He couldn't miss how her voice changed from cold efficiency to a purr of sound. Based on Sophie's expression, she couldn't miss it, either. Yeah. Somehow, he'd landed himself in Giselle's sights.

Without thinking it through, he very deliberately scooped Sophie closer and dropped a quick kiss on lips parted in shock, not anticipation. He'd meant it to be an impersonal peck. Only the softness of her lips registered, as did her barely audible inhalation, and he blinked down into sparkling eyes and lost his train of thought for the amount of time it took her to get over the surprise.

Line definitely crossed. He lifted his head before she could push him away. "We'd better go get those chickens."

Calling her an endearment was tempting, but after that kiss, doing so would be akin to sprinting over the line and all the way to the North Pole, where Santa would probably put him on the permanent naughty list. So instead, he sent Giselle a friendly wave and, a hand at Sophie's back, careful not to touch, hustled her away.

Thankfully, she didn't start hissing and spitting at him like Snowball until they were out of eyesight of the woman still at the gazebo.

"You want to explain all that?" she asked through clenched teeth.

"Giselle was flirting."

"And?"

"Now maybe she won't bother."

Sophie's steps slowed until he had to stop or he'd leave her behind. "So . . . instead of dealing with one flirty woman, you needed to make a spectacle of kissing the new girl in town, in front of everyone shopping today, to throw the other woman off the scent?"

Not exactly how he'd put it. He stuffed his hands in his back pockets, trying not to feel like a schoolboy called in front of the principal. "I didn't make a spectacle. You're fine."

"You kissed me in the most public place possible other than maybe the steps of Town Hall. On a raised platform at the heart of the shops." She crossed her arms and tapped a boot-covered toe, eyebrows raised in challenge.

"A peck." He shrugged. "No one will think anything of it if they saw it at all. You're making too big a deal of this."

"Uh-huh. Gossip is the hallmark of small towns. People are always interested in everything their neighbors are doing."

She wasn't entirely wrong. Now a crook of guilt snared inside him along with a confusing swirl of offense on his own behalf. What was wrong with being seen kissing him anyway? "I'm sorry if I put you in a tough position."

"Apology accepted." She stalked past him.

"But I won't apologize for the kiss," he called after her.

He'd never seen a spine go so straight as she turned wide eyes his way. Daniel tossed her his most cocky grin, guaranteed to make her lips pucker with irritation. "It was nice," he said simply. *And I wouldn't mind doing it again, properly.* He kept that last bit to himself.

Then he walked past her, with her jaw almost in her lap, to the site. As soon as he walked outside through the still-open hotel interior, he got his first sight of his men chasing down three white hens. Levi hadn't been kidding. They were fat.

White feathers floated around everywhere, and the place sounded like a barnyard in revolution thanks to the frantic squawking of both birds and men. Levi himself had folded his massive form in half, sort of skip-running with hands out in front of him as he tried to corner one screeching, flapping hen.

A feminine laugh from behind him had him turning to find Sophie watching the situation with a wide grin, her husky chuckle about the sweetest sound he'd heard in a while. Then she turned that grin on him, as though including him in her amusement, and something strange happened around the region of his heart. As though that smile lassoed him and drew him in tight.

Before he had a chance to inspect his reaction more closely, Sophie, shaking her head, walked over to a spool of insulated wire.

His eyebrows tried to crawl into his hairline as he watched her use wire cutters to cut off a length; then she bent one end like a handle and the other end like a tiny shepherd's hook. Perfectly calm, unlike the chickens or his crew, she positioned herself in the center of the yard.

"Herd them to me," she called.

Levi didn't even look up, just changed the direction of his hunched-over skip-run. As soon as his chicken was close enough, Sophie reached out with her hook and snagged it by one leg, lifting it right up into the air, where she got a better hold on it with her free hand. Then she gently took it by the other leg, unhooked the wire, then tipped it upright with a hand under its belly. The chicken stopped flapping and settled right into her.

Sophie Heidt. City girl and a chicken whisperer. Who knew?

Every man on his crew, Daniel included, stopped what they were doing to stare at her slack jawed and bug-eyed.

"That's quite a trick," Daniel managed.

Sophie didn't smile, but he got the impression she was holding one back. She pushed the one captured chicken into his arms, then proceeded to do the same with the other two. Holding on to the last one, she hitched her chin at him and Levi. "Let's go put these gals back in their coop."

Levi just shook his head with a grin and fell into step beside Daniel. "Boss, you might want to marry that one before someone else does."

Based on the derisive snort from the woman in front of them—clearly, she wasn't completely over that kiss—Sophie had caught that.

Unable to resist, Daniel called after her. "Did you hear that, Soph? How about marrying me?"

Only the instant the words were out of his mouth they didn't taste quite so teasing. Which, in and of itself, was absurd. He hardly knew her, and something about him rubbed her the wrong way, and she had the potential to make his job harder, and . . . well, so many reasons.

"You should be so lucky," she called over her shoulder.

For Levi, Daniel managed a chuckle, but he still couldn't help thinking about how soft her lips had been when he kissed them, or what that small gasp had stirred inside him, or the strange feeling that she'd hooked him the same way she had those chickens.

They hadn't stood a chance, and Daniel suspected he didn't, either. Trouble every which way he looked at it.

The chickens and I had made a deal when they first moved in for the petting zoo. Since they produced eggs and were confined to their coop, I'd promised they could stay. A rooster would have been a different story. One lived next door, and that sucker was mean. And loud.

But if Sophie was going to let Mr. Muir's stupid birds into my house—who had cooed all night long since they'd arrived, by the way, and taunted me any time I was outside their door or perched in the tree outside their window—I was going to let her know how unhappy I was about it.

The hens happened to be the only birds I could get to, so I made my point with them.

I waited up in one of the trees, where I could see where the chickens went after I opened the door to the coop. Just in case no one noticed and I needed to bring them back myself. Foxes and coyotes still roamed the open land around the inn, and both Emily and Mrs. Bailey used their eggs in their cooking. Couldn't have them come to harm to make a point.

Watching those big men run around like . . . well, like chickens with their heads cut off . . . was about the funniest thing I've ever seen. On the other hand, I should've figured that Sophie would know exactly what to do. She's the efficient type.

From my perch I watch as she brings them back to the coop, where the door is still wide open. She looks around for a bit, and when she crouches over the very deliberate paw-print I'd left in the mud beside the door, I know she knows.

With a hiss of sound through her teeth, she puts the chicken she's holding down inside the coop, takes the other two from Daniel and his friend, who haven't said anything, does the same with them, then shuts the door. Then, without a word, she marches off toward the house.

No doubt in search of me.

I would try to beat her there, but Daniel is standing almost directly under me, and it's too good a chance to pass up.

"What was that about?" his big friend with no neck asks.

Daniel frowns, staring around the ground. "I'm not sure."

He takes one step.

Just a little closer, I urge him silently while I prepare to pounce. This isn't the first time I've dropped onto his unsuspecting head. This is going to be fun.

Another step and he crouches down by the gate. "Snowball," he mutters.

Then he jerks his head back to look straight up into my eyes, horror filling his gaze.

With a war cry I drop from the low limb, flailing in the air and aiming right for his shocked face.

Chapter 6

The soft patter of rain against her office window was the last thing Sophie wanted to be hearing. It had been going on for days now. A constant *rat-tat-tat*. Not hard, just unending, soaking the ground.

The rain was making everyone in the house antsy. The guests, who were less inclined to go out. Mrs. Bailey, who was having to feed more mouths at lunch and dinner with the guests staying in. The shopkeepers complaining about the slowdown in foot traffic. Snowball, who seemed to be in a snit probably because her fun had been curtailed. The one and only time Sophie caught her going outside, the little cat took exactly four steps before turning back to the house, shaking her paws with every dainty step back.

Sophie herself wasn't sad. This gave her a chance to try a few of her activity ideas out on the guests, who seemed more than willing to participate. Even rain clouds could have silver linings.

Just not for construction, it seemed. Thankfully, Daniel's crew had finished the roofing, which meant several of them could work on the inside trim, which, apparently, usually got completed when they did the outside trim since it required the same materials and equipment. But since the rain meant working outside was off the table, they'd split things up. Anything to make progress was good in her mind.

The sudden distinct banging of a hammer on a nail happening somewhere in the house had her hands pausing on the keyboard, back going straight.

What on earth?

She pushed to her feet, and Snowball jumped down from her lap in a scowling, "you woke me up" kitty way.

"Sorry," she murmured, only half paying attention, then hurried out the door and followed the sound, which was coming from upstairs.

Except a flash of movement in the dining room caught her eye and she paused to peep inside.

Levi and Henry, another of Daniel's crew, stood with their backs to her, holding a length of Christmas garland she knew was supposed to go up all around the house over the doors. Item 121 on her checklist that Sophie planned to get to. Later. That and decorating the bare Christmas trees that had been delivered a few days ago and stood, unadorned, in their stands in each downstairs room.

She had a little more time to do that, because the annual guest tree lighting ceremony wasn't for another week.

"We can't put nails in the door," Levi was telling the younger man with the patience of age and experience. "Sophie would kill us."

"She definitely would," Sophie agreed.

Both men swung to face her with twin expressions of guilt. "Hey, Sophie," Levi said. "I hope we didn't disturb you. Daniel said he'd take it out of our paychecks if we made too much noise."

Ironic given the hammering going on, and who she suspected was behind it.

"You're fine." She offered a sincere smile. "There's a box

of adhesive hooks with the decorations. Use those to hang the garlands."

"Told you." Age went out the door as Levi dug his elbow into the younger man's side.

Sophie stuffed down a chuckle, mostly because she was still grumpy. Daniel hadn't spoken to her about doing anything inside the house today, and he darn well should have. She had games lined up in less than an hour. "Speaking of . . . where is your illustrious boss?"

Levi's eyebrows went up in a way that told her she wasn't successful in hiding her exasperation. "In the attic," he told her.

With a wave of thanks, she turned and hurried up the flights of stairs to the upper floors, then up the hidden narrow staircase that led to the attic. Sure enough, there he stood, hammering away, back to her.

She was in no mood to admire the muscles on display with each swing, or the steady confidence with which he worked. Instead she crossed her arms and cleared her throat pointedly when he was between swings.

He jerked around, then let out a sharp breath. "You scared me."

"You're working on the attic," she said. Her tone alone should be enough warning that he was already on thin ice.

He glanced around as if trying to figure out what the trick was to the question. "Yes?" The questioning lilt almost had her sniggering.

"And your guys are hanging Christmas decorations," she said next.

He opened and closed his mouth a few times. "I feel like if I agree, something bad is going to happen."

"You missed a step."

His brows lowered. "There's a broken stair that needs fixing?"

"No, a different kind of step. Something you should have

done before getting started on any of that." Her tone was one a preschool teacher might reserve for a particularly unruly toddler. "Can you think what that might be?"

A flash of irritation crossed his features, but she was still too exasperated to give him any slack.

"We didn't start until after breakfast was finished being served," he said. "So I know we aren't in Mrs. Bailey's way or disturbing sleeping guests."

"I'm glad you thought that part through, or I'd be more than merely annoyed right now." Maybe she was being too hard on him. Still, if she didn't make her point, he'd do it again. "But you still missed a very important part."

"Didn't you need these things to be done? Might as well take advantage of the weather and get to it."

"I absolutely agree."

"Then what?" If he hadn't been holding a hammer and nails, she got the impression he would've tossed up his hands.

Sophie took pity on the poor guy, softening her tone. "You should have checked with me first."

Instead of contrition, the darn man smirked. "*That's* what's got you so bothered? Jeez, Soph. I thought I'd really messed something up."

Would anyone blame her if she stomped on his foot? No. That wouldn't work. Steel-toed boots. Maybe she could take that hammer away and throw it at his thick skull. "Yes, that's what's got me so bothered."

She dropped onto one of the covered couches in a heap, giving up in the face of his confusion. Dust flew up all around her, and she coughed hard, then brushed off what landed on her.

Daniel belted out a laugh, and she couldn't help the answering chuckle, even if she was still frustrated. She must look ridiculous.

Sobering, though his lips were still twitching, he crouched

in front of her and dusted his hand across the top of her head. "That's better," he said after a minute. Then tipped his head. "I thought I was helping."

Sophie considered her words with care.

Yes, he *was* helpful, which put her in a tougher position, because she *did* appreciate it. But the way he walked all over her without even a blip of realization that he might be causing her problems was amazing. Yes, he was a friend of the family and trying to help, but *she* was in charge, and he couldn't seem to wrap his head around that. A bulldozer was more subtle.

"I appreciate the help and the thought, really I do," she said finally.

"But . . ."

"But . . . What if I had an activity planned for the guests today?"

"Do you?"

"Yes, but that's not the point."

Lips twitching in the most frustrating way, he propped his elbows on his bent knees and gave her a steady look. "What is the point?"

"The point is . . . you should have thought to check with me before beginning any work inside the house." She frowned. "Or anywhere else that's not the construction site for that matter."

"I checked the calendar."

Her irritation fizzled like wind falling out of sails, leaving them flapping and limp. He'd checked the calendar? The one she'd put up in the foyer on an easel so guests could see what times various activities were occurring. She shook her head both at herself and at him. Nice to hear that someone was using it.

"I was about to change it and had let most of our guests know during breakfast. You'd know that if you *talked* to me." Was she being unreasonable to ask that? She didn't think so. "Next time, please don't start anything without asking me first. That's all I ask."

He held up both hands in surrender. "You have my word."

Progress. "Thank you." She paused, wanting to be fair. "And thank you for the help."

Pushing to her feet, she brushed more dust off her slacks before carefully making her way down the narrow stairs, now worrying that she'd been too hard on him. After all, he *was* helping her in his own very merry Daniel kind of way. Except, this was at least the fifth time she'd asked that he check with her first if it didn't have to do with construction. The other four times had been hints, trying not to come off like a control freak. Maybe the direct approach was better with him.

"I noticed the Christmas trees are still bare." His voice stopped her halfway down the stairs.

She paused to find him leaning over from the top and watching her. "It's on my list," she said.

"I could move it to my list and get it done today. Henry and Levi won't take long with those garlands."

Her first knee-jerk reaction was to politely refuse, but Sophie stopped herself. Why did it bother her so much to accept his offers of help? Because this *was* a big help. She didn't have time and that would be one huge thing less to do.

She hadn't been like this at the hotel. The massive staff worked together as a team, sort of like Santa's elves. Each with his or her own job to do and the ability to step into other roles if required.

Maybe her Malcom episode had impacted her way more than she'd realized. She hated that he was still influencing her life, even tangentially. Only one way to fix that, try harder to be easier on the man still watching her. "That would be nice. Thank you. Although, let them know we'll be using the front living area from eleven to noon?"

"Will do. And don't mention it." The grin in his voice told

her he knew exactly how hard accepting his offer had been for her.

"What's going on at eleven?"

"Playing a game." She tried to play it cool.

Apparently, she failed. His slow smile turned her stomach into a series of knots. "You look excited."

She couldn't help perking up. At her old hotel, she hadn't got to do this kind of personal interaction. Maybe she was being silly, but she'd been looking forward to it ever since she'd come up with the idea. "I hope the guests think it's fun."

"I'm sure they will."

With a nod of thanks, and vowing to give Daniel a bit more slack, Sophie headed back down to her office, but a quick check of the time told her Giselle would be there any second, and she wanted to be done with that meeting before the game started, so she went to the front stairs instead.

"What is that racket?" an irascible voice sounded from behind her on the landing.

Mr. Muir.

Guest-friendly smile pinned in place, she walked back to his room to find him poking his head out the door.

"One of our handymen is fixing a few spots in the roof from the attic side," she explained. "He should be done shortly."

"I would hope so," the old man snapped. "Some people are trying to sleep."

Sophie, having already checked the time, kept her expression polite with more difficulty than usual. Back-to-back Daniel, Mr. Muir, and Giselle was like running a gauntlet of fire. "Lunch will be served in about two hours," she said. "He'll be done by then."

He'd better be.

Not giving Mr. Muir more chance to air his grievance, she

hurried away, only to get an earful of Giselle's voice from the foyer. "Well, then, where is she? I have a meeting and my time is limited."

"I'll go check, ma'am," poor Levi, who wasn't remotely involved with the Christmas Market, was saying.

His expression of relief as he glanced over Giselle's shoulder to see Sophie coming down the stairs reminded her of her brother's face every time he'd gotten out of homework in high school.

"I'm here," she called out, and Giselle turned a now-familiar pinched face her direction.

"I thought we agreed to meet at eleven thirty."

"It's only five after, and I had a guest to attend to," Sophie answered as serenely as possible, already reaching for a calm she was far from feeling.

Before Giselle could comment further, she stepped past her down the hall. "Let's go talk in my office."

She pulled up her chair to find Snowball curled up there, a pure puff of white with her tail curled around hiding her paws, snoring tiny little kitty snores. She hated to disturb her but had no choice, pushing her gently onto the floor. The cat took one look at Giselle and, instead of wandering away, sat herself down by Sophie's feet, watching the woman with keen interest. The same way she studied any birds that dared to land in the trees around the house.

As soon as they were settled, Giselle started in. "We need to enlarge the gazebo."

Sophie, hands on her keyboard ready to take notes, paused.

Maybe Santa is testing me this year and my present under the tree is going to be a winning lottery ticket as a reward.

She sent up a quick prayer for the patience of the saints, then gazed across the desktop, wondering how she could possibly word a response to that request in such a way that didn't give away her real opinion.

"Why?" she asked instead. As good a place to start as any.

"We have three different dance troupes coming to perform at different times throughout the Market, and that stage just isn't going to be big enough."

"Can they perform to the side of the gazebo?" she asked in what she thought was a reasonable voice.

"Where will all the shoppers and audience stand?" Giselle sniped, not rude . . . yet, but flirting dangerously with the edges of it.

Think fast or this is going to go where you don't want it to. "I—"

"Hi, Giselle," Daniel said, strolling right in as though he owned the place. "How's the Christmas Market planning going?"

The woman across the desk from her went through a miraculous transformation—from impatient frowns to the sweetest smile and fluttering lashes in less time than it took Santa to pop down a chimney. "Well, we have hit a few last-minute snags," Giselle said, pursing her lips prettily.

Given the natural downturn to Sophie's own lips, if she ever tried a move like that, her face would look like her lips got painted on upside down.

"I'm sure you'll work them out to everyone's satisfaction." Daniel's gaze darted to Sophie. She couldn't tell if he was trying to include her in the conversation or checking for the amount of time left before she lost it.

But he was underestimating her ability to deal with these kinds of situations—except when it came to him for some odd reason. She was merely thinking through all the possible solutions, discarding each as she went along. A tiny growl at her feet and his gaze dropped to find Snowball sitting there, staring at him with a feline predatorial stare.

To give the man credit, he didn't run, though he did back toward the door a careful step. For once, Snowball didn't attack. Instead, she held that steady gaze on him, tail swishing, and waited.

"While I have you here." Giselle put a hand on his arm, reclaiming his full attention. "When can we expect those decorations to go up, because I have an idea."

Another one? Terrific.

The thought popped into Sophie's head unbidden and she frowned at herself. When had she turned into the Christmas Grinch? She used to have a lot more fun, and a lot more patience, and a lot more . . . holiday spirit.

"What idea is that?" Daniel asked, pulling her out of her thoughts.

He'd come down to get the guys started on decorating the Christmas trees. That had gone over with Levi and Henry like Rudolph's nose with all the other reindeer before he saved Christmas, but they were, grumblingly, getting it over with. Which was when he'd heard Sophie's voice—the tone he was starting to realize was her most hotel manager-y—followed by Giselle's.

So he'd risked life and limb—he honestly wasn't sure which woman was scarier—and popped his head in to interrupt.

Only now he had Giselle petting him like he was Snowball, while the cat in question continued to watch him with the intensity of a polar bear stalking a baby seal. A hungry, bloodthirsty polar bear. How he wasn't all scratched up already was a minor Christmas miracle.

"So I was thinking . . . wouldn't it be adorable to make the decorations themed?" Giselle's eyes sparkled with her enthusiasm. Idly he compared how that did nothing for him, meanwhile Sophie's glares got his heart pumping.

"Themed?" Sophie parroted.

He didn't even need to look over to know that she was less than enthusiastic about the idea already.

He could go a couple different ways with how he reacted right now. Step in and choose a side to support. Which was easy enough. Giselle didn't need any more encouragement where he was concerned. Or . . . he could keep his mouth shut and let Sophie handle this, which, given the conversation they'd just had, was probably what she'd prefer.

Hard call.

For once, he made himself button his lips around helpful words and wait. Hardest thing he'd ever had to do.

"Oh yes," Giselle continued blithely on. "I was thinking along the lines of The Twelve Days of Christmas."

Daniel had to turn a snort into a cough, sliding an amused glance in Sophie's direction to find her listening with that friendly professional thing she could pull off so easily. Though he suspected a slight twitch to her lips even as she ignored him.

Where had they left off again? Oh right, the three French hens.

"Just think," Giselle said. "We could have little birds and golden rings and things in all the decorations and maybe bring in dancers for the lords a-leaping and whatnot."

"While that sounds . . . adorable," Sophie said slowly, "I'm afraid it's a little late to start on something so detailed. Perhaps next year."

Giselle waved a hand with more bling on it than the crown jewels. "I'm sure it would be simple enough to add to what we already have."

"The Webers have already selected the decorations they want for the stores," Sophie pointed out gently. "And it does have a theme, all quite Victorian."

Now she'd reverted to using the carefully kind tone of voice she reserved for guests. A tone she never used on him, allowing him to see her annoyance. Only, instead of feeling slighted, a part of him, deep down, saw that as her being more real with him than anyone else. He'd take a real but irritated Sophie any day over polite and distant.

For a flash, Giselle's features hardened in such a way that her undisputed beauty dimmed, her bright green eyes narrowing. "I'm sure the Webers' decorations are lovely, but if this is what the committee wants—"

"In that case, the committee can arrange *all* the decorations, including procurement and installation." Sophie, who might start glazing over with frost if the chill in her voice was any indication, still managed to hold on to that polite thing she did.

"There's no need to throw your weight around." The way Giselle said that, even Daniel couldn't miss the implication that Sophie didn't have any to throw around in the first place. Like she looked down on Sophie, who'd taken on all these extra things to help out people she barely knew.

He rolled his shoulders under the sudden anger that flared in his gut, along with a level of protectiveness toward Sophie that sent a jolt through him at its intensity. Probably because they were, if not partners in this mess, at least allies of a sort.

"That's not what she's doing, Giselle," he said, trying for a placating tone. Having grown up with the woman, he knew that when she didn't get her way, Giselle had a tendency to get even.

She blinked, then turned the motion into a simpering bat of her eyelashes. "Of course, I didn't mean that."

Yeah, right.

"I'm sure you wouldn't mind adding a few more items to the decorations as you're doing them. I'm happy to do all the work to find them. It would be so special . . ."

Maybe Giselle was unfamiliar with the concept of time. Did she seriously think they had enough time to procure or even make the additional items needed for her idea, let alone get them up? In the middle of construction and everything else?

"Are you sure you can squeeze this into your own schedule?" he asked, taking a page from Sophie's book and turning it around on Giselle.

That earned him a little laugh and a glance that said she appreciated his concern. "Oh, this is all I have on my plate. My parents are organizing our traditional Christmas party at the manor, and I've completed all my Christmas shopping early."

What luck for him and Sophie.

"Unfortunately, Daniel and I aren't quite so free," Sophie broke in, finally seeming to pull herself out of the silent simmering he suspected had been happening.

She moved out from behind her desk and moved to his side, slipping her hand through his arm. He wasn't sure the other woman caught the mischievous twinkle suddenly glinting in Sophie's unusual eyes, but he braced himself for whatever was coming next.

Sophie turned her wide-eyed concern on Giselle. "I mean, you wouldn't want us to disappoint Miss Tilly and the rest of the town by not being able to hold the Christmas Market at all, would you?"

"Why on earth wouldn't you hold it?" Giselle demanded.

Sophie gave her a woebegone shake of her head. "Deadlines are so tricky with the weather lately, and obviously our focus is the construction completion. I'm not even sure Daniel and his crew will be able to get the original decorations up in time."

Her wide-eyed innocence almost had him believing he couldn't get the decorations up, until he remembered that she wasn't stretching the truth. But threatening the Christmas Market? Sophie had to be bluffing. Right?

Then she pinched his arm where Giselle couldn't see, and it took everything in him not to yelp.

"Errr . . . we *are* swamped," Daniel said. Which wasn't a lie. "And the rain isn't helping. It'll be a close thing."

Giselle glanced between them, her face turning an alarming shade of red. "But the town moved the Market here because Tilly assured us the grounds would be ready. The Market is already starting later than we wanted, after Saint Nicholas Day. All the other larger towns started in November."

"Yes, of course," Sophie said. "And we will do our absolute best to stick to the schedule. However, at this late point, adding any new plans will only slow us down further. Don't you agree?"

Giselle stared at her with tight-lipped crossness.

"But since the decorations about to go up already have a Dickensian feel, how about we make that the theme. *You* could even track down a few caroling troupes who dress up in the period to wander the shops singing." Then Sophie perked up as though brilliance had just struck. "Even better, if you could find actors willing to dress up as *A Christmas Carol* characters and maybe act out parts of the story. I'm sure you'll think of something wonderful."

"Yes, well . . ." Again Giselle glanced between them. "I suppose that could work."

Sophie beamed. "Wonderful. As soon as this rain lets up, Daniel and his men will have those decorations up. You'll see. I'm sure it's going to be lovely."

When Giselle said nothing, Sophie gave a nod that seemed to cap the conversation. "Was there anything else you needed today?"

"No, I'd better go start calling around for carolers and actors." The words came out pure snipe.

Sophie waited, appearing not to notice, as Giselle gathered her things.

"I'll be back at the end of the week to see the decorations." Giselle tossed the words out like a threat.

"I'll let you know if weather delays things further," Sophie said, solemn-faced. "Oh, and I'll think about the stage sizing issue for the gazebo as well."

The gazebo had a sizing issue? He wisely kept his mouth shut.

As soon as the thud of the front door closing behind Giselle sounded, Sophie let go of his arm and stepped back. "Thanks for letting me handle that," she said, suddenly sounding weary.

He gritted his teeth around the strangest urge to wrap her up in his arms and kiss the top of her head and tell her they'd get through this.

"I would like to think that her heart is in the right place," he said in a wry voice.

Sophie gave a crack of laughter that made him want to earn even more of the sound. "Why didn't she think of these things last spring? Tilly assured me that the committee had been on board for months and that most of the details had been ironed out."

"Giselle might volunteer on committees, but I'm pretty sure she's never the one who does the actual work," he commented. "My guess is this was more her idea than the committee's."

"Maybe so." She tipped her head to the side.

They were getting along. This was novel. No scowls or debates over who was in charge. He should walk away now, while they were still on an almost pleasant roll.

"Which reminds me . . . the fencing thing. I keep meaning to tell you."

That didn't last long. "Tell me what?"

"That we'll need fencing up around the construction site. For safety purposes."

"We have yellow tape up to designate no-go areas," he said. "I was told that would be fine."

"But what if a small child wanders off?"

She did have a point there, much as he hated to admit it because it was just one more thing. "I'll look into it."

"Thanks." Her shoulders dropped visibly. Was he really that difficult to talk to?

"I will say, I'm surprised you didn't jump at Giselle's new theme." The teasing words just sort of fell out of his mouth.

He was rewarded when she chuckled. "I've been watching for calling birds everywhere I go."

Daniel grinned and tucked that nugget away for another time. "We probably *could* have put up the extra decorations."

He almost expected a frown, but after a pause, she just rolled her eyes. "Don't you start, or I'll sic Snowball on you."

He gave a small start and dropped his gaze to find the cat hadn't moved, nor had she stopped watching him. Resisting the urge to bare his teeth at the little horror, he backed out of the office. "I'd better go."

"Oh." Sophie blinked. "Of course. And I have to figure out where dance troupes can perform without it being a liability."

With a wave, he closed the door behind him, but stood there, only semi-registering the wood grain as he thought about their interactions so far today. The thing was, he'd been enjoying being on the same side as Sophie for once. They made a good team when they managed to be on the same side at least.

Temporary fencing was an added cost, one more thing coming out of the bottom line of both his budget and his time.

I curl up in the velvet-covered chair that sits in the corner of Sophie's office. The one that should be in a beam of sunlight right now, except for the darn rain. Chin resting on the tops of my paws, I close my eyes, but I can't help thinking . . .

Daniel had been nice to Sophie. Helpful even, with Jack Frost's evil twin sister. Anytime that woman comes over, Sophie ends up looking tired by the time she leaves. But the way she stared at the door after he left, I'm not sure what she's thinking.

I like Sophie. She has strange ideas about keeping me in the house, but she's a great nighttime snuggler, sneaks me treats from the kitchen, and lets me curl up on her lap while she works. I think I'll add her to my list of favorite humans, which means I'd like to see her happy.

Lukas and Emily are happy now that they've found each other. Maybe what Sophie needs is to find love.

I'll have to think about that more.

Chapter 7

———✦———

A horrible quacking noise roused Sophie from sleep with such a start that Snowball leapt to her feet, blue eyes startled and wide awake.

"What was that?" Sophie asked the cat.

The quack sounded again, directly outside her window. A dying duck maybe? One that hadn't made it south for the winter. Or . . .

She shoved the curtains aside and looked out to find Daniel, Levi, Henry, and Louis, another one of his crew, standing outside with what appeared like kazoos in their mouths. As soon as she appeared, they grinned and blew in their ear-torture devices. Loudly.

Sophie fumbled with the locks on her window for a good twenty seconds, then managed to get it up and shoved her head outside.

"Are you crazy?" she whisper-yelled.

Daniel grinned and indicated the four of them with a gallant wave. "We are four calling birds here to spread the good news."

Four calling birds. She bit her lip and bent a schoolteacher look on them. "If I was on the first floor, I'd be tempted to climb through the window and bop all four of you with those ridiculous bird callers."

Either that, or let the laughter bubbling up inside her out, and that wouldn't do at all. No need to encourage this kind of silliness.

All four men grinned, Daniel's grin maybe the biggest.

"Are you drunk?" she asked, putting a wealth of mock suspicion into her tone and squinty eyes.

Two of the others sniggered. Levi had the good sense not to.

"Just for that . . ." Daniel said. All four of them inhaled dramatically, lips poised over their bird caller thingies, prepared to make a racket all over again.

"Stop. Stop." She shook her head. "What's the good news?"

He blew out a long breath, like bagpipes suddenly deflating, but then grinned again. "We wanted to let you know that we have finished with the Christmas decorations in the shops."

Tempted as she was to take that information and whoop for joy—maybe Giselle would back off finally—Sophie didn't. "We have guests still sleeping, Daniel Aarons."

To give him credit, he did grimace, but then shrugged. "Worth waking early to see the glory of what we have completed. Come out and look."

"Later," she insisted.

The way his face fell, she felt the same as she had when she was six years old and Jimmy Dougan had called her pretty in a dress she hated and, at an age where she had no idea what to do with her embarrassment, she'd retaliated by kicking him in the shins. "I have to shower and dress, and there are a few things to do here first."

"Spoilsport," he called back. At least he'd had the sense to lower his voice. "We're going to get a later start on construction, just so you know."

Wait. Had they been up all night?

She didn't get the question out and he kept going. "Not by

too much. We have to take advantage of this." He waved at the sky.

Sure enough, sunlight was streaming through the bare trees, lighting up the crystalized dew on the ground and setting everything aglow in shades of pinks and soft blues thanks to the sunrise.

"Let's go, guys." They did a military-style about-face that might have even been practiced and, bird calls to their lips, marched away with merry, annoyingly loud tweets that thankfully faded.

Slowly, Sophie shut and locked her window, then glanced at Snowball, who sat on her bed. She was smiling before she knew it. "Four calling birds," she said. Why should that warm her up from the inside like a potbellied stove? Because he'd made her part of the celebration, maybe.

The cat darted a glance outside as though hunting for the infiltrators in the tree outside her window, and Sophie laughed, feeling easier than she had in a long time, even if they did get complaints from guests, then went to get herself ready since she was now wide awake.

She went to the dining room and scooped herself up breakfast. On the way to her office to eat it, an irascible voice sounded from the landing above her.

"What on earth was all that racket?" Mr. Muir asked.

She lifted her gaze to find his leathery face contorted in a scowl, one directed at her. She thought quickly through her options. Luckily the gentleman's window faced the other side of the house. Crossing her fingers behind her back, Sophie lied through her teeth. "Racket? I didn't hear anything?"

He snorted. "Then you must sleep like the dead, because a bunch of birds woke me up at the crack of dawn."

Containing her giggle took maximum effort. "It must've been a few late migrators getting an early start," she reasoned. Then held up her plate. "Mrs. Bailey is treating us with her world-famous cinnamon rolls this morning."

"Huh. I'm a ham and eggs man myself," came the tart reply.

Mental note to ask Mrs. Bailey for a few ham-and-egg–related breakfasts over the next week or so. "Well, these are worthy of a taste. What plans do you have this morning? Anything you're looking forward to seeing on this visit?"

Mr. Muir's expression buttoned up tight, which gave her the sudden impression that he had no intention of talking about himself. Confirmed by his next words. "We'll see. Those damn birds got my doves all flappy, so I may need to sit with them a while."

Another mental note to pay back Daniel for this. Except a twinkle of mischief and fun went with the thought, rather than irritation. Maybe she'd finally shed her Scroogeness, because her heart was lighter than it had been in . . . months probably. Even in the middle of so much work she barely had time to breathe.

"How about I bring my computer up and I'll sit with them for a while if you want to go out?"

Mr. Muir eyed her closely for a minute. "You've got better things to do today than sit with my birds."

"I'm going to be sitting around my office anyway. I can do that from anywhere."

He hesitated, expression wrinkling up in such a way she wasn't sure what he was thinking. "No need," he said.

Rather than pursue it, she nodded and waved, but got only a few steps toward her office when a "Thanks for the offer, though" floated down to her.

Knowing he couldn't see her, she didn't bother to keep her eyebrows from shooting straight up, a pleased grin pulling at the corners of her mouth. "Anytime," she called back.

Progress on all fronts.

She might have rushed through breakfast and paperwork as quickly as she could. She did want to see the progress on the decorations.

THE TWELVE DAYS OF SNOWBALL 89

Hurrying to the back door, Sophie pulled on the plain black rubber rainboots she'd invested in—which did not look at all fashionable with her festive red layered skirt and usual white blouse, but got the job done protecting her from splatters—and tromped herself over to the shops. She wanted to double-check it all before Giselle had a chance to inspect it. At least, that was the excuse she gave herself for the hustle.

Emily had been sugarcoating it when she'd called the woman particular.

Giselle had blown up over the fact that a wedding ceremony had been booked on the grounds just before the Christmas Market opened. Sophie'd silently agreed with her on that one actually, but Tilly had done the booking.

At least for the gazebo situation, she'd agreed on a less permanent solution of setting up a temporary dance floor at the far end of the shops. A brilliant solution on Sophie's part, if she patted herself on the back for a second.

The most recent was the issue of parking. The Webers had chosen to go with clearing a field toward the back of the shops, unseen from the road, but they hadn't paved it. With the numbers being predicted for the Market, Giselle wanted to try to pave the parking and enlarge it. Thinking of the time and disruption that would take, Sophie had countered with people parking in town and being bussed in. That one had required Miss Tilly calling in from the hospital to back Sophie.

Sophie hadn't won all the encounters.

Giselle had managed to convince someone in town to erect a small, temporary ice-skating rink on the grounds. The location of which was what had precipitated the need for the fencing around the site. At least Daniel was on top of that part. A special license for the sale and consumption of alcohol had also been approved. As had the layout of the temporary booths being brought in for the extra shops and activities. A layout that involved taking up more of the already small parking area.

Sophie rounded the corner and stopped so abruptly her boots skidded in the mud. Luckily, she managed to keep a shred of her dignity and didn't end up in a heap on the ground. She just couldn't help it. The decorations . . .

"Wow," she murmured.

Maybe he'd earned that calling birds stunt this morning.

Beribboned garlands of evergreen boughs hung in sweeping ropes down the storefronts, and matching wreaths decorated the old-fashioned black lanterns spaced every twenty feet down the main thoroughfare. A matching Christmas tree took pride of place, towering over the gazebo, which had also been bedecked in the garlands and bows. She could also see that the Christmas lights had been strung across the tops of the buildings and around the top of the gazebo. The place was lovely in the daylight but would be stunning at night.

The Crown Liberty had been elegantly beautiful this time of year—all golds and silvers and modern—but if she was honest, she preferred Weber Haus's style more. A traditional Christmas.

"They really did work all night," she said to herself, because no one else was standing anywhere close. A good thing, too.

He'd done it. In the middle of construction, which had been delayed even more, Daniel had managed to keep that promise. But at what cost to himself and the guys?

Guilt tumbled through her like catching an edge on her skis and landing hard in the snow before sliding down the mountain. She wished she'd known. If she'd been doing her job right, she would have checked up on them at the very least. As a decent human being, she should have been out here helping, or at least providing them something like hot chocolate.

The sound of a familiar deep voice got her feet moving.

Sure enough, Daniel, looking as fresh as newly fallen snow and not like he'd been up all night, was standing on the other side of the gazebo with a host of other people she didn't recognize. Primarily women, all laughing at what he was saying. A head taller than most of them, he stood out easily. He was, of course, in his usual work gear—jeans, flannel shirt with the sleeves rolled up, tool belt, and work boots.

Boots that had spent more time than she initially wanted sitting by the kitchen door while he "helped" with things around the house on those rainy days. Which is why most of the interior of the house was done with being decorated as well, the Christmas trees in each room and the garlands over the doorways all up. All that was left were the outside lights on the house; then all the decorating would be complete.

Not today, though. Today, after he and his crew finished work on the site, they deserved a little time off. Time they probably couldn't take, but she was going to insist. Tilly would agree with her, she didn't doubt.

Daniel threw his head back and laughed at one of the ladies with him. That same woman, who was holding a baby, made a questionable decision and handed it to Daniel while she rifled through an oversize bag hanging from the back of her stroller. Rather than hold it like a tainted football or try to hand it back, though, Daniel brought the child in close, said something she couldn't catch from so far away, then lifted the infant's shirt and blew raspberries on a round belly, eliciting squeals of delight. No doubt that beard tickled, too.

Sophie's steps slowed.

She'd already realized that she'd judged him too harshly. Standing there making a baby laugh, suddenly he transformed from pushy know-it-all into a pretty darn adorable mountain man.

Oh. My. Gosh. See him playing with a baby and you melt like Frosty the Snowman on a summer day.

Sophie straightened abruptly and rolled her neck as if that might rid her of such silly thoughts. *So what if he made a baby laugh? Get over it.*

Pasting a polite but hopefully pleasant expression to her features, she crossed to where he was standing. He happened to glance over the infant's head and spotted her. With what appeared to be practiced ease, he handed the babe back to its mother, who apparently had better maternal instincts than Sophie had given her credit for, then waved her closer.

"Sophie, I'd like you to meet Clara Schmidt, a friend from way back."

"I heard Miss Tilly hired a hotel manager for the inn," Clara said as they shook hands. "That's good. She deserves to relax a little."

"Not likely," Sophie and Daniel said at the exact same time. She ignored the smile he shot at her, still shaken by her reaction to him and the baby.

"I only got to spend time with her during my interview and my first day here, but I get the impression that Tilly Weber is a force all her own."

Clara laughed at that. "You're not wrong." Then she waved around them. "Aren't the decorations just gorgeous?" She turned a guileless brown gaze to Sophie, who flicked Daniel a glance only to look away when she found him watching her with an oddly intent light in his eyes. One that sent a nervous thrumming through her.

"Absolutely," Sophie agreed, and turned to Daniel. "I'm seriously impressed."

"It was nothing."

"You worked all night," she insisted. "That wasn't nothing."

His cheeks turned slightly rosy. Had she made him blush? Hard to tell under that beard and standing in the cold.

Clara, meanwhile, glanced back and forth between them with wide-eyed curiosity.

Unfortunately, Jannik Koch chose that moment to show up, oozing into their small circle. Blond and good looking, in a cookie-cutter sort of way, he'd gone to school with Clara and Daniel and Giselle. He'd also inherited his construction business from his father. When Daniel had started out, more than one client had seemed close to signing a contract before Koch Construction had swooped in with a lower bid.

The man immediately focused on Sophie. "You must be the new manager for Weber Haus," he said, and held out a hand.

Sophie shook it as she introduced herself, and Daniel had to keep himself from smacking Jannik's hand away from hers.

The blond man finally acknowledged Daniel. "How is the construction moving along?"

"Fine." Daniel didn't miss Sophie's speculative glance.

Jannik turned a smile her way. "I, too, am in construction."

"Oh?" she asked, not sounding all that interested.

"If you have problems with this one"—he hitched a thumb at Daniel—"let me know, and I'll get my crew out here."

"Jannik," Clara sort of gasped. "Don't be rude."

That only earned her a smirk. "Was that rude?" Jannik asked. "Sorry. I didn't mean to be. Nice to meet you, Sophie." With a wave they left him alone.

"What was that about?" Sophie asked.

Daniel shrugged. "Competing business is all."

"Oh."

When neither of them said any more about it, sure enough, a second later, the questions started coming from Clara. "So, what made you decide to leave the city to come here?" she asked Sophie.

"Clara," Daniel said with a small frown, as if he was defending Sophie's right to privacy.

"It's okay," she said to him, then turned to Clara. "I decided a change of scenery would be nice."

Only Clara grinned. "I left here after college for the same reason, but truthfully that was because Jason, my husband now . . ." She gave her baby a cuddle. "Broke my heart."

Way too close to the mark. "But you obviously worked things out," Sophie said, trying to keep the conversation focused on Clara.

The other woman beamed. "Yes, he came after me and apologized." Then she gave Sophie a speaking glance that was in itself a warning. "Should we expect any love-sick men to show up and steal you away again?"

"I sincerely hope not," was all Sophie could think by way of reply. She had no idea what she'd do if Malcom showed up here. Most of the first things to pop to mind would probably land her in jail.

Her response only had Clara cocking her head with added interest. "So, there *was* someone—"

"Good grief, Clara," Daniel muttered, looking to the skies as though he might find a muzzle up there.

"What?" she asked.

"Just because you're deliriously happy in love doesn't mean every single person you meet has to be, too."

Rather than be offended, the other woman snorted. "You're just punchy because Giselle Becker has been sniffing around."

Sophie laughed. She couldn't help herself.

He shot both of them a glare. "I'd better get to work."

"I'll go with you," Sophie said. "Nice to meet you, Clara."

"We should meet for lunch sometime," Clara called after her.

An offer of friendship.

One she could have easily breezed over, agreeing that would be nice "sometime." But maybe it was beyond time to start acting like she'd be here longer than a summer camp holiday. Sophie paused and returned to the waiting mother and exchanged cell phone numbers with her. "Thanks," she said. "See you later."

Then she hurried after Daniel, who hadn't waited, probably not realizing she wanted to go with him. She fell into step beside him and he tossed her a surprised glance. "Need something construction related?"

"Actually, I wanted to thank your crew in person for the hard work and send them home for a well-earned break."

He stumbled to a halt. "Sorry, what?"

She glanced around, confused. "What?"

"Who's sending *my* men home?" he asked.

Oh, heck. Now look who was stepping on toes and ruining the clearly tenuous connection she'd thought they'd built. Time to backpedal quickly. "You, of course. But I thought I'd offer it as a thank-you for this." She waved back toward the shops.

"*I'll* make that call," he insisted.

She held up both hands. "Of course. Just a thought."

After a long pause, he gave an abrupt nod and continued on. Only she didn't follow. Maybe she should just let it go. He could pass on her thanks.

He paused and turned, jaw still hard, but with raised eyebrows. "Come on. They'll appreciate the thanks bit."

Sophie stayed quiet the rest of the walk to the new wing. She paused at the table at the front of the building to grab a hard hat, adjusting the inside strap thingy first as she'd seen him do, then hurried after Daniel through the open building only to run right into his back with a muffled *oomph*.

"Ouch," she grumbled. "Brick walls have more give than you."

When he didn't respond, she peered around him only to gasp. Something had run through the area—if she didn't know better, she would have guessed maybe a miniature tornado or a stampede of reindeer. The equipment was haphazardly scattered across the ground, many with chunks clearly broken off, and a whole stack of siding had been broken into pieces.

"What in the world?" The exclamation popped out of her mouth.

"Don't say a word about fencing," he shot at her through clenched teeth.

"I wasn't going to," she insisted as she turned to Daniel.

But she stopped anything else she might have said as she got a good look at his expression. Anger, of course. But under that she got the impression that he was . . . hurt.

Heaven knew what it would take to replace the material, let alone any equipment that might have sustained permanent damage, which only set his schedule back further.

He stood there, staring at the scene, clenching and unclenching his fists. Maybe if she hadn't messed up their friendlier footing just a second ago, she might've tried to make him feel better. She had the strangest urge to curl her hand into his and lend him a bit of solidarity. She knew that kind of alone all too well.

"And if you say one word about the Christmas deadline—"

"Not at all," she said, trying to ignore the twinge of hurt that he thought she was that kind of person. The kind who might try to twist the knife.

The hell with it. She stepped closer and slipped her hand into his, tension sort of easing out of her when he didn't jerk away from her touch. Instead, he curled his work-roughed fingers around hers.

"Where are the rest of the guys?" she asked when he didn't say anything.

"They should be here soon."

"Has this happened before?" she asked next.

He gave a nod. A single, sharp move that told her more than words might have. "Not at this site, though."

"Do you know who?"

His hand twitched in hers and he looked down, almost seeming surprised to find their fingers linked. Letting go, which she tried not to take as a rejection, he ran his hand through his hair. "My best guess is another contractor who resents a new business in town."

Made sense. Sophie'd been tempted to take a baseball bat to Malcom's office before she left out of sheer resentment. Except Daniel's work more than spoke for the fact that he had earned this job. Malcom had not.

"They must've done it while we were decorating last night," he said. "I can't believe we didn't hear or see anything." The self-blame lay thick over the words.

"Will insurance take care of anything you need to replace?"

He nodded again.

Sophie hadn't known Daniel long, but this closed-off reaction, like he'd shut down his emotions, wasn't good for him. Why some part of her suddenly felt responsible for helping him snap out of it she had no idea. Before she could process the emotion, her mouth was already open and words were coming out.

"Do I need to make a few calls?" she asked next.

That was only her opening salvo, using their usual conflict to poke at him. She didn't like seeing him so much in his head.

Her words were enough to get him to turn away from the wreckage and face her, eyes narrowed, arms crossed. "Of course not," he said. "I can handle this."

The slump to his shoulders disappeared in that moment and the glitter in his eyes told her he'd returned to fighting form. Good. She could deal with him better like this.

"*There's* the Daniel I know." She flashed him a grin and he cut himself off with a huffed laugh. He searched her expression, and the irritation suddenly drained out of him, his arms dropping to his sides.

"You totally Jedi mind-tricked me."

The construction-owning mountain man had an inner geek? She wasn't sure if she should let herself like that about him. She was starting to like too much about him. The last thing she needed was a man. Or a distraction. He counted as both.

"Are you ready to snap out of it and get to work?" she asked.

"I'm ready to throw one of those bricks at you."

"Then call me Master Yoda."

He snorted.

"What the hell is going on out here?" Levi's gruff voice sounded behind her, interrupting whatever Daniel was going to say.

He stopped beside them, the other guys filing out of the building behind him, all staring around with a range of emotions—mostly anger—crossing their scruffy, work-worn faces.

"Again?" Levi asked, directing the question to Daniel, who said nothing.

She'd have to ask him about that other incident, but now was not the time. "I know this only adds to your workload," she said. "I'll get out of your hair. But dinner on me tonight after you're done?"

He couldn't get mad at her for that offer, could he? She'd make sure she arranged it on his timetable.

Daniel didn't say anything as she backed toward the door leading away from him. Something in his gaze sent the oddest fluttering sensation through her belly. Like earlier when they'd been with Clara and the baby, or . . .

She didn't want to give in to the fluttering or think about what that look meant. Getting through these unusually tough weeks was what needed her focus. Six weeks since her life imploded and she'd walked out on her job and into a new mess, and she was damned if she wasn't going to make this work. Daniel didn't need her attention, just his work and the impact of that to her own.

She waved a hand at the mess, well aware she was babbling now. "Both as a thank-you for your decorating work last night and maybe to make up a little for . . ."

Levi glanced between them. "That'd be real nice," he finally said. "We'll be there."

She shot him a grateful smile, then, driven by Daniel's indecipherable stare and her bewildering reaction, she turned and tried not to appear as though she was hurrying away.

Even if she was.

The coincidence was just too much to take. Jannik showing up like that the same day Daniel had been vandalized. He had to have been there to gloat.

Exhaustion slowed Daniel's movements. That and the rapidly dropping temperature as the day had gone on. This must be what hypothermia felt like, turning his muscles sluggish and his mind stuffed with cotton. Still, he pushed through it as he worked beside his men to put away all their equipment for the night. After two endless days of work, of course he was physically tired, but, if he was honest, mostly he was tired from the mental hoops of figuring out how to protect his job site and his crew.

He'd never had to before. This was a small, quiet town with very little crime. Everyone trusted everyone else. Heck, he'd bet most everyone didn't even bother to lock their doors at night. He knew for certain the Webers didn't, leaving the inn open for guests to come and go.

If Jannik was responsible, hopefully he wouldn't risk trying it again. He had to know Daniel would set things up so he'd be caught. If, however, this was the work of bored teenagers, he'd find that out, too.

The one other time this had happened, last spring, he'd brushed it off as stupid kids messing around. But two job sites being vandalized was too coincidental . . . he just couldn't risk it.

They put as much of the equipment and materials as they could inside the small moving truck he'd managed to rent over the lunch break, but a lot didn't fit. The rest remained inside the building, sheltered from the elements, but protecting all of that would be hard to do with no doors or windows yet installed, giving any intruders multiple points to enter and exit. So many ways to do more damage. Tonight he'd stay here—camping was nothing new to him, though it would be as cold as the North Pole with a cold front blowing in. Tomorrow, he'd work on setting up a security guard and fencing around the job site.

He dragged a weary hand over his eyes.

Levi clapped him on the shoulder. "At least we've got a hot meal waiting for us."

Right. Sophie.

He hadn't let himself think about how she'd needled him out of the foul mood that had struck with the force of a thunderbolt the second he'd seen the destruction. Had that been her trying to help him? Or payback for the kiss he wouldn't apologize for? Or maybe for the calling birds wake-up call this morning?

Although she'd sent Mrs. Bailey over with a rolling cart sporting carafes of coffee and hot chocolate not long after she'd left them, so he honestly had no idea what was going through her head.

As he followed the guys through the now-closed shops to the back door to the kitchen, he wasn't sure if he should thank her for snapping him out of it . . . or get a little payback himself. The strings of white lights set a glow around the shops, and all of them slowed their steps to appreciate the view. He had to admit, the place looked fantastic.

At least he'd gotten this much right. And completed.

One less thing on his never-ending list of things to get done. No more distractions, that was for sure. He couldn't afford any. People were relying on him to get this done. Usually, he ate up being depended on like that. But tonight . . . Tonight he just wanted to go to bed and wake up after the New Year had come and gone. Then, hopefully, Pete would be better, and Christmas would be over, and the construction would be complete, and he'd get the contract with George Becker for the next big thing.

He wasn't quite sure Santa had that kind of miracle up his red sleeves, though.

Rather than have all of them tromping through the house, Daniel opened the door but stayed on the top step. A peek inside found Sophie sitting alone at the small kitchen table, working away on that tablet of hers that she didn't seem to go anywhere without. Dark smudges under her eyes—ones that hadn't been there the first day they'd met—told him the strain she was under, and his first instinct was to offer more help. Only he couldn't. He was as snowed under as she was after today's latest setback.

The scent of something meaty, and he hoped filling, smacked right into his grumbling stomach, which gave an extra appreciative gurgle.

The door creaked as he leaned in farther, and Sophie lifted her head. "I was about to come out there and drag you boys away," she said with a tired grin.

"We had a lot of work." He gave an inner wince because that had come out more snarl than comment, and Sophie's smile dimmed.

"Of course," she said. "Well, come in. Everything's all ready for you."

Taking his boots off, he left them outside by the steps, then went inside, his men copying the action until all of them crowded into the space, watching Sophie flit back and forth. She went from the fridge pulling out large bowls of pasta salad and fruit salad, to the stove to pull out several loaves of bread and something that appeared to be a vegetable casserole.

He couldn't have peeled his gaze away from her if he wanted to. And he didn't want to. She looked so . . . different. Very un-Sophie-like. For the first time since he'd met her, she was wearing jeans that looked soft as butter and lovingly clung to her figure, and a sweatshirt with the neck cut out 80s-style, slipping off one shoulder. Not to mention no shoes, her bare feet with the cutest toes ever, peeping out from the hem of her jeans. She'd also left her hair down. Much longer than he'd guessed, hanging to the middle of her back in soft waves.

This Sophie—rumpled and easy—he might not be able to resist kissing again.

And hadn't he just been thinking that any and all distractions from his goals needed to be put aside? Sophie definitely counted as a distraction.

"Reel your tongue back in, boss," Levi teased in a low voice that thankfully she didn't seem to catch.

Daniel's only acknowledgment was a grunt. "Can we help?" he asked.

"Nope," she said. "I've got it." Like she did with everything.

She placed all the food between the stacks of plates, bowls, and utensils already on the large butcher-block table in the center of the kitchen. "There's beef stew on the stovetop." She waved a hand. "Everything else is here. Help yourselves."

With a hungry groan, his men fell on the food, ladling hunks onto their plates and into their bowls. Sophie had left the door to the dining room open, shooing a few of them in there; others sat at the stools at the center table, and some took seats at the smaller kitchen table.

Sophie, herself, didn't get anything to eat and refused to sit, even when several different guys offered her their seats. "I already ate," she said, waving them away. "And I feel like I've been sitting all day."

He found himself leaning against the counter beside her, bowl in his hand, plate with everything else on the counter behind him, suddenly feeling more human than he had all day.

"This is great," he said. "Thank Mrs. Bailey for us."

Sophie paused, so quickly he almost didn't catch it. "Sure."

But he *had* caught it. Daniel frowned, glancing around the room at the food she'd laid out. It certainly smelled and tasted like Mrs. Bailey would have cooked it, but . . . "Did *you* make the food tonight?" he asked softly.

Instead of answering him, she cleared her throat and raised her voice. "I should have brought you guys something last night when you were working on the decorations in the shops. They look incredible, by the way. Thank you."

Several of his men mumbled their appreciation, the others lifting a glass around their chewing, and Sophie settled beside him against the counter.

He opened his mouth to ask again, but she beat him to it. "Were you able to get much done today beyond cleaning up?" she asked.

No expectation in her eyes, just asking the question.

He blew out a breath of pent-up worry. "We got at least a half day in," he said.

Her wince didn't contain judgment . . . more like understanding. "You should take tomorrow off," she said.

Daniel was shaking his head before she finished. "Can't. It's supposed to be another sunny day, and we've had enough rainy days off."

"But you've worked so hard the last few days."

"It'll all come out in the wash. Don't worry."

"But—"

"Sophie." He tried to say it softly but knew by the way she bit her lip that it had come out more as a bark. With a determined effort, he tempered his tone. "Trust me to know what I can do and what my men can do. Okay?"

After a moment, she reached over and squeezed his arm. "Fair enough."

Levi's chair scraped across the floor as his foreman got up

to return to the stove for seconds. "Best stew I ever tasted," he said.

"I'm pretty sure we have Sophie to thank for the food," Daniel said. "Isn't that right, Yoda?" He turned to find her wrinkling her nose at him in consternation with color rising into her cheeks.

"My wife would love this recipe," Louis piped up from the dining room.

That got her to quit as she arranged her face into a kind smile. "I'm happy to write it down for you," she said.

Which elicited a round of "me too" requests from most of the other guys and had Sophie laughing. "I'll email it to Daniel, and he can send it to you, in that case."

"Where'd you learn to cook like this in the city?" Levi asked.

"She's no city girl, the way she handled those chickens," Henry said around a huge bite, his words garbled.

"Actually . . ." Sophie said. "One of my favorite things to do in the city was to go to pop-up cooking lessons. Chefs from all over would open their kitchen to a limited group and show them how to make a dish."

The others all nodded, but Daniel leaned down to murmur softly. "You didn't answer the question about the chickens or if you ever lived outside the city."

She raised her eyebrows. "That was a question?"

He shoulder-bumped her softly, not pushing it. Sophie was clearly a private person who didn't like to talk about herself. No matter how much he wanted to know more.

"Actually," she said suddenly, voice lowered so only he could hear, "I grew up on a dairy farm."

"That wasn't so hard," he teased.

"You assumed city girl," she answered. "It was sort of fun to watch you be so wrong."

First sharing, now teasing—yep, definitely a distraction.

"You didn't need to go to all this trouble," he said under the general talk the guys fell into.

"I felt bad, not thinking to offer something last night."

"*I* signed us up for the decorations," he said. "You didn't, and we will get paid for the labor."

"Still . . ." She shrugged. "I felt guilty that they were up so late and I didn't help."

Daniel paused, giving her a closer look, noting the color in her cheeks. Huh. Turned out Sophie Heidt was a bit of a softie. Somehow, he wasn't remotely surprised by that fact.

Not wanting to embarrass her more, he sought around in his head for a change of topic. "Where's the devil cat tonight?"

I stare at Sophie's door, which is locked. I know because I already tried my trick of jumping up to hang on the handle until it opened. But I'd just slid right off. In the meantime, I can hear the people talking downstairs. Daniel, in particular.

Sophie apologized before she locked me in here earlier, saying something about not trusting me to stay away from Daniel.

My tail swishes once more before I finally lie down, resting my chin on my paws, to watch the door. Sophie and I are going to have to have a talk.

No one locks Snowball in a bedroom.

Chapter 8

Standing in the kitchen surrounded by Daniel and his entire construction crew should not have any effect on her ability to breathe. Try telling that to her lungs, which, for some odd reason, decided that they wanted to see if she could survive on less oxygen, tightening up, like squeezing the air out of a plastic baggie before you sealed it up.

The sensation only got worse as the guys thanked her and started leaving out the back, headed to their cars, while Daniel stayed behind.

"I'll help you with the dishes," was all he said.

He proceeded to go to the sink and start rinsing off plates and loading them into the dishwasher which, thankfully, Mrs. Bailey had emptied before she'd gone home. Sophie made a mental note to set an alarm to get up and empty it after it had finished running so the kind cook didn't have to worry about it in the morning.

Something about Daniel standing there, broad shouldered, doing something so domestic with the ease of obvious practice, struck her as . . . comfortable. As though they did this all the time.

Shaking off the dangerous sensation—dangerous because Malcom wasn't all that long ago and as much as she adored Weber Haus, this wasn't where her career would stop—she started collecting the leftovers and putting the food into smaller containers and away in the fridge.

"So . . ." she said, scraping her useless brain for any kind of topic that might be neutral ground. Silence never did sit well with her. "Did you always want to do construction?"

Then made a face at the bowl of limp leftover salad she was dumping into the waste bin. Probably not the best topic to hit on given the pressure and the deadlines.

For once, he didn't make a thing of it. "From the first toy construction set my parents got me."

That was cute.

Nope, she hastily corrected in her head. *Not cute*. Even Malcom had a cute side to him. Like a fluffy snow-topped mountain that decided to be an avalanche.

"I loved working with wood and started building furniture and then worked summers helping frame and roof houses. I got a degree in construction engineering, then started my own business."

Just like me. Single-minded, her mother called her. She glanced over her shoulder, eyeing Daniel more closely. Maybe he was the same.

"I bet that's a lot harder than you're making it sound," she murmured, turning back to her task and eyeing the bowl of what was left of the fruit. Was it worth keeping, or should she take it over to the petting zoo animals tomorrow? Definitely the animals. She dumped the contents into a baggie and moved on to the stove.

"The business side wasn't easy," Daniel admitted. "I had a hard time getting a loan right out of school, so I started smaller than I wanted, mostly general contracting work and handyman stuff."

She was struggling to lift the massive stew pot and not drop it when a pair of strong arms came around her.

"I'll tip, you use the ladle to scrape it out," Daniel said, his breath stirring her hair, which she'd left down for once.

The last bit of air puffed out of her, but she managed to hold herself away from him, mostly, while at the same time doing what he'd said. When she finished, he put the pot back down on the stovetop but didn't let go of it, trapping her between his arms, her back to his chest.

"See," he murmured. "Those muscles you secretly admire so much come in handy every once in a while."

If she weren't trying so hard to not lean into him, she might've laughed at that. Instead, she faked irritation that, in truth, wasn't remotely readily available to her, and gave a dramatic roll to her eyes while elbowing him away. "The last guy I dated didn't have many muscles, but he seemed to get along just fine," she said.

Then clamped her lips shut, wishing she could scoop those words back into her mouth and swallow them whole. Only now that the comparison was in her head, she couldn't help but note the differences between Malcom and Daniel.

"Is that so?" he asked, curiosity rife in his voice.

She wrinkled her nose at him, refusing to keep that topic open.

Two men couldn't be more opposite.

Malcom was the masculine version of pretty and all charm. He could keep a bee from stinging him with that smile of his. That or blind them with his brilliant white teeth. He was the kind of handsome that women's gazes, and some men's, had followed anytime they were out together. She'd been proud to be on his arm, to stare down those covetous others with a proprietorial glance.

But Daniel . . . Daniel was something else. Bigger, brawnier than Malcom. Rougher, definitely, though she suspected that beard didn't hide a soft jawline. More like a chiseled face that would elicit its own kind of appreciation from the opposite sex. And hands that were callused but capable.

Malcom was fool's gold, all polish and veneer on the outside, but nothing more than a lump of iron sulfide on the inside, whose only use seemed to be to blow things up.

If Malcom was fool's gold, then Daniel was the real thing. She mentally blinked at her thoughts.

Wait? Did I just compare Daniel Aarons to gold?

In her head, she practically stumbled over herself to walk that back. In comparison with Malcom, Daniel definitely came off the better man. Not hard to do. That was all.

"So, you had to start small?" she prompted, trying to get them back on track.

"Yes, a few friends encouraged me to try crowdsourcing to get started, but I didn't feel comfortable with that idea."

"What about it? Having to rely on others?" That totally fit the Daniel she'd been interacting with since she got here. The "I can do it better than you" guy who seemed to think everyone else needed his help.

And okay, sometimes they did. She did.

A clunk of metal on granite and she turned to find him with a hand fisted on his hip, made slightly incongruous by the yellow rubber glove now leaving a wet, sudsy mark on his jeans. "Is that really what you think? That I'm that guy who shoves in and makes everyone do things his way?"

"No!" she hurried to assure him. Only honesty had her wrinkling her nose.

Daniel narrowed his eyes, and she spun away to hide her expression from him.

"You *do* think that." The incredulity in his voice might've made her laugh if she weren't worried about hurting his feelings.

A quick peek over her shoulder had her mashing her lips together in an adorable expression somewhere between disgruntled, shocked, and reluctantly amused.

"Only at first," she assured him, because he'd know she was lying if she waffled now. "And I was probably oversensitive to it because of Malcom."

Now why on earth had she let that pop out?

"Malcom?" He paused, eyeing her intently. "So that's his name."

She turned fully to face him, leaning against the countertop, arms crossed.

"So . . ." he said when she didn't speak. "This is the not helpful guy, right?"

Not long ago, yesterday even, she would've cut this conversation off, not wanting to share the most humiliating episode of her life. Only . . . maybe it was the coziness of the kitchen and doing dishes together, or the fact that he'd opened up to her a bit already.

"He took my dream job."

Daniel moved closer, to lean against the counter beside her, feet crossed at the ankles. "How'd he do that?"

At his prompting, the story just sort of poured out of her. "You know how in school the aptitude counselor talks to you about careers that match your interests and talents and whatever?"

He nodded.

"Well, mine told me I was most well suited to a job in the hospitality industry or possibly nursing." Positions that involved interacting with many people because Sophie loved people.

"You chose hospitality." By his expression, he seemed genuinely interested.

Not even her family had listened so intently, not that she'd shared a lot of the details with them. Sophie shrugged. "I have a small thing about blood that involves fainting at the sight of it."

His lips twitched. "I can see how that would be a problem."

She'd crossed nursing off the list and moved on to the other. "Anyway, after talking to her I went home and searched the term 'hospitality' and found degrees in hotel management, one of which just happened to feature a picture of the Crown

Liberty, one of the oldest and most beautiful and historic hotels in the country."

"Is that where you worked?"

She nodded. "I fell in love with it on sight. We even took a few family vacations to stay there."

Probably for the first time since everything happened, the thought of the hotel made her smile. Daniel's gaze dropped to her lips, and an answering warmth fizzed through her veins. She might even have been tempted to do something about it, except he pulled his gaze up. "So you always wanted to work there."

Right. Her story. "I was thirteen. I sat down and drew up every step I'd have to take to become the manager of *that* hotel."

"You and your lists," he teased with a twinkle in his eyes. "Not the owner, though?"

She huffed a laugh. "No, I'm a realist." Were his eyes always that bright? The golds and greens glinted in the depths of the browns.

"So what happened? Why aren't you there?"

"I worked my tail off first to get in as an employee at the Crown Liberty, and then to climb the ladder. I'd been waiting a few years for a manager position to become available, and it was mine. I had earned it . . ."

Suddenly she realized that the worst of the bitterness surrounding this episode had dulled. Maybe time and the distraction of all the work here had helped. Admitting that the man in front of her was part of that . . . she couldn't go there yet.

"Then the Malcom guy happened?" he asked.

She cleared her throat. "He's the owner's son. Except I met him through the hotel, but he never told me that part." And somehow it hadn't come up with anyone else, either. "We worked closely together, and I shared all my ideas for the hotel. Then he passed them off as his own and took the position I'd been aiming for . . ."

"Since you were thirteen years old."

If she hadn't known better, she would've sworn Daniel was angry, though his expression didn't change.

She shrugged. "More fool me."

He gave a hard shake of his head. "You're not a fool, Sophie."

"Yes, well . . . I quit and started fresh here."

"Determined to prove yourself capable on your own and not let some man take credit for your work," he murmured, more to himself than her.

"Something like that."

He searched her gaze for a long moment, and she had no idea what was going on in his head. "So that's why you didn't want me around?"

She hesitated. Partly, but his brand of help had taken some getting used to. "Maybe so. Even if you did come across as a know-it-all determined to watch my every move and make sure that not only did I not mess with your situation, but I didn't mess up anything here, either."

"That doesn't sound like me at all." He grinned and she grinned back.

Just like that, the tension of the last months, and her wanting to prove herself in her new role, and everything else sort of melted away. The problems were still there, but the boulder of doubt and worry growing like moss in her stomach had been rolled away.

"Thanks for telling me." Daniel shoulder-bumped her, in a pals kind of way, then moved back to the sink. "I'd better get this finished."

"I can do it. You've got to be tired."

"I'm almost done."

Rather than argue, she picked up the bowl he'd discarded and dried it with a towel.

"*You've* clearly been successful with your dream," she

tried after a long stretch of silence. "Though you said it started slowly. I guess a girl didn't come along to derail you."

"Not yet," she thought he muttered, but wasn't sure.

He set another bowl to the side. "Honestly, I'm still building a client list. I started with a smaller crew than this, a few of the guys I'd worked with before. Mostly little jobs to begin with. A lot of fixing things or helping to upgrade homes, then my parents wanted to retire and build a home on land they'd purchased years before. They hired us. What I did there brought in more jobs by word of mouth."

She couldn't mistake the note in his voice. The pride. As if he was saying without words that he'd earned the business he'd built with quality work. Maybe not as fast as he wanted, but he'd considered that way the only right way. Which she was sure it had been, from his point of view.

"Then you got the shops remodel and now the hotel extensions, which must have been great for business."

"Thanks to the Webers, yes."

Sophie couldn't contain her small frown at that, Malcom's perfect-toothed smile flashing in her mind. It really was all about who you knew. "Do you feel guilty getting the job because of your personal relationship with them?"

Sophie dropped what she was doing and clapped her hands over her mouth. No matter what, Daniel hadn't deserved that. "Don't answer that. It was . . ." What? How did she justify being so horribly rude?

Silence greeted the question and she lowered her hands and turned to find him scrubbing at the pot with a little extra oomph and shoulders so stiff he could've turned into a nutcracker before her eyes. He finished the pot, placed it quietly on the dishtowel he'd spread out on the countertop, then turned to face her. "I'm not your ex."

Even when they'd first met, she'd never heard that hard voice from him. She'd really messed up. "I know you're not."

"Thanks for that, at least." Daniel shook his head and sent her a wry grin that didn't come close to his eyes. "Good thing you didn't say yes to my marriage proposal when the chickens got loose, I guess."

The words were so not what she was expecting that she snapped her mouth closed. She honestly couldn't untangle her emotions or her thoughts at this point.

"It's been a long couple of days," he said. And suddenly he looked tired, shoulders slumped slightly and shadows under his eyes. "I'll see you tomorrow."

Before she could say anything, he walked out of the kitchen. She could see his shadow as he put his boots back on outside, then left.

Sophie blew out a hard breath, only it didn't rid her of any of the tension coiling through her muscles. She felt like she'd stolen Christmas.

"Good job, Sophie Heidt," she muttered to the empty and now-clean kitchen.

Not her best moment. One that would require a bit of groveling next time she saw him. Maybe a lot of groveling.

Daniel stomped his way to his truck where he'd left it close to the site. When he'd gone out to get the rental truck for temporary storage, he'd also picked up a tent and sleeping bag from his house, along with a few odds and ends to make camping on-site doable. Despite the exhaustion dragging at him, the built-up tension from the way his conversation with Sophie ended had left him on edge. Like a soda bottle shaken up but the lid remaining on. He'd probably need to bleed off that energy before he could call it a day.

At least I know why Sophie doesn't want me around. She sees me in the same light as her ex.

Daniel put all that extra energy into carting the gear to the site and setting everything up. For extra warmth, he started a small fire, and though he was tired as Santa's reindeer after an entire night flying around the globe, he still couldn't turn off his mind enough to go to sleep.

All while trying to figure out why Sophie's words were bothering him so much. In general, he didn't care what others believed about him. He had family and friends who loved him, a crew he'd handpicked whom he enjoyed working with every day, and a business he was proud of. Even in high school, he hadn't been that kid who needed peer approval, happy to do whatever made him personally happy.

The thing was . . . he genuinely liked Sophie.

Sure, she'd been prickly with him at first, and still had the ability to derail his project. In addition to the covered walks, she'd also questioned access points to the building and paint colors and even the plan for the elevators, all of which she'd seemed to drop, but still . . . trouble. Plus, he'd bet that she still didn't want him checking up on her.

But she was one of those rare truly good-hearted people. With everyone else at least.

He'd seen it in the way she was kind to the guests, hardworking, and the type of person who stepped up when others needed her. No matter her personal connection to them or not. She could have told Miss Tilly that all she was willing to do was manage the inn, which was all she was contracted to do, but she hadn't done that.

No doubt she hadn't told him all the gory details of what happened with the guy who stole her job, but since they'd been dating, then probably her heart was involved. That didn't make it fair for her to paint Daniel with the same brush, but at the same time, he got it.

"What on earth do you think you're doing?" Sophie's voice snapped through the cold darkness.

Daniel jumped but didn't get up from the camping chair he'd dropped into beside the fire as she moved into the circle of light cast by the flickering flames he'd been staring moodily into. Which wasn't him. This woman, in a short amount of time, had sure managed to twist him up.

"Until I can arrange a better solution," he said in his most reasonable, least bossy voice, "someone needs to be here to keep an eye on things."

She crossed her arms trying to contain a visible hard shiver, and part of him wanted to offer a blanket but reminded himself she wouldn't appreciate that. She'd leave in a minute or two anyway.

He eyed her closely. "How'd you know anyway?"

"I saw the light of the fire from my window."

"Oh. Sorry."

"It's freezing," she said. "You can't stay out here."

"I have a sleeping bag rated for the Arctic in winter." Only a small exaggeration. "I'll be fine."

"But you won't get very good sleep."

"I'll be fine," he repeated instead.

She breathed through her nose like this was a personal affront to her. "I thought you installed cameras today?"

He had, but who had told her about it? Her mouth twisted in what might have been a smirk if her teeth weren't starting to chatter audibly. She hunkered over, arms crossed to try to hold in her body heat.

"I did, and my phone is set to wake me up if the cameras catch any movement. But my house is too far away to get here to stop anything. Same thing with the police in town."

"So you're going to . . . what? Fight them if they show up again?"

He flicked a glance at his tent, where he'd stored his favorite baseball bat, but decided not to mention that. "I figured my presence would be enough of a deterrent. It's only for a day or two until I can get fencing up around the place and possibly arrange some sort of guard."

An expense he hadn't budgeted, but it wouldn't be for long. Just until they wrapped things up.

"What if you stayed in the house?" she asked.

A ripple of surprise had him peering at her face more closely. There'd been no inflection in her voice, and her expression gave him no clue what she really thought about that offer. "I wouldn't want to be a burden," he said slowly.

That earned him an adorable puckered frown that reminded him of Snowball in a funny way. If he didn't know better, he'd say Sophie actually cared.

"You didn't cause other people to be vandals," she said. "Besides . . . I would get in trouble if you got sick from exposure, got into a fight, or got injured because you were too tired to work safely. As manager, I'm ultimately responsible for those on this property. Insurance is a nightmare for those types of things. Not to mention possible lawsuits."

That was it? She'd be liable, essentially. "You think I'd sue Miss Tilly?"

Sophie winced. "Of course not. I—" She cut herself off and shook her head. "You can stay in Lukas's room until you figure this out. I'm sure he won't mind."

Daniel held in a grunt of doubt at that. While he and Lukas were on good footing now, it had taken most of the year to make the man believe that Daniel wasn't still interested in Emily.

Sophie spread her hands wide in appeal. "You can sleep in a nice, warm bed and still be close enough if your warning system lights up. Win-win."

No matter her personal motivation, that *was* a heck of a lot better than the camping idea.

"Fair enough," he said. With a groan, he levered himself off the ground, his bones protesting after having frozen in place in that position.

Dumping the jug of water he had for brushing his teeth and whatnot on the fire, he then kicked dirt over the embers. Sophie was still standing there instead of running back to her own nice, warm bed.

"Can I help with anything?" she asked.

"No, I'll leave this up." He waved at the tent. "Take it down in the morning. I just need this." He reached inside and grabbed his toiletries bag and his cell phone, wallet, and keys. "Let's go."

They were both quiet all the way back to the house. It wasn't until they got to the back door and Sophie took off her rubber boots that he realized she'd been out there in fairly thin pajamas, the pants tucked inside the boots and the top covered with her jacket. Not a very warm one.

"You're going to get pneumonia in those kinds of clothes, Sophie."

As soon as the words were out of his mouth, the tone he'd used had him cringing. Maybe he *did* sound like a bossy know-it-all. He'd honestly thought she'd been joking, but maybe she hadn't. Did he do that all the time?

Sophie, though, didn't turn an irritated frown his way. All she said was, "I know. I already ordered warmer clothes."

"Ordered?" he asked, following her inside. "Why not go shopping?" Didn't all women love to shop?

"No time," she said. "I'll do that when the Webers are back."

Had she even made it off the property since arriving? He hadn't thought of that. Granted, work had kept him occupied all hours, but even he had managed to have a night at his favorite bar with friends.

He glanced at her face, wondering if she was lonely. New to town and never leaving the Weber Haus property. Maybe he should ask her to dinner—

Brilliant idea, Aarons. When you're both beyond busy and can't afford any distractions. He dropped the thought like a hot potato.

Together, they padded softly up the dark back stairs, going carefully because she hadn't wanted to turn on any lights in case it disturbed guests. They stopped at the same time, outside a door. She pointed at it. "This is Lukas's room."

"I know."

She glanced away, took a step farther down the hall, then paused and stepped closer. Tipping her head back to look him directly in the eyes, she opened her mouth, then paused as if gathering her words.

"I want to apologize," she said finally, the words softer than any she'd used with him since they'd met. "I viewed you through the lens of my own history and problems and unfairly judged you because of it. You would never do what Malcom did to me."

Daniel had no idea what to say to that. Because he *had* used his connections to get this job. No arguing with that. It hadn't set well at the time, which was probably why he'd reacted the way he had.

But, more than that, what if she was right about his tendency to take over? He'd heard his own tone of voice only a few minutes ago. "It's okay. I get it actually."

"Really?" She searched his gaze as though she didn't quite believe him.

"Sure. Heartbreak can lead to all sorts of crazy. Liesa Hiddleston broke my heart in high school and I never could eat jelly donuts again after that."

Her eyes lightened in color, sparkling at him in the dim hallway as a small smile tugged at her mouth. "Jelly donuts?"

"Yeah." He heaved a dramatic sigh. "It was our thing."

Sophie bit her lip, which only made him want to pull that real smile from her. The one that lit her up from the inside.

Before he could think of something to say, she went up on tiptoe, bracing herself with her hands on his arms, and kissed his cheek.

Was it just his imagination, or did she linger? Sinking back to her feet slowly, eyes on his, the air between them turning . . . heavy. Electric.

Maybe he was more tired than he'd thought.

Because he was fairly sure kissing him for real was the last thought on her mind, and it should be the last on his. "What was that for?" And why was his voice coming out lower, gruffer?

"Because I jumped to conclusions where you were concerned."

"So that was . . . another apology?"

Her eyes narrowed, but still sparkled at him. "How many do you need?"

"Well . . ." He drew the word out with a grin, and she rolled her eyes.

He hardly registered the creak of a door nearby. "I guess now is a bad time to give you another shot at that marriage proposal, then?"

Suddenly, with a snarl that sounded like a miniature tornado siren, a streak of white shot down the hallway and attacked his feet.

"Snowball!" Sophie yelped, then leaned over and scooped the little cat up.

Snowball didn't stop hissing at him, though, waving an ineffectual paw in his direction.

"Stop that." Sophie tapped her lightly on the nose, enough to catch her attention, and the threatening noises cut off as the cat turned wide blue eyes on her.

"I'll take that as my cue to go to bed," Daniel said wryly.

Sophie lifted her gaze to his, expression unreadable. "Oh. Okay. I'll see you tomorrow then."

She disappeared down the hall and into her room, Snowball dead-eyeing him over her shoulder. The snick of her closing door sounded pretty definitive.

Thwarted by his feline nemesis yet again.

* * *

Sophie sits down on the edge of her bed, still holding me against her, petting my fur soothingly, but I can tell she is distracted. The petting isn't up to her usual standard.

Then she holds me out in front of her, eye-to-eye. "I think you might need to rethink your issues with Daniel."

What is this now?

I frown at her.

And she frowns back. "I mean it. I know he can get all . . . nosy . . . and bossy. But so do I. And it comes from a good place, I think."

His personality isn't my problem with him. He almost ruined Emily and Lukas, and they're so happy now, but it could have gone differently. All my good work getting them together spoiled. Cats don't forget. People think elephants have long memories, but cats have nine lives.

"Try to be a little nicer to him?" Sophie implores.

I'm not making any promises.

Sophie puts me down and flops back on the bed. "And now I'm talking to a cat as though she understands. This has to be the strangest day ever."

I hop up on the bed and curl into a tight ball against her side. Sophie shuffles over onto her side to face me, bringing up her legs and tucking me into the curve of her body. "I think for Christmas I'm going to ask Santa for a new dream," she murmurs sleepily.

Together, we fall back into the sleep that Daniel—I assume he was the reason she left in such a hurry earlier—woke us up from with that fire.

Chapter 9

Sophie walked the downtown of the nearby town of Braunfels doing her best to enjoy the scrap of time she'd managed to steal for herself. A chance to explore the shops here, comparing them with those at the inn, as well as explore the town itself, which she'd seen only as she'd driven through on the way to Weber Haus her first day.

She would not, repeat not, think about Daniel and that kiss, and how he'd smelled so good up close—sort of woodsy and manly—and the way his beard tickled her lips. Because it had been a peck on the cheek. Nothing big. Just an apology.

So stop thinking about it.

She forced herself to focus on her surroundings instead. Braunfels was lovely, with a wide main street lined with side-by-side two-story buildings used for shops, restaurants, and other entertainments. A small river meandered through on the back side of the shops, and the town had added a river walk along it.

Sophie fully intended to explore that part on a better weather day, but for now stuck to the street side. She raised her eyebrows at the sign for the tattoo parlor and the karaoke bar, noting them as options to include in their list for guests. One never knew what guests might be interested in regardless of age or any other outward appearance.

A shiver chased itself across her skin as a wintry blast of air sped down the sidewalk, smacking her in the face and flinging her hair about. With a distracted hand, she gathered it to the side and tucked it under her scarf while she leaned into the wind and plodded along. The first things she should get were winter-appropriate clothes for herself. Spying a ladies' store, she slipped inside, enjoying the warmth and the Christmas music softly piping through the sound system.

Not "The Twelve Days of Christmas."

"Sophie?" She raised her head from unwinding her scarf to find Clara standing at one of the racks looking back at her with a welcoming smile.

She returned one of her own. "Clara."

"Snuck away for Christmas shopping?"

She nodded, and Clara beamed. "Me too! I've got Jason watching the munchkin for an hour or two. Would you like to join forces?"

Sophie struggled to recall bumping into someone she knew in the city in the first shop she stepped in, let alone being immediately asked to join that person. A handful of the better memories of small-town life struck her, and she warmed to the petite woman in front of her. "I'd love to."

"Great! What are you shopping for?"

"For now . . . warmer clothes for me."

Clara eyed her current ensemble. "I see what you mean. This will be fun!"

"What about you?"

"I needed a mommy break." She winced. "Should I feel guilty about that?"

"I don't have kids yet, but I should think that you'd be a better mom if you take care of yourself, too."

Clara gave a little sigh of relief. "That's what I thought." Then she pulled her shoulders back, a sparkle entering her eyes. "Right. I'm done with my holiday shopping. How about we get you outfitted, then grab lunch?"

A few hours later, Sophie was both thrilled to have found a new friend in Clara and more than satisfied with her haul. Plus, she'd been introduced to a terrific lunch place that served the best meatballs in a white sauce served over rice. Perfect for a cold day.

After a hugged goodbye and a promise to get together again in a week or two, they'd gone their separate ways. Sophie still had some gift shopping to do. Maybe something for Daniel, too. . . .

No. They weren't there yet.

She battled the wind back to her car to stuff the bags inside before she did a bit more shopping, for gifts this time. She'd just closed the trunk when her cell phone went off and she had to fish it out of her purse.

"Hello?" she answered, a tad breathless.

"Hi, Sophie, it's Tilly Weber."

Her greeting made her smile. She'd recognize Miss Tilly's deceptively frail voice anywhere. It didn't match the lady's personality at all. An incongruous marriage of impressions. "How is Emily's brother?" she asked.

"That's what I wanted to tell you. Peter is awake, thank heavens. He has to stay in the hospital another few days as they run more tests. He may have a bit of temporary amnesia, at least surrounding the incident that landed him in here. We're not sure yet."

"That's unfortunate, but I'm so glad to hear he's awake. That's what's important."

"Yes, it is."

They paused.

"So do you have an idea of when you might be home?" Sophie asked next. She ran her gaze over the shops as she walked by and noticed a children's store that appeared to carry half clothes and half toys. She'd pop in on her way back to the car and get presents for her nieces and nephews.

Maybe drop by the postal office and get them mailed, too, if the store had any wrapping.

"Probably we'll stay while he's still here," Tilly was saying. "I'm guessing at least another week."

So after the Christmas Market. Sophie made a face. Not that she'd say anything whatsoever to Tilly, but she wouldn't mind having them back sooner than that, either. "Thanks for letting me know."

"Of course, sweetie. While I have you, is there anything for me?"

Sophie considered bringing up the covered walkways, but now wasn't the time. She'd wait until Tilly was back and suggest them as another phase, later down the road if open sidewalks proved to not be enough. As Daniel had suggested.

See. I can listen to others.

She'd been doubting herself lately, even though she'd led a large team at her previous hotel. She'd been better about delegating there. *I let Malcom impact me more than I should have, but no more.*

Instead, she kept her talk to the Market and other doings that wouldn't require Tilly's input too much. "Well . . . I think I figured out a larger space for the dance troupes. According to Giselle, the gazebo isn't big enough."

Tilly snorted. "That woman would make Santa swear."

Sophie cleared her throat to disguise her sudden attack of giggles. "How would you feel if I brought in a temporary dance floor and set it up at the end of the shops. The ground is paved and flat there."

"Sounds like the best solution, but I'd prefer the town pay for it. They knew the limitations when they asked me to hold the first annual Christmas Market at Weber Haus. Since the other option was the town square, they would only have been able to run it for one weekend, but out where we are, they can go for weeks."

That was a tidbit of information Sophie hadn't had previously. This hadn't been the Webers' idea—this was the town's. Ammunition for dealing with Giselle.

"How is construction going?" Tilly asked.

Sophie grimaced. "We've had quite a bit of rain, unfortunately, but they're doing everything they can."

"If we need to push back or cancel reservations, then we'll have to deal with that. But that's on us. Don't let Daniel work those boys off their feet."

"I'm sure he knows what his crew is capable of."

Even Sophie paused as the words—which put her in mind of Miss Schreiber, her prim, proper, and much-hated teacher from grade school—left her mouth. She was sticking up for Daniel Aarons. Funny how things could change.

"How are things between you two?" Tilly asked suddenly.

Sophie paused, frowning at the shop window in front of her—mostly tools and hardware—though not really taking it in. "Fine, of course. Why do you ask?"

"Because I'm pretty sure Daniel's particular brand of teasing means he likes you."

He likes me? Her heart fluttered like a caged bird at the idea. *As a person? Or as in likes-likes?*

She didn't dare ask for clarification. This was her boss after all. "He's been a . . . big help."

Tilly's snigger came as a surprise. "You mean he's been stepping all over your toes with those monster boots of his in his effort to help."

Sophie chuckled. "Something like that, but I haven't been exactly easy on him, either."

"It's how he shows he cares. Takes getting used to."

"Well, of course he cares about Weber Haus. You're his friends, and Peter is his best friend."

"Those two boys used to run all over the town together, a tornado of mischief that would sweep through leaving chaos in their wake, though never mean-spirited. Daniel was an only child after his brother died, and I think his parents were just happy to have other children for him to hang out with. They gave him a bit more rope than most."

His brother had died? Sophie tried to imagine losing one of her siblings, and the pit that formed in her stomach at the mere thought could have swallowed the town whole with grief. And that was just a thought. "I'm sorry to hear that he lost his brother."

"Yes." She could picture Tilly nodding. "Tragic. Leukemia when Drew was only ten. Daniel was twelve at the time and took it hard."

Sophie's heart squeezed tight at the image Tilly painted, especially knowing Daniel now—so confident and capable and unbothered, other than when she insulted his way of getting his business started. She had to take shallower breaths for a second.

That kind of experience changed a man, especially at that age.

"So the next time those boots are aiming for your toes, maybe try a little sidestep and walk beside him instead," Tilly said.

"You're telling me to go easy on Daniel Aarons?" Sophie asked slowly.

"I'm telling you that boy is one of the good ones."

Yes, he is. Though, as far as Miss Tilly was aware, Sophie's only interaction with Daniel involved the construction. So why was she saying this?

"Did Daniel complain about me, Ms. Weber?"

"Stubborn must be drawn to stubborn." Sophie thought that was what Miss Tilly muttered on the other end of the line but couldn't be sure.

"Sorry?"

"Of course not." Tilly came across more clearly all of a sudden. "When he's called, it's only been with updates and to check on Peter."

Guilt sprang up all over the place, like a leaky hose with too much water pressure. His best friend had been in a coma, and all he wanted to do was help. That had been a silly question to even think, let alone ask.

"I'll try to go easy on him," she promised in a contrite voice.

Sun. Finally. It had only been days, but it had felt like forever, thanks to the delays.

Sun, along with a significant drop in temperature, which likely meant any more precipitation was going to be snow instead of rain. While that was semi-easier, it didn't help them do the trim around the outside of the building.

So Daniel's number one goal while the weather held was to get the outside as close to completed as possible, especially around the base of the building, where snow might pile up in their way. Swigging hot coffee from the carafe Mrs. Bailey had insisted on sending him to work with when he'd come up to the house on his lunch break to check in with Sophie, he thought over what needed to be done. Maybe the cook had seen his disappointment that Sophie was out and taken pity on him. He strolled up to the table with the plans, sounds of his crew back to work after their break hurrying his steps, and reached for his helmet, only to pause at the sound of his name.

"Aarons."

He turned to find Jannik standing on the other side of the fencing that had gone up around the site. Daniel was almost tempted to immediately check that nothing had gone missing or been broken overnight. The last time this guy had turned up was after the vandalism.

"Can I do something for you?" he asked.

Jannik shook his head. "I'm here with my wife while she shops." He indicated the fencing with a wave. "What's all this about?"

Daniel had a hard time not narrowing his eyes at that. "Sophie insisted we needed it up so that any Christmas Market shoppers didn't wander into a dangerous area."

"Ah." Jannik nodded as though totally on board with the idea. "Smart of her."

"Right. Well, if you'll excuse me . . ."

"Of course." Jannik wandered away, and Daniel watched until the guy turned the corner of the barn and disappeared.

What was he up to?

Turning back, he paused again. Tiny mud-splattered pawprints had been tracked across his pristine blueprints. It had to be recently, because those hadn't been there during the first half of the day. The first direction he looked was up, cringing as he did, even though a tree branch wasn't hanging over his head this time. He'd barely avoided a claw to the eyeball last time, so he wasn't putting anything past that darn cat.

Sophie was not going to be happy to learn that Snowball was still getting out, probably because the rain had finally stopped. He'd have to keep an eye out for her in case she needed to be herded back home.

The ring of his phone had him pausing again and reaching for where he left it on the plans. Seeing the name on the screen, he answered quickly. "Hi, Miss Tilly."

"I thought you'd want to know that Peter is awake."

Air punched from his lungs only to whoosh back in just as fast. Daniel slumped against the makeshift desk in relief. "That's terrific news."

Worrying got him nowhere, and he hadn't allowed his thoughts to tumble about like socks in a dryer while they'd been waiting for news . . . but this was Pete.

The toughest man he knew had been in a coma in a hospital far away, and that old edge of quiet desperation kept creeping up on Daniel despite his efforts not to think about it. When Drew had died, all he could do was stand by and watch. Helpless to even ease the pain for his little brother, who'd swelled up like a balloon before he'd wasted away more every day.

Daniel had promised himself that he'd never give in to that helplessness again. At twelve he'd had no idea that life didn't exactly stop serving up rough situations. Being here, instead of there with Peter . . . he couldn't decide if that had been worse or better. Distracted by the amount of work being thrown at him, but not there for his friend. Not directly at least.

"How is he?" he asked.

"Madder than an elf who misplaced his tools." That he could hear the amusement in Tilly's voice was a good sign.

He chuckled. If Pete was already being his usual self—irritated with any kind of coddling and hating being the center of attention—that was a good sign. That gnawing tension in his chest eased a fraction more.

"You want to explain to me again why you needed my help getting on Sophie Heidt's good side?" Tilly segued without warning.

Daniel paused to catch up, gripping the phone a little harder. That had been fast. "Let's just say I got off on the wrong foot with her and I'd like to be on the right foot."

"Asking for help with a woman isn't like you, Daniel."

"Sophie is a tough nut to crack, but she's doing a fantastic job here," he hastened to add. "You hired a good one." Not for the first time, he wondered if they'd manage to keep her around long, though. He got the impression that Weber Haus was a stepping-stone to wherever she was going next, though she clearly loved what she did. Especially around the guests, when she practically glowed. But compared with the Crown Liberty—which he'd looked up on his phone . . .

Maybe they needed to give her a better reason to stay . . . and something in him wanted her to stay. Not that he was willing to put his finger on why quite yet.

"Well, I could tell that for myself, but thank you for your approval."

He grinned. Then paused. "She didn't suspect anything, did she?"

"Give me a little credit," Tilly scoffed. "Sophie is also clearly a woman with her own thoughts, so I'm not sure I moved the needle for you any. But I did what I could."

"That's all I can ask. Thanks, Miss Tilly."

"My pleasure, kiddo. I'll call again when we know more about Peter," she said.

"I'd appreciate that."

"Oh . . . don't hang up yet. You there?" she asked.

"Still here."

"I've been meaning to talk to you about covering the walkways."

Daniel gripped his phone harder. She hadn't. Sophie hadn't gone around him to Tilly with that like she said. When she hadn't brought it up again, he'd assumed she'd thought better of it. After all, she knew their deadlines.

"Why don't we get closer to finishing the main building, and then we can discuss that," he said, trying to keep the frustration from his voice.

"Of course."

After a few more pleasantries, they hung up.

"You asked an old woman to help you make a good impression on a girl?"

Daniel swung around to find Levi standing in the still-doorless opening, arms crossed, and with an expression that said he couldn't decide if he was about to laugh his head off or wanted to frown with disapproval.

Daniel shrugged. "Things will go better if she and I can be on the same team." And she could stop meddling with *his* job. If anyone should be sensitive about that, he'd think Sophie would, given everything she'd told him.

"She made you dinner last night," Levi pointed out. Disapproval seemed to be winning out. From one of his own men and a good friend. Starlight-colored eyes and feeding his men had gone a long way to winning them over, apparently.

"She made *all* of us dinner last night," Daniel said in return. He had no delusions that was for him.

His foreman and friend shook his head as if he disagreed, but didn't argue.

"She implied that I've been sticking my nose in her business too much," Daniel said. He wasn't about to mention the nepotism remark. She'd apologized for that.

Levi glanced away and shifted his feet, and Daniel wished he hadn't said anything.

Only now he couldn't unsay it. "You agree?"

"I'm sure you're just trying to help her get her footing." Levi looked anywhere but at Daniel.

"But you agree?"

Levi sighed. "When we first met and you hired me on, you had a tendency to . . . lecture."

"Lecture?" Daniel tested the word out and tried to think back to those days.

Levi had gotten into gambling debts and hung out with a rough crowd, but *he* was the one who'd declared he was trying to turn his life around. All Daniel had done was try to point him in the right directions to attain that goal.

Levi's mouth tipped up in a grin that was half amused and half unsurprised. "You remember the conversation that went along the lines of me saying, 'If I want your help, I'll ask for it; otherwise, back off.' "

Oh. Yeah.

"I can see that you do."

Daniel ran a hand around the back of his neck. "But I listened and we're good now. Right?"

Were they good? Or was Levi with him only for the steady work? That would hurt more than he was willing to admit.

"We're great, man. The reason I bring it up is to point out

that, while your heart is always in the right place, your brand of help can be a bit . . ." Levi's turn to run a hand around the back of his own neck as he searched for words.

"In your face?" Daniel supplied.

Levi blew out a long breath. "Yeah." He shrugged. "Someone has to want your help to appreciate it."

And for someone like Sophie, who'd been burned by a "helpful" person in her life, it had to be worse. Which begged the question, why would she go behind his back on the covered walkway thing.

Daniel leaned back against the table, arms crossed, and thought about that for a long minute, Levi giving him the space to mull it over.

"I guess everyone deserves the benefit of the doubt," he said finally.

Levi clapped him on the shoulder, then walked away.

So Daniel wants to get in good with Sophie, huh?

I scoot back into the shadows of the room where I was listening from, careful to tuck my tail in close to my body as Daniel and the big guy he's friends with come through the building. They pass by without seeing me, of course. I'm a great hider.

I creep along stealthily behind them and jump up onto an open windowsill to watch Daniel while I think about what I just overheard.

If Miss Tilly was willing to help Daniel with Sophie, maybe I should think about it.

I think Sophie could use a real friend. I mean, she has me, but a human one would be good, too. She seems so lonely sometimes. If Daniel is willing to try—and asking Miss Tilly for help sounds like trying to me—well then . . .

I let go of a deep sigh. Maybe—I can't believe I'm thinking this—but maybe I should be a little bit nicer to him, too.

Chapter 10

The blare of his alarm clock came way too early in the day, and Daniel was tempted to snatch his phone from the bedside table and chuck it at the wall.

Winter was almost officially here, so the mornings were dark regardless of what time he woke most days, but the alarm tied to the site had gone off at three in the morning to tell him something had activated the motion sensors. Nothing had shown up on the video feed, though. Worried that Jannik had figured it out—he was convinced the man was involved in both instances of vandalism to his sites—he'd wrapped up in a jacket and boots, grabbed his trusty baseball bat, and run over there. To find a raccoon messing around, her eyes glittering in the glare of his flashlight.

At least it hadn't been Snowball, because then he would have felt obligated to chase her to kingdom come, no doubt risking his own life and limb, or, at the very least, his skin to her claws, to get her back inside. Otherwise, Sophie would be worried sick when she woke up.

But that wasn't the only reason he groaned now and hit Snooze.

He'd successfully avoided Sophie for the last few days as he'd thought over things and cooled off about the walkway thing. He'd even come to the conclusion that adding those to the project was really Tilly's call in the end. They all understood the impact on the guest bookings, though maybe he'd let Sophie know about the potential impact on his own business. After their chat in the kitchen, before he got offended, if anyone would understand, she would.

He'd come to another realization. Distraction or not, he was interested in her. No use denying it. While he wasn't entirely sure what he wanted with Sophie yet, he just knew he didn't want them at odds. So, in the spirit of the season, he'd decided to come up with a way to declare a truce.

He still wasn't sure if what he had in mind would make things better or worse, because now he was second-guessing himself, and he never did that. Not ever. A waste of time, he'd always believed. You make a decision, you follow it through, case closed.

Snooze went off and he groaned again, shifting around in the bed.

Then something sharp speared into his toes, which had been sticking out of the covers trying to find a balance of body temperature. With a yelp he jerked away from the pain. Scrambling, he sat up and fumbled around to flip on the bedside lamp, having no idea what attacked him, to find Snowball sitting on the other end of his bed.

Daniel dropped his head in his hands, even as he kept a close eye on the cat. "Snowball. What was that for?"

Instead of hissing or growling at him, though, the tiny cat tipped her head to the side and gave a small meow. Almost like an apology.

That was . . . new.

"I'm going to choose to believe that you thought my toes were mice."

Another meow and he'd almost swear she'd understood

him. Which was way over the line of ridiculous. Maybe he was more exhausted than he realized. With a sigh, he dropped back against the headboard with a thump and rubbed the sleep out of his eyes.

He took his gaze off her for only a second, but when he dropped his hand, it was to find Snowball had come closer to lie down beside him. Maybe cats could sense when people needed to be given a break?

He didn't try to pet her, though. That would be asking to be scratched, and while he had his moments like everyone else, he wasn't *that* dumb.

"I'm trying, Snowball. I really am," he said, more under his breath than to the cat.

A glance showed her listening, ears pricked, blue eyes trained on him, with a curious lack of evil sparkle for once.

Compelled by an odd urge to share the thoughts chasing around in his head like a dog going after his own tail, he reached over to the bedside table and picked up a small black box. "I got this for Sophie for Saint Nicholas Day," he told the still-listening cat. "What do you think? Too much?"

He opened the lid, well aware that having no human audience was a good thing right this second, and showed her the gift inside. "Do you think she'll like it?"

To his surprise, Snowball lifted a small white paw and patted the box, then gave a meow that he swore sounded like "Good job."

He had to remind himself that Snowball loved shiny things. Heck, last Christmas the kitten stole Lukas's mother's engagement ring and gave it to Emily, causing all sorts of misunderstandings.

Daniel replaced the lid. "I hope she doesn't think it's too much. Or stupid. Or . . ." He shrugged, then grinned at Snowball. "I feel like I can talk to you about this, because you're the only one who knows her well."

The little cat snuggled down on her belly, paws peeking

out from the long white fur that puffed out around her, attention still fully on him.

"If you and I are on better terms now," he said slowly, "you think you could help me with Sophie? Because . . . I like her. A lot."

More than a lot if he was honest. He wanted to get to know her better, learn what made her laugh and think and what she found interesting, what she did with her free time, if she ever took any. But she was so closed off . . .

And now I've been reduced to asking the devil cat for help.

Pathetic. Right. Putting the box back down on his bedside table, he slid out of bed gingerly, careful not to disturb Snowball, who seemed content to lie where she was.

After getting ready, he headed downstairs, Snowball hot on his heels, practically tripping him as they went down. At least she wasn't attacking his legs. He had a good idea he'd find Sophie in her office. Construction started early, always, but she seemed to be on the same schedule. Which worked well for the timing of this little visit.

Fresh start.

Rather than barge right in, he knocked softly, aware that most guests in the household were still sleeping.

"Come in." Her voice sounded faintly startled.

When he opened the door, her eyebrows lifted slowly as if the surprise crept up on her. "Daniel?" The question in her voice clearly wondering why he was stopping by at this time in the morning.

"Hi." Now that he was questioning every second word out of his mouth, he had no idea where to start.

Something soft brushed against his jean-covered ankles and he glanced down to find Snowball winding around his feet. She gave a small chirp, then pranced over to where Sophie was sitting.

"I see you've made friends with the cat," Sophie said, silver eyes sparkling with humor.

"I'm not sure why," he admitted. "But we seem to be on better footing."

"Because she's such a sweet kitty." Sophie leaned over to run a hand over her soft fur, then tickled her under the chin, Snowball leaning into the touch, her face a study of bliss.

Daniel wouldn't go quite so far as to call the devil cat sweet. They might be on a temporary truce after all. Maybe she was just drawing him closer to go for the jugular. Still, he had no intention of disturbing the delicate peace between them by saying that out loud. That cat understood human. He was almost sure of it.

He cleared his throat. "Speaking of better footing, I wanted to apolo—"

"Don't you dare." Sophie got to her feet so fast, Snowball had to skitter out of the way of her chair, which rolled haphazardly to the left.

"I'm . . . sorry. What?"

Sophie grimaced as she came around the desk. "I've been wanting to apologize for days."

"You already did," he said.

She blinked.

"That kiss on the cheek in the hall." That had been an apology, hadn't it? Or maybe he was getting every single one of his assumptions wrong these days.

"That doesn't count."

It didn't? He couldn't help the smile tugging at his mouth, but honestly, he might never figure this woman out. And that was okay. She kept him on his toes. For sure, he'd never be bored around Sophie.

"You don't have to apologize," he said, instead of laughing like he wanted to. "I've been informed by several folks close to me that I have a tendency toward being an interfering ass at times."

That only made her wrinkle her nose. "Not how I'd put it,

and I was being too sensitive. I've also butted in on the construction stuff."

"Not really." This was not going the way he'd planned. "But I'm sorry for my part in things all the same, and I'll try to be better."

She gave her head a hard shake, her ponytail flying. "That's just it. You shouldn't have to change who you are—and you have been very helpful and kind—because one guy made me a bitter, hate—"

Daniel put a finger to her lips. Something in him couldn't stand to hear her knock herself down.

"How about we agree that we were both wrong, both right, and could both do a little better in the communication space? Sound good?"

Wide silver eyes stared at him a second before she nodded. "I'd like that," she said, her lips soft against his skin.

He had to curl his hand away from her, clenching his fingers into fists, before he did something stupid, like ruin the decent progress he'd made by kissing her. Hard. That hotel guy must have been a total jerk.

"In the spirit of starting fresh . . ." He pulled the small box out of his pocket and held it out. "Happy Saint Nicholas Day."

She blinked at the box but didn't reach for it. "You got me a present."

Why wasn't she reaching for it?

"Nothing big," he said. Uncomfortable didn't begin to cover this situation he'd gotten himself into. "My family celebrates this holiday." He waved a hand. "And this seemed . . . appropriate. For us." Mental grimace. "I mean not us, as in us. Because we're not—"

The hole at his feet kept getting wider and deeper with every word.

"Here." He took her hand and laid the box in her palm.

"Open it later." Then he backed out of the door. "Have a good day. Only two more days before the Christmas Market opens, right?"

"You too." Her voice floated down the hall after him as he walked away like a total coward.

Sophie dropped heavily into the chair behind her desk, staring at the small box that she'd set on the desktop as though it might be a snake that could strike at any second.

Daniel had gotten her a gift.

Because she'd made him feel bad for the ways in which he'd helped her and implied he'd used his connections to get a job he didn't deserve. She honestly had no idea how to feel about that beyond guilty. The emotion itched under her skin, making it feel too tight.

"Mrrrrow," Snowball said as she hopped up on Sophie's desk and nosed at the little package, then batted it toward Sophie as if to say, "You open it."

Carefully, Sophie lifted the lid, and a surprised laugh burst from her lips.

"What a goofball," she told the cat as she lifted a necklace from out of the box. Then laughed again. A thin gold chain supporting not one, not two, but . . . "Five gold rings," she murmured.

Snowball tipped her head to the side as though confused about why that was so funny. Sophie ignored her and attached the chain around her neck.

As gestures went, this was a sweet one. Suddenly that itching, tight sensation eased, leaving her feeling lighter than she had in a long time.

Humming a little Christmas tune that was drifting her direction from the shops behind the house, she went back to work. Giselle was coming by today for one last check, then they'd be ready to go for the Market starting Saturday, which would run through the day before Christmas Eve. Dealing with whatever last-minute demands she had no doubt were coming her way was going to take all the patience of every saint in the world pooled together, she suspected.

It was probably concerning that anytime Giselle showed up, Sophie mentally hummed the theme song for the Wicked Witch of the West in her head. After all, the woman was just trying to put together a lovely event in such a way that the town wanted to continue holding it annually.

Doesn't make her any more pleasant to deal with.

With Giselle at least, Sophie was fairly certain that her irritation was justified. More so than with Daniel. Still . . . she reminded herself that she was a professional and could handle anything thrown at her.

She wasn't sure how long she'd been working on the monthly numbers and projections for the new wing for the hotel chain with whom they now partnered. Swimming in numbers was never her favorite part of the job, which meant they took an inordinate amount of her focus. She'd rather be out greeting guests and helping them find fun activities and hearing about what they'd enjoyed throughout the day. Vaguely, as she'd plodded her way through spreadsheets, she'd been aware of the soft sounds of guests moving around the house, getting breakfast, and leaving, the weather about as lovely as it could get for December.

A sudden thump followed by swearing in a familiar, irascible voice had her up and out to the foyer in a hurry. The first thing she saw were the branches of a massive fir tree lying across the main staircase and blocking the hallway like a drawbridge.

"What in heaven's name is this?" she asked no one in particular. "Mr. Muir?"

I hope to high heaven that he's not been injured.

"It's my Christmas tree, of course," came the grumpy response, and she blew out a silent breath of relief.

She dropped her head in her hands, glad he couldn't see

around the thing any better than she could and discover her reaction. On a deep inhalation, she raised her head back up. "We have a ton of Christmas trees in the house," she pointed out in her best friendly-but-firm voice. "We're doing the lighting ceremony in a few days. You should come. I think you'll enjoy it. We turn on all the tree lights and sing carols and enjoy Mrs. Bailey's treats and mulled cider." Apparently, the treats were usually from Emily, but they might not make it back in time, so Sophie had made other arrangements.

A snort sounded from somewhere between the branches. "You didn't get the right kind."

Sophie scrunched up her eyes. Did she dare ask? "Right kind of what?"

"Tree. *This* is the kind that's supposed to be used."

Given that they had a different type of tree in each common area of the downstairs—five in all, including a white spruce, a blue spruce, a Douglas fir, a balsam fir, and a white pine—she found it statistically impossible that at least one wasn't close enough to what he was thinking. Unfortunately, this conversation was happening after the fact, too late to stop him.

"What type is this?" she asked out of sheer curiosity. Maybe she was picking up habits from Snowball.

"A Scotch pine, of course." As though that were obvious.

She tipped her head, studying it, though the thing was essentially sideways.

Before she could even ask, he was explaining, still invisible through the branches. "The color and branch strength are similar to the trees you have, but this one retains its needles better. You'll be vacuuming nonstop with those other ones."

She was not remotely prepared to debate the merits of Christmas tree types. "And where do you propose to put this one?" she asked.

"In my room."

Lord, give me patience. "I doubt this will fit in your room along with the bed and the birds, Mr. Muir. Perhaps we could find a different—"

"This is *my* tree. I'll put it where I want."

Having this conversation through the admittedly lovely-smelling pine needles clearly wasn't working. Sophie gingerly scooted under the lowest branches and squeezed herself between its bulk and the floor and wall to find Mr. Muir standing on the other side, at the bottom of the staircase, scowling at her as though she were about to haul his tree away to the Island of Misfit Toys.

She swallowed a laugh that wanted to escape. "I'd like to point out that, while this may be your tree, Mr. Muir, it's not your house."

His lips flattened, eyes glinting dangerously, and she held up a hand. "However, let me get someone to help get it upstairs. *If* it fits, I'll let it slide. *This* time."

She was turning into a regular marshmallow where this man was concerned. Given the satisfied smirk he shot her, what's more, he knew it.

Pulling out the walkie-talkie she'd gotten into the habit of attaching to her waistband, she held down the button. She opened her mouth, then paused, a spark of mischief she hadn't felt properly in ages igniting in her. At her grin, Mr. Muir's eyebrows lifted, but she ignored him.

She pushed the button again. "Partridge. Come in, Partridge. This is Gold Rings."

The walkie-talkie crackled, and then deep laughter came over the line as though Daniel had pushed the button down mid-chuckle.

"Go ahead, Gold Rings," he said between chortles.

Her own grin threatened to break out over her entire face. Not proper for a hotel manager to be that enthusiastic. She managed to stuff it back down. "Turtledoves needs help hauling a large tree to his room. Can you spare a man for a few minutes? Over."

"Turtledoves?" Mr. Muir murmured.

She caught the sparkle in his eyes and felt safe that he wasn't objecting, just questioning.

"Be right there," Daniel came back. "Over and out."

She ignored the small flutter to her heart and the frisson of hope that he'd be the one to come help. Just because he'd bought her a necklace—come to think of it, she should thank him for that—and they'd both cleared the air didn't mean she had to look forward to his company. That would be taking the holiday spirit a bit too far. Wouldn't it?

As they stood and waited, the tree suddenly started shaking, a scratching sound coming from within the thick branches.

"What on earth?" Mr. Muir muttered.

Sophie already had a decent idea what was happening. Digging through the fronds that trembled the hardest, she made her way down until she came face-to-face with a pair of bright blue eyes.

Snowball paused in sharpening her claws on the tree trunk—something she'd shockingly not done to any of the other trees—and stared at Sophie with a mixture of innocence and frenetic energy. Sophie tsked and the cat's little ears flattened. Then in a very slow, entirely deliberate show of defiance, she scratched one unsheathed paw, then the other, down the trunk of the tree with what were no doubt quite satisfying little pops of sound.

"Come here, you naughty thing." Gently she reached into the tree.

But Snowball clawed her way around the other side of the sideways lying trunk, practically hanging upside down and also unreachable from this angle. Sophie gave a little *grr* of frustration and changed positions. Only when she got close enough, the dang cat moved again.

"Snowball," she warned in a dire voice.

The kitty shimmied her way farther down the trunk, in the opposite direction, of course.

"Stop that," Sophie snapped, softly.

After all, a guest was watching this performance, no doubt with keen interest, as her backside waved in the air and the rest of her was buried in a fluffy, yet extremely prickly, Christmas tree. With a lunge of superhuman effort, she snagged the little cat around the belly.

"Ha! Gotcha!"

It still took both hands to disconnect those sharp claws, multiple times actually, as she pulled Snowball out of the tree. Halfway out, a tell-tale ripping sounded, and Sophie paused, mouthing a few swear words where no one else could see or hear. She was pretty sure her favorite—and most expensive—silk blouse was ruined.

"Would you like help?" A laughter-filled male voice sounded from the direction of the dining room at her left.

"Nope," she said through gritted teeth. "I've got her."

She managed to back the rest of the way out of the tree without further incident, still clutching the cat, only to encounter a pair of bright hazel male eyes so filled with laughter they dared her to join him.

Sophie chuckled reluctantly even as she shook her head.

"I told you," Daniel said. "Dev—"

"Shhh." Sophie tucked Snowball in close and covered her ears. "You just got on good terms with her," she told him. "Don't ruin it."

Daniel managed to sober his expression, but the way his shoulders shook, she knew he was laughing. Probably at her for such a silly notion, but she couldn't help it if she wanted them to get along.

She didn't dare glance down for fear of seeing how badly rent her blouse was. "I'll pop her up in Miss Tilly's room, then go change. Can you take this tree and see if it will fit in Mr. Muir's room?" she asked. "If it does, help him get it set up. I'll be right back."

Before either man could say a word, she did the splits, for

once more than happy that her uniform here was more slacks and fewer skirts, to get around the tree and up the stairs, hurrying the rest of the way to Tilly's room. "Stay out of trouble," she told the cat, and closed the door in her affronted little face. As soon as she hit her room and looked in the mirror, she couldn't contain her wail. The rip was across one shoulder and *not* at a seam.

Irreparable.

Only she didn't have time to worry about it, dropping the offending garment in the trash and changing into a new one, this one gold. It went with her new necklace and made her eyes pop. She didn't have time for more than a cursory glance to make sure everything was in the right place before hurrying back to her guest.

As she neared Mr. Muir's room, a series of grunts sounded from within, along with several nervous birdy twitters and the flapping of wings. The turtledoves didn't seem too thrilled with whatever was going on in there.

"How's it coming?" she asked, popping her head into the open doorway.

Then had to clamp a hand over her mouth to keep full-on laughter from breaking free.

The tree, while not so tall that it couldn't stand upright, was fat. So fat that, even though Daniel was doing his best to shove it into a corner, uncaring if he smooshed or even broke a few branches apparently, Mr. Muir would still be sleeping with pine needles fanning across the foot of his bed.

"Um," she said, searching for an appropriately professional response. "I think it's a little too big—"

"It's fine," Mr. Muir snapped.

Right. Okay. "Well, if Daniel could maybe push the furniture a little out of the way so it doesn't get scratched or stained with sap, I guess I'm okay with it."

The two men must've been arguing about her decision, because Mr. Muir shot Daniel a look that smacked of "I told you so." She was surprised the words didn't pop out of his mouth.

Daniel merely shrugged.

"But if you come to stay with us again next year," she said next, "no trees. You'll be lucky if I let you in with the birds."

Daniel's turn to shoot the older man a triumphant look.

She ignored them both as Mr. Muir grumbled his acknowledgment. "You okay without me?" she asked Daniel. "I have that meeting with Giselle, and I don't dare be late."

"Yeah, I'll be down when I'm done."

"You don't have to," she offered. Just an offer. Because she honestly didn't mind a buffer between her and jail time for assault.

He eyed her across the room, between branches of tree, his expression telling her clearly that he wanted to be pushy about it and was consciously holding himself back. "Are you *sure?*"

If he could try that hard, so could she. "Actually . . . I wouldn't mind a little company."

"Make up your mind, young lady," Mr. Muir said, letting his arms rise and fall back to his sides in exasperation.

Instead of shooting her a cocky smirk like he'd done with Mr. Muir a second ago, Daniel simply nodded. "I'll be there."

The glow that went through her, starting in her heart and radiating out, was disproportionate to his offer.

Am I falling for Daniel?

She gave herself a mental shake. Too soon, too much, and after Malcom, too everything else. Friends was the best they could be, and friends didn't glow. So no more of that.

She left the two men to the task of figuring out that ridiculous tree and made her way downstairs.

Glaring at the back of Miss Tilly's door isn't going to change the fact that I'm here as punishment.

I've been so good about those darn Christmas trees, which

are just right for scratching on. Except I'd remembered from last year how I'd get in trouble when I did. Plus, while I'm not a big kitty—Lukas calls me a runt, and Emily says that means I'm a survivor—I am bigger than last year. I admit that I did try to climb up into one of these trees the first day they were up and got stuck.

But Mr. Muir's tree is the exact right size. . . .

Only, Sophie pulled me out of it and called me naughty. She'll be lucky if I help her with Daniel from now on.

I slide my gaze to the bathroom, where there happens to be a hole in the wall that lets me climb up to the attic. Once there, I can jump from the stairs and hang off the door handle to open it and get out that way. It would serve her right if she were to come back and find me missing.

Instead, I hop up on Miss Tilly's window seat and curl up, watching outside. I may like a little fun, but I'm not mean, and Sophie worries.

I'll wait for her, and then show my displeasure by sleeping in Daniel's room tonight. Maybe I'll even get a better hold of one of those little mice that were sticking out of his blankets this morning.

Chapter 11

─────── ✦ ───────

"What are you going to do about all that poop!"

Daniel winced as Giselle's distinctive, high-pitched warble—not quite a screech, though that was debatable—resounded through the house. Poop? What on earth was she talking about?

Sophie's softer voice, though he recognized that firm, friendly thing she did, floated down the hall as he hurried toward her office, wondering if he'd have to bodily put himself between the two women. "Well, if it's in the parking lot—"

"You're not going to leave it there for people to step in and track through the Christmas Market? It starts *Saturday*." As though Sophie wasn't already more than aware of that fact. If Giselle's voice went any higher, only bats would be able to hear her.

Despite wanting to rush in and save Sophie from aural evisceration, Daniel made himself pause at the threshold and knocked. "Sorry I'm late."

Giselle spun to face him with an expression hovering on feral. "Where the hell have you been?" she snapped.

Daniel paused again, only halfway into the room. "Doing my job," he said in a low, no-nonsense voice that sometimes worked to get Snowball not to attack him when they were on bad terms. "And I don't appreciate being spoken to like that."

Giselle opened her mouth to blast him, then pulled herself up short, probably at his expression. She visibly collected herself. "We have a *huge* problem."

"Involving poop . . ." he said slowly. "What happened? Did the sewer line erupt or something?"

Her eyes narrowed to slits, his humor clearly misplaced. "*You* have geese."

Ah. Now the situation was coming together for him. As majestic as the birds were, they also created a minefield of oversize bird droppings when they decided to take up residence on a property. "Where?"

"The parking lot." She pointed as though he could see through the house.

"Well, that's not such a big deal—"

"The buses in from town will be dropping off in that area. That *can't* be the first impression people have. This is the first year with the Christmas Market," Giselle explained through clenched teeth. "It has to be *perfect.*"

Daniel glanced past Giselle at Sophie, who twitched a shoulder in a shrug. He took that as permission to be the one to deal with this.

"Let's go out and check the damage," he said, stepping back to usher Giselle through the door. "Then we can decide how to handle it."

The three of them bundled up and made their way outside, only to pause on the front porch and stare.

"It's snowing," Sophie said, then glanced at him, a question in her eyes. He knew exactly what she was wondering— whether or not this was going to cause further delays with construction. He grimaced and she gave a resigned nod. No doubt she'd ask for specifics later.

"Oh no!" Giselle wailed after a long beat of silence. "No one will want to come out in snow."

THE TWELVE DAYS OF SNOWBALL 151

"More than they would in rain, though," Sophie tried to comfort.

Her effort only resulted in a glare tossed over the other woman's shoulder. "And what about the vendors? They won't want to sit in the cold outside."

She faced forward to march away and Sophie stuck her tongue out at the back of Giselle's head. Daniel coughed to cover his laugh and Sophie waved at Giselle, clearly giving him permission to take a shot.

"I'm pretty sure that everyone involved already planned on cold since it's December," he pointed out.

"You give them too much credit," Giselle snapped back.

Sophie clamped her lips together, and if he didn't know better, he'd say that she was about to lose it. Only, of course she didn't. "Don't forget all the space heaters we've brought in," she said softly. "And the bonfire in the field. The hot chocolate and coffee vendors will help, too."

Giselle's shoulders dropped by a hair. "Yes, that's true. I *did* plan for those things."

Actually, Sophie had planned for those. Daniel had been in on that particular meeting because Giselle hadn't wanted to pony up the money.

She continued blithely along. "I didn't think we'd need them, it's been so warm."

Warm and wet. What would she have done if that type of weather had continued and rained out the Market entirely?

"Let's deal with one thing at a time," Sophie suggested now.

As soon as they made it to the parking lot, even with the fine dusting of snow already frosting the ground like a sugar donut, Daniel could see the problem. Geese had taken up residence in the mowed grass strip along the edges of the dirt lot . . . and pooped all over the place.

Geese. With difficulty, he held in his first comment, aimed at Sophie in particular.

"They shouldn't stay long," he assured both women. Because even Sophie was staring at the scene with dismay in her eyes. He could practically see her mind cranking over how the heck she was going to clean this off.

"They look settled to me," Sophie murmured as Giselle stated something similar.

"It's not nesting season. They're flying south still. This is just a rest stop." He hoped.

That's when a flicker of movement behind one of the cars caught his attention. A white fluffy tail sticking straight up. Snowball.

He left both women staring as he quietly—as much as possible in his thick boots—scooted around the car. He scooped the little cat up right as she went to spring. "Not yet, Mighty Mouse," he told her.

Snowball tucked into his arm but still straining to peep around his bulk at the geese, no doubt sending them death glares, he turned back to Sophie and caught her wince. Yet another Snowball escape.

"What about the poop?" Giselle demanded, eyeing the kitten with disdain.

Instead of addressing her, he looked at Sophie. "I have an idea. It involves the fire department."

She raised her eyebrows, confusion flitting across her features before realization seemed to dawn that he was asking her permission before he acted. They'd get this communication thing figured out eventually.

"Any help would be appreciated," she murmured.

Like watching the silver thaw of winter into spring.

Tempting to see if she'd thaw even more with a kiss. Not a quick peck, like before, but an honest-to-goodness kiss. He could easily picture wrapping her up in his arms as the snow fluttered around them. Her lips would be cool at first but warm up quickly. Like the rest of her.

You only just got on friendly footing, he reminded himself, shoving the image and what it did to him away. Drowning it out with the fact that they were in a parking lot full of geese, poop, Snowball, and Giselle. He wasn't sure which was more dampening.

He had no intention of ruining the progress he'd made by being stupid. Or hasty.

"Got it." He pulled his cell phone out and dialed. Not the emergency line but directly into the station.

Luckily the voice on the other end was one he recognized. "Bert? Daniel Aarons."

He listened through the man's greeting.

"I've got a bit of a situation here at Weber Haus that I'm hoping one of your crews could help with if they're not currently busy?"

"What's that?" Bert asked.

Snowball squiggled in Daniel's grasp and he almost dropped the phone as he adjusted his hold on her.

"Daniel?" Bert's tiny voice sounded.

He got Snowball situated and put the phone back to his ear. "Sorry about that . . . Is there any way you could come spray geese droppings out of the Weber Haus parking lot? We've got the Christmas Market starting soon, so . . ."

Bert gave a bark of laughter. "I think we could do something about that."

"Terrific." He gave both women a thumbs-up.

"Probably better to do it now so it might have a chance to melt. It's only going to get colder as the day goes into night."

Bert wasn't wrong.

"We'll bring sand to scatter over it, too, just to be safe," the fireman added.

"Sounds good. Thanks, buddy."

"My wife has a booth at that Market," Bert said dryly. "She'd have my hide if she discovered I didn't do something to fix any sort of problem."

After goodbyes, Daniel hung up and stuffed his phone back in his pocket, facing both women. "That was the fire department. They'll hose it all off and lay sand over the area so it doesn't turn into an impromptu skating rink with the temperatures dropping."

Sophie's smile was everything he needed to finish his day happy. "Thank you," she said. "I never would have come up with that."

"Small towns," he said. "Everyone helps each other."

"Not how I remember growing up. Our town was more about interfering," she murmured. Offering a sliver of a glimpse into her life.

"Braunfels is special," was all he said. Then he glanced at the large birds taking naps in the grass. "I'll run the geese off before the truck gets here."

"Giselle and I will go inspect the booths which are being set up today." She tried to tug the other woman away, but Giselle ignored her and stepped up to Daniel, eyes glittering.

"You saved the Christmas Market," she breathed dramatically. "How can I repay your kindness?"

Even without looking at her, he still caught Sophie's volte-face and had to tuck his answering laughter down deep.

"Not needed," he said. "I only made a phone call."

She took his free hand, which he'd left hanging at his side after tucking his phone in his pocket. "Actually, I've been meaning to set up a meeting with you and my father. He's purchased a large piece of land and is thinking of making it into a country club. I'm sure he'd want the best for the construction."

Daniel stilled. So that's what the secret project was. A country club. The mayor would love that idea. A project like that would probably involve multiple buildings over the property. Except he didn't want it tied to Giselle and him, so he tried to think of the most diplomatic way to deal with that situation. "I'm happy to speak with him, of course."

More than happy. This was an opportunity he couldn't pass up. Mr. Becker owned more land and opened more businesses than anyone else around town. Getting on his roster of construction crews could be huge for Daniel. Only he didn't want Giselle as part of the package.

She lit up like a Christmas tree. "Wonderful. How about dinner? Tomorrow night?"

That's not what he'd meant, but he couldn't see any way out of it. "Let me know when and where."

"I'll pick you up. How about six?"

He wouldn't be done with work at that time. Not on their current frantic schedule. "It would be better if this could wait until after the New Year."

"Dad wants to get started as soon as possible," she said.

Right. "Then let's make it eight. I'll meet you there."

"I guess that will work," came the ungracious answer, followed by a laugh he was sure was meant to distract him from her rudeness.

"Let's go see the stalls," she said to Sophie, who'd been waiting in silence through the entire exchange. Then walked past her, clearly expecting her to follow.

Only instead of following, Sophie walked over to Daniel, so close he swore her body heat permeated their layers of clothes, warming him with her presence. Snow fell softly around them, glistening in her hair and on her eyelashes.

"Play along," she whispered, her back to Giselle.

With what?

Before he could ask, she went up on her tiptoes, hands fluttering to his chest to balance as she avoided squishing Snowball and laid her lips over his in a kiss that stole his breath and his mind. Giselle, and the geese, and the cars, and the snow faded into the background as he focused on the softest lips brushing against his so sweetly.

He reached for her, wanting her closer, wanting to deepen the kiss, only she stepped back to twinkle up at him. "Six geese a-laying," she murmured, and waggled her eyebrows.

Daniel huffed a laugh. So, she'd counted, too.

"Want me to take her?" she offered, reaching for the cat.

He held back. "No, she's going to help me with the geese."

Sophie held up both hands. "As long as she's back in the house after you're done, I don't want to know." With that, she turned back to Giselle, smiling despite the other woman's hard stare.

Uh-oh. He'd have to watch out there. For both his sake and Sophie's.

"Most of the vendors will arrive this afternoon to set up before the grand opening," Sophie was saying as they walked away.

As they passed a tree that would take them out of sight, she glanced back over her shoulder at him. And winked.

I shouldn't have kissed him. What was I thinking?

Only Sophie knew exactly what she was thinking. She was thinking about wiping that flirtatious smirk right off Giselle Becker's face. In her head, she'd been helping Daniel put up a front that he wasn't available, but really, she'd been wrestling the green-eyed monster in her own breast. Hopefully, she hadn't messed up things for that opportunity with Giselle's dad.

The thoughts chased their tails through her mind. Round and round and round.

She'd managed to hold her turmoil at bay while she and Giselle walked through all the temporary booths already in place, talked with the crew in the process of setting up the sound system, and also checked on the temporary dance floor already laid out.

Which Giselle had declared to be "Not as good as a stage, but what can one expect in a small town?"

Silently, Sophie had thanked the powers that be that she'd managed to convince Giselle to go with the plastic one rather than the hardwood. Wood warped if it got wet, and also, she'd been warned, tended to be slicker indoors, let alone out-of-doors. She'd pictured dancers slipping and sliding, broken legs, and lawsuits.

Midway through their inspection several loud blasts—that she was pretty sure involved a shotgun—sounded, making everyone jump. A few seconds later, a flock of large birds appeared in the air, flying away.

Thankfully.

Conflicting relief and irritation had a fistfight for her attention. The man had said *nothing* about a shotgun. She sure as heck hoped he wasn't aiming directly at the geese. What if he hit Snowball by accident?

"Don't worry," she said, even as she ignored her own advice, worrying away in her head. She'd aimed her words at the crowds of people nearest her, mostly vendors and shop owners peeking out of their tents and doorways. "Just clearing out some geese."

At least she'd been right there to reassure them.

An hour later and she'd seen Giselle off with even more relief than watching those darn geese fly off, then made her way back to her office, where she'd flopped into her chair. Spent. The head of the Christmas Market committee was an emotional vampire if she'd ever met one, sucking away every ounce of energy Sophie had started the day with.

She jumped when Snowball hopped up on her lap and rubbed her head into Sophie's chest, begging for petting. Expelling a pent-up breath, she smiled. "I'm glad he didn't shoot you," she said. "Did you have fun chasing the geese?"

Snowball butted her again, demanding her pats. Which Sophie was happy to give, though in a distracted manner as she thought about that kiss.

It had started out for show, for Giselle—and yes, the jealousy crawling under her skin—but despite all that, it had felt . . . real. *He'd* felt real. The firm warmth of his lips against hers. The tickle of his beard. The way he'd reached for her and she'd wanted to step closer, wanted to deepen the kiss. Wanted more.

Only that wouldn't be fair to either of them. They were finally on good terms. So she'd stepped away, trying not to acknowledge the hole of disappointment that action had left in the center of her chest.

She absently rubbed at the spot now. "Daniel is a pretty good kisser, Snowball."

The kitten's head shot up at that, perking up with interest. Then she tipped her head to the side. All ears.

"It was a casual kiss, but . . . oh my." Sophie gave a low whistle.

Giving in to a momentary lapse of weakness, she closed her eyes and relived the sensation and how her heart had tumbled around inside her like a mouse in a wheel.

"Knock, knock." An amused male voice had her jack-knifing up, Snowball tumbling off her lap to land on her feet on the floor.

Sophie stared at Daniel warily. Had he heard any of what she'd been saying—stupidly—out loud to the cat?

For her part, Snowball trotted over and rubbed against his legs until he leaned over and ran a hand through her fur. Then, looking exactly how the proverbial cat with the cream would, sat beside him, and Sophie would swear the tiny cat was smiling at her.

"Giselle gone?" he asked.

"Yes. She and the rest of the committee will be here tomorrow for a final check. They'll come early Saturday morning to get ahead of the crowds before we kick things off."

A minor miracle they managed to get everything ready, in time, in the end. Of course, a wedding ceremony was also happening tomorrow on the grounds, which had nothing to do with the Market. A bride with questionable decision-making skills had apparently pictured an idyllic winter wedding. Outdoors.

At least she'd get a white wedding if the snow held. Hopefully, it didn't do more than the softly falling thing that was still going on outside Sophie's window, crystalized flakes clinging to the edges of the glass and catching the light. A crew would be coming in to set up for the ceremony this afternoon, but maybe waiting for the morning would be better, given the weather. Not that she had much control over their timing.

When New Year's was over, Sophie had every intention of taking a few days off and sleeping straight through. No doubt Tilly would give them to her if she asked after the start she'd had.

Daniel leaned against the doorframe, socked feet—why was she starting to find that habit adorable?—crossed at the ankle, arms crossed, and pinned her with a searching gaze. "Want to explain that kiss?"

Relief that he apparently hadn't overheard her warred with the sudden tightening in her gut as that question hit her with the subtlety of being run over by Santa's reindeer on landing. He'd put her right on the spot. Kissing him had been entirely unprofessional, and yes, the jealousy, too. Not that she'd ever, ever admit such a thing to him.

Giving herself a minute to collect her thoughts, she got up and circled the desk to stand in front of him, needing to not be sitting and at a disadvantage for this particular chat.

"I was helping you with Giselle," she said, proud of how reasonable she sounded.

His expression didn't change, but by a hard glint in his eyes—there, then gone—she would have sworn he was unhappy about that explanation. "Helping?" he promoted.

"You're the one who didn't want me to leave you alone with her," she pointed out. "And you kissed me that first day. I assumed . . ." She waved her hands in an "and so on" gesture.

"So you decided that kissing me again was a good idea?"

"Sowing seeds of doubt in her mind for that meeting with her dad."

"But that's with her dad," he pointed out. "Not Giselle."

Poor, misguided man. "I'll lay good odds that she'll be there, too."

Daniel sort of grunted at that. Not an agreement, but not a denial, either. *Because he knows I'm right.*

His gaze didn't waver from her face, and it took all her willpower to stay still under his scrutiny.

"The necklace looks nice," he said suddenly. Then reached out with a finger to trace the delicate gold circles, brushing the skin at the base of her throat and sending warmth spiraling through her ahead of a wave of tension that sparked at the edges.

"It was a lovely gesture," she said.

He dropped his hand and she could take a breath again. Amusement flickered across his lips, amusement that disappeared quickly. "I'm glad I got it to you before the geese, or we would've been out of order."

Sophie forced a chuckle at that. "I can't believe there were six."

Which was kind of perfect because she already had a swan situation coming tomorrow and, laughing to herself, had planned a bit of a surprise in exchange for Daniel's four calling birds stunt.

"Actually, there were eight," he said, interrupting her thoughts.

Her eyebrows shot up. "Oh?"

"I spotted two more in the woods. Probably a good thing, or I'd be worried that Weber Haus is about to turn into a zoo at the rate we're going."

We're. He'd included himself in her rather dodgy game of The Twelve Days of Christmas, as though they shared this funny, silly secret. Snowball, too. She'd been there for all of them in some way.

Warmth washed through her again . . . because she liked being on the same side as him, she realized suddenly. She'd enjoyed it today, going up against the woman Sophie was starting to think of as her own personal nemesis. Tag teaming the things that needed to be done for the Market.

Enjoyed it maybe too much.

Because that's how she'd thought of herself and Malcom. A team. Working at the same place with similar goals and only wanting what was best for the hotel. Look where that landed her.

You've loved working here, a tiny voice sounded at the back of her mind.

That hadn't been her plan or her expectation. Give her all, of course, and enjoy the experience as much as possible. But this was supposed to be a small stop on her bid for the next big thing. She wasn't prepared to like it here. Not ready to settle. Not ready to give up her original dream. Definitely not ready to trust a man with . . . any part of her.

"I need to get back to work," she said, giving a mental wince at how brusque she suddenly sounded, even as she moved behind her desk and took her seat. "I'm sure you do, too."

Another flicker of emotion in his eyes was quickly masked and she lowered her head to stare at her computer screen, not really taking it in but pretending to.

"Yeah." She was horribly aware of him in the room. Like all she had to do was glance at him to set a spark to the tinder.

After another beat, or maybe more, he levered off the door. "See you later, Sophie."

She waved a casual hand, not lifting her gaze as though already absorbed. Then, as soon as he was gone, dropped her head to the desk, only to pull up with a gasp as her hair caught in the clasp of her necklace.

With fumbling fingers, Sophie took it off, along with a

hunk of her hair that came with it, and stared hard at what exactly had snagged. A knot in the chain. She tried to undo it with her fingernails for a few seconds, then, needing to bleed off her residual tension anyway, left the necklace on her desk and went to get tweezers.

I watch Sophie, noting the frown burrowing between her brows and the way she's staring at her computer but not doing anything, then turn my head and listen to Daniel's plodding tread as he leaves the house.

These two humans clearly need my help. The question is, what should I do?

I mean, making friends with Daniel was a great first step. The fact that he let me chase the geese while he shot that gun to help me get rid of them . . . Best. Day. Ever.

Other birds and vermin take warning.

But being friendly with them both isn't enough. They need to spend more time together. Without the Wicked Witch.

Sophie leaves suddenly, but I don't follow her, still trying to figure out the next thing I should do to bring them together.

I glance around her office, thinking hard. Then my gaze lands on a glint of gold on her desk and I smile to myself.

I *do* love shiny things.

Chapter 12

Daniel wielded a paint gun with proficiency when required, and given their delays and deadlines, his taking on that job *was* required. Masked with glasses and gloves, he was working his way room by room through the interior of the new hotel. The bottom half of the walls would be wood paneled in all the common areas, so he only had to spray to a line there, but the rest of the rooms would all be white. At least they wouldn't have to worry about the edges with the white crown molding up against colored walls showing every tiny mistake.

Not that his crew made mistakes.

At this rate, guests would be able to move in long before the outside walls were done because the interior was coming along so much faster than the exterior. Not that Tilly or Sophie would allow that. Frustration bubbled, and he took it out on the wall with the paint. Hammering would be better for his blood pressure right now, a way to dispel the built-up energy gathering in his muscles.

He was *supposed* to be working outside. Granted, they had been out there for a good chunk of the day, but then the snow had started falling in thicker clumps, and they'd moved the action inside.

"You missed a spot," Levi yelled over the sound of the hissing paint.

Daniel blinked himself back to awareness and swore under his breath. At this rate, they'd definitely take finishing this job away and give it to Jannik. He was tempted to swing the paint canister at Levi, but they couldn't be messing around right now. Even if his head wasn't totally in it.

The entire workday—with a maddening lack of self-control—he'd thought through that kiss and then the "chat" in Sophie's office afterward. He'd hardly even noticed the increase in snow until Henry asked if they should move things inside.

Daniel exhaled long and slow.

He could still feel the press of Sophie's lips against his, soft and sweet. The curve of her waist as his hand slipped under her thick jacket, which hadn't been buttoned. The coffee taste of her, extra sweet as though she'd added more sugar than coffee. The way those starlight eyes had sparkled up at him for a heartbeat, drawing him into her, before she'd frowned—at herself? at him?—and stepped away.

A connection.

This wasn't hormones or an inexplicable, temporary attraction. This was more. Deeper. Stronger.

An urge to share himself with her and hold nothing back struck hard, despite their rocky beginning that they still weren't entirely past. Even so, he knew, in his gut, that opening up to her would feel . . . right.

The sight of her wearing his gift had already been an unexpected sucker punch. Most people with any modicum of a heart would do that out of politeness. But dang if he hadn't lost his breath for a moment. He wanted to kiss her again, only without his beard getting in the way, and make her smile like she had before that frown. He wanted to make her smile all the time. Know her, every part of her.

Only the kiss she'd given him hadn't been a connection for her. It had been for show.

He'd tested that reality out, daring to touch the necklace and wanting to let his fingers linger over the heat of her skin, trace the dip at the base of her neck. Thankfully, he'd held back, but mostly because she'd pulled away.

Knowing a tiny bit about her ex-boyfriend situation, and the opinion she had about Daniel being overbearing, there really was only one thing he could do. *Not* push himself where he wasn't wanted.

With the Christmas Market starting soon and nothing else for him to help with there, all he had to focus on was construction. True, they currently lived in the same house, but he didn't have to linger if he bumped into her. He could tell her updates over the walkie-talkie. Otherwise, he'd let her have the space she'd so obviously wanted from the beginning.

"Boss?" A shout from outside on the ground level had him turning off the paint gun so he could walk over to the still-glassless window and poke his head out.

"What?"

Snowball.

With one hand, Henry held up the tiny white cat, who seemed perfectly amenable to being held that way, not making a fuss. If anything, she looked . . . smug.

"She had this in her mouth." Henry held up his other hand and something gold glinted in the bright spotlights they'd turned on as day had turned to an overcast and gloomy dusk.

"What is that?" He asked the question even as the pit in his stomach told him exactly what.

"A necklace. Probably from one of the guests or maybe the shops."

Not if it had five gold rings.

"Hold on to the cat and I'll be there in a sec."

He didn't wait for Henry to respond as he turned back inside to Levi, who was still painting. Daniel gave a slashing sign across his throat. "Time to close up shop for the day. I need to take Snowball back to the house. You got this?"

"On it," Levi said. "We'll see you up there for hot chocolate and cookies."

Daniel paused midway out the door and backed up. "Says who?"

"Sophie. She invited us via the walkie-talkie around lunchtime. I forgot to let you know. Sorry."

So much for his good intentions to give her space. Did she want him gone or want him around?

Best to stick with his plan of staying away, otherwise this merry-go-round he'd gotten on with her might give him motion sickness.

Or you're love-sick.

He shoved that voice way to the back of his mind and put a rock on it to pin it down as he made his way down to Henry and took Snowball, who didn't protest and, in fact, snuggled into him. Not one to look a Christmas miracle in the mouth, he made his way back to the main house, paused at the back door to shuck his boots, and went to find Sophie. He couldn't exactly avoid her for this part.

After this, *then* he'd stay out of her way.

He skidded to a stop inside the door at the sight of Mrs. Bailey at the stove stirring something in a massive pot. At the bang of the screen door behind him, she jerked her head around and grinned.

"The crew done for the day?" she asked.

"They're breaking down and locking up and will be here in a second. You didn't have to stay to do this." He knew she had a large family at home waiting for her.

Mrs. Bailey clucked her tongue. "Sophie is giving me a little bonus to stay an extra hour, and I could use it. I've got my eye on a new grill for John. The hot chocolate is ready. I'll get out the cookies when the men come inside."

"What's this for? Did she say?"

She nodded, hand on her ample hip, as she watched the pot she was stirring. "Saint Nicholas Day. On such short notice, hot chocolate and ginger cookies were the closest I could get to the more traditional fare."

Sophie's idea? She'd gone and done something thoughtful for him and the crew on a day when she was run-off-her-feet busy? Well . . . enlisted Mrs. Bailey's help, but still.

"That's nice," Daniel said slowly. Because how did he go from that to showing Sophie the necklace she'd obviously thrown away. "Where is Sophie?"

That got Mrs. Bailey clicking her tongue again like a mother hen at her chicks. "She's on the front lawn arguing with the people setting up for the wedding tomorrow."

There was a wedding tomorrow? On top of everything else? Whose brilliant idea had that been? And why hadn't Sophie mentioned—

He cut that thought off. Sophie didn't have to mention anything to him. This was part of her job.

"Well, I found this little dickens out at my construction site." He held Snowball up, then put her on her feet gently. "Keep an eye on her while I go see if Sophie needs help?"

"Of course."

He grabbed his boots from outside.

Mrs. Bailey's voice followed him out the swinging door to the hallway and into the foyer. "That poor girl could use all the help she can get."

I'm doing everything she'll let me. Which wasn't a lot. Except maybe giving her space wasn't what she needed right now.

The merry-go-round started spinning again.

As soon as he was outside, Sophie's voice reached him, and he caught sight of her back turned to him as she faced someone obscured from his view by a pine tree. Hands on her hips didn't bode well, or the tense set to her shoulders. Even more telling was the still-calm but clipped tone of voice, different from the calm steadiness she used when dealing with Giselle or Mr. Muir. Daniel sat on the top step, putting on his boots, and shamelessly listened in.

"But if we put everything out tonight," Sophie was saying, "it'll all be covered in snow by tomorrow for the wedding."

"I'm sorry, but I can't do anything about the weather, lady." The guy didn't sound remotely sorry. More harassed than anything.

Sophie half turned toward Daniel, waving at the house. "What if you left the chairs on the front porch, where they'll stay drier, then come back tomorrow to set them up? The guests shouldn't start arriving until mid-afternoon. Plenty of time."

The man shook his head. "I have three other events to set up for tomorrow. I'm sorry, but I can't help you."

Daniel stood up and stepped around the pine tree right in time to see Sophie's expression slide into her professional kindness thing. "No," she said to the man she'd been speaking with. "I understand."

She glanced around and caught sight of Daniel, nodded in a friendly enough way, then turned back to the event guy. "Let's do this then . . . You set up the arbor and the row stands and leave the chairs on the front porch," she said. "I'll set them up tomorrow myself before the florist gets here to decorate."

The other man shrugged. "Up to you."

She watched him leave, then turned to Daniel, and suddenly he could see exactly how tired she was. Her shoulders slumped, her expression no longer bright but exhausted, made worse by faint purple marks under her eyes. "Are you done for the day?" she asked. "I had Mrs. Bailey make the crew some treats—"

"I saw her inside. The guys will be there in a bit."

THE TWELVE DAYS OF SNOWBALL   169

She managed a wan smile that only made him want to put his arms around her and snuggle her close and take away any burdens that he could. Except the necklace was burning a hole in his pocket and he still couldn't get the way she'd pulled back—twice—out of his head.

"We can help with the chairs tomorrow," he found himself offering.

She shook her head. "I can't ask you to do that. They shouldn't take me too long. It's not a huge wedding. Only fifty guests."

He grunted at that. "I can't believe you allowed a wedding to go on here the day before the Christmas Market opens."

"Talk to Miss Tilly," she said wryly. "Thankfully, it's only the ceremony and outside with their own decorations. The reception is in town." She paused. "Which reminds me. They also have their own event planner. I think I'll call her and enlist chair duty help."

At least she planned to ask *someone* for help. Even if it wasn't him.

"Sounds good." Maybe he should just put the necklace in her office and be done with it, not add to her day.

But something about that didn't sit right. So instead he pulled it out of his pocket and showed it to her. "Snowball brought me this."

Sophie gasped and snatched it from his grasp. "Thank goodness."

That at least was a better reaction than he was expecting. If puzzling.

She gazed up at him, eyes wide. "It has a knot in the chain, and I went to go get tweezers to fix it, and when I came back it was gone."

Daniel grinned, mostly because the pit in his stomach disappeared. Mostly.

"I've been searching all day." Sophie's voice was as close

to a wail as he'd ever heard. Over a necklace. Not over the chairs or the snow or the rain or Giselle or geese poop, but over losing his gift.

Relief, sharper and sweeter than he would have expected, disintegrated the rest of that pit.

"Snowball loves shiny things," he managed to say while keeping a straight face.

"She *was* in the office when I left." She plonked her hands on her hips, expression as fierce as the cat's ever got. "That sneaky kitty thief."

Daniel's relief came out as a laugh that was probably too loud, but he didn't care. "Let's go warm up with hot chocolate."

She snaked her arms up around her neck and put the necklace back on. "I'll fix the knot later. When Snowball isn't anywhere nearby."

Which only made him smile bigger—probably looking like a complete fool.

Sophie peeked over her shoulder as she towel-dried the large pot the hot chocolate had been warmed in to watch Daniel packing up and putting away the cookies. It was hardly a clean-up that required help, he could have easily retreated to his room, but he'd hung around to help while the rest of the crew went home.

This time they worked in a sort of contented harmony. Like they did this all the time. Why did this make her picture what life would be like with him around all the time, sharing their days and dinners and . . . nights?

"Are your parents waiting for you to celebrate today?" she asked to distract herself from thoughts she had no business thinking. Besides which, it suddenly struck her that he'd said today was a family tradition.

Snowball suddenly jumped up on the counter beside her

and Sophie scooped her up and put her back down on the floor while Daniel turned to face her, leaning against the counter. "They're on an extended holiday cruise this year. An anniversary present to themselves."

"Over Christmas as well?" she asked.

"Yes."

She finished with the pot and put it away, thinking that over. "I hope you have people to celebrate with this year."

He cocked his head. "You sound like you care."

Sophie made a face that made him laugh. "I'm *trying* to be a friend," she pointed out.

Again, Snowball jumped up and Sophie put her back down.

"Implying that I'm not making that easy." He laughed again.

Snowball jumped back up and Sophie made a sound in her throat. Only, this time, Daniel crossed the room and scooped the cat up. He held her in front of his face, nose-to-nose, but Sophie noticed with a secret grin, at a safe distance from sharp claws and teeth. "What do you want?" he asked the cat.

Snowball meowed, and a surprised laugh burst from Sophie.

"I swear she understands us perfectly," she said.

"I think she does," he murmured, eyeing the little cat with narrowed eyes. "I think she wants us to do something."

Sure enough, he lowered Snowball to the ground and she meowed again, then trotted to the door, where she looked over her shoulder at them in apparent expectation.

Daniel grabbed Sophie's hand and tugged her after him. "Let's see what she wants."

She let him lead her out of the kitchen following Snowball into not the main living area but into a smaller sitting room. Cozier, tucked into the center of the house with no windows, it sported a simple, cushy love seat and a wingback chair. Two opposite facing walls showed off lovely built-in shelves with a library that boasted a darn good assortment of reading.

Snowball hopped up on the armchair and curled up there. Then, when they didn't move, she raised her head and chirped another meow at them.

Daniel grinned and looked down at Sophie. "I don't know about you, but I wouldn't mind relaxing for a second."

Actually, that did sound pleasant. More than pleasant. They both stepped inside.

"When is the tree lighting ceremony?" Daniel asked, eyeing the smaller Christmas tree—this one a blue spruce with lovely color—that his men had decorated.

Snowball had taken over the armchair, all curled up and comfy in a heartbeat, forcing them to sit together. They both plopped down on the love seat, and she tried not to be horribly conscious of how close he was sitting or the way their knees were pressed together. Sophie dropped her head back, closing her eyes, and just let go of the tensions of the day on a long exhale. She should be a nervous knot with him here, but instead, she found herself . . . content. "The lighting thing was supposed to be this weekend, but I might wait for the Webers to get back."

"That's a nice idea."

She hummed noncommittally.

"Do you have any family Christmas plans?" His deep voice washed over her, adding to the peace of the moment in the nicest way.

Sophie didn't open her eyes as she shook her head. "They're used to me spending holidays at the hotel," she said. "It's the busiest time. I go pay visits a few weeks later, which is nice because it isn't quite as . . . frantic."

"But lonely for you on holidays."

She managed a tired grin at that. "Hard to be lonely when I'm so busy and usually surrounded by travelers and guests.

Although, I think next year I'll have my parents, or maybe my older sister and her family, come stay here for Christmas. Best of both worlds."

Daniel was silent for long enough that she wondered if he'd fallen asleep. Lifting one eyelid, she peeked at him, only to find him relaxed—socked feet up on the coffee table, hands folded over his stomach, leaning back into the cushiness of the love seat. Yet the way he was staring off into space, as though seeing nothing, and the firm set of his lips . . .

"You okay?" she asked softly.

If her eyes had been closed, she would have missed the small start he gave, followed by the way his lips twisted. "I was just thinking."

Not about anything very happy, she'd bet.

As if she'd spoken that aloud, he shook his head, smiling a little, though it seemed sad. "Just one of those random thoughts, you know?" He paused, sort of collecting himself. "My brother was big on Christmas trees. Sort of like Mr. Muir, actually. Drew loved the entire process—picking out just the right tree to go with the ornaments we had and spending time together as a family to decorate it. He would have loved how Emily puts a different tree in each room of Weber Haus."

He rolled his head to the side, hazel eyes scanning her face. "I'm guessing someone told you about my brother."

She didn't bother lying, but she wasn't going to push him to talk about it, either. "Only that you lost him when you were a kid."

"Is that why you were suddenly easier to work with?" The frown that followed the words turned so fierce, he almost didn't look like himself.

Sophie grimaced. "Was I really that terrible before?"

"No." But he didn't look away, waiting for the answer to his question.

Sophie shifted to look him directly in the eyes. "Not because of that. No, though I do feel for you about that."

To give her hands something to do, she grabbed one of the decorative pillows and hugged it, pulling at the fringe.

"You're going to have to put aside the Malcom thing eventually."

Sophie blinked, mostly because he'd caught what she hadn't said. "I am."

"Good." He reached out, stopping her plucking with a hand over hers. "And I'm glad you see what a wonderful guy *I* am now."

The wag of his eyebrows was what did it, pulling laughter from her in a way she hadn't experienced in a long, long while.

Too long.

His deep chuckle and visible enjoyment of her reaction only kept her rolling longer. Still chuckling, cheeks aching, she calmed to find Daniel grinning tiredly at her.

"Should I be offended that you found that so funny?" he teased.

She shook her head and they both quieted, happy to just sort of *be* there together. She wasn't sure how long they stayed that way, but it was comfortable, nice even.

"Drew was ten when he died, and I couldn't do anything about it." Daniel's voice, though soft, suddenly settled heavily between them. The smile had faded from his mouth, shadows filled his eyes.

Sophie stayed quiet. He'd gone back to those memories, and maybe he needed to say this.

"I remember how my parents had to make me leave the hospital every night there at the end. I didn't want to go because then Drew would be all alone and scared. He didn't like the way everything beeped in the room."

Sophie's heart clenched at the picture he painted, the pain in his voice, sending an answering ache through her, and she twisted the hand still under his to link their fingers together, needing him to know that she saw his pain.

Only, Daniel hardly seemed to notice. "I even snuck back at night. They'd find me asleep in there the next morning, and I'd get in trouble for leaving home and scaring them. But I didn't care and snuck back out again the next night."

"Sounds like Drew had a pretty awesome big brother."

That pulled a lopsided half smile from him. "He was a handful. He needed someone to watch out for him."

Sophie could immediately see in her mind's eye a younger version of Daniel dealing with bullies, or consequences of boys being boys, picking up the pieces for his brother. No wonder the man had an "I can fix it for everyone" complex. Because for the one person who mattered most, he couldn't.

Sophie let go of his hand and pulled out her phone. "This is Angela," she said, showing him a picture. "My baby sister. I'm second youngest."

They were standing in front of her old hotel, arms wrapped around each other, laughing at something Angela had said, though Sophie couldn't remember what. A snide comment no doubt, knowing her sister.

Daniel studied the image. "Your handful?" he asked.

She hummed an affirmation. "She keeps everyone on their toes. Right now, she's on a backpacking trip around the world and I worry when she doesn't check in each day, even though she warns us when she can't. It does something to who you are as a person," she said. "to have a person like that in your life. Makes you grow up faster, be the responsible one."

He snorted. "I went the opposite direction for a while after Drew died," he said. "Pete reined me in."

"I've heard a few murmurings about that." She grinned. "You'll have to tell me a few of those stories someday."

And just like that, they were friends. Really friends, and not just trying.

Then she went and ruined the moment with a massive yawn that stretched her face until her ears popped.

Daniel chuckled. "Sounds like bedtime."

She lowered the hand she'd covered her mouth with and gave a rueful groan. "Yeah."

He levered himself up and Snowball gave a squeak of protest, raising her head to glare at them as though they were ruining the evening she had planned. Then Sophie squeaked, too, as he suddenly leaned over her, hands on the love seat on either side of her shoulders, his face inches from hers. "For the record," he said in a voice gone low and gruff, "your ex was an idiot."

Eyes wide, she tried to keep her heart from taking off at a gallop and flying away into the night like one of Santa's reindeer. "I agree." She licked her lips. "And for the record, I bet you were your brother's hero. I bet you still are."

He grunted as though she'd knocked the wind right from him.

"If I kiss you," he said, "I want you to know it's because I would like to kiss you and for no other reason than that."

Oh heavens. I'm not ready for this. For someone to look at her as if she was precious and wanted. As if he needed a taste to keep going. What if . . .

"I think I'd like that," she whispered.

His lips settled against hers, soft and lingering at first. Then raised as he seemed to check her expression before returning to plunder, his kisses turning harder, more insistent. Oh boy, could Daniel Aarons kiss. This wasn't like the other quick pecks they'd shared, though those had been nice, too.

This was . . . something else.

Anticipation and need and tenderness all rolled into a beat that echoed in her heart and made her want to hurry up and slow down all at the same time. Made her want to linger even as she wanted . . . more.

His lips gentled against hers for one last brush. Then he lifted his head, smiling down into her eyes.

"Better get you to bed, young lady," he said in a husky drawl that only sent another wave of heat blazing through her.

He reached down and hauled her to her feet. "I'll put out the lights down here," he said, and gave her a little push toward the door. "See you tomorrow."

That turned out much better than I'd hoped when I led them into the sitting room. I've found lots of people kissing in there this year. The canoodling room, Miss Tilly calls it. I'd hoped getting them in there might result in that, but you never know what humans are going to do.

I follow a dreamy Sophie up the stairs. If I could, I'd give myself a pat on the back. These two figured it out way faster than Emily and Lukas did, but it's obvious they wouldn't have gotten there without my help.

Job well done, me.

Maybe I should find another couple who need my assistance. After all, my efforts so far speak for themselves. Clearly, humans need me to help them fall in love.

Chapter 13

───────◦❦◦───────

Daniel hadn't dropped by this morning, and Sophie had to admit . . . she missed his face.

Which was silly. In the same way she'd hated staying at home alone at night when she was a kid—an irrational kind of silly. They'd lived in the country and knew all their neighbors, so there had been no reason for her fear. Just like she had no reason she should miss his face. Even if it was a cute face. At least she assumed so, under that scruff.

He was still staying in the house and she knew he was nearby, working hard on the construction because—thank goodness—the snow had stopped. The sun wasn't out, which was probably a good thing, or the wedding would turn into a mud puddle in a hurry. Though, she'd sort of expected to see him pop in at some point while the chairs were being set up. Not that she'd needed help.

She stood now on the top stair of the front porch watching the florist and his team work. They were wrapping lovely garlands of red roses, white Christmas chrysanthemums, and starbursts of stephanotis around the arbor under which the couple would stand. Smaller standing sprays were being placed at the ends of the rows. A red weatherproof carpet would be rolled up the aisle and another one placed under the arbor, to protect the bride's and bridesmaids' dresses and shoes no doubt.

Sophie had to give it to the bride and the wedding coordinator, especially with the snow, it would look lovely. The pictures would no doubt be striking, as long as the people in the pictures didn't look miserable with cold. She hoped they'd planned on a short ceremony.

A honk sounded from the inside of an open van that had been backed up the drive, and Sophie grinned, hardly able to wait to see Daniel's reaction. Two could play at the game Snowball had started that first day with her partridge and pear tree. Okay, three were playing if you counted the cat, Sophie, and Daniel.

"Am I late?" a deep voice asked from behind her.

For a second, she couldn't breathe.

This had *never* happened with Malcom—or any of her boyfriends. The sensation of air whooshing from her lungs, leaving her winded, and, frankly, stunned, because he'd shown up. Because he hadn't left her to deal with this alone.

"The bride's brothers showed up," she said, not turning her head to address him directly, her gaze still on the florist. Then, the thought of last night's kiss and a bout of unaccustomed mischief sneaking up on her, she mentioned, "Good-looking group of guys, and so polite."

"Hooray for them."

Was that a growl in his voice? She bit back a smirk.

"I guess since you don't need me here, I'll be along my—"

"Actually, there's something you should see first."

Finally, her breathing functioning properly now, she turned her head to look at him. Directly into warm hazel eyes.

Don't look at his lips. Don't look at his lips.

He smiled. She looked. And her breathing went all hooey again.

This was going to be a problem if she didn't get herself

under control. She pictured collapsing in a heap at his feet every time he entered a room, and had to hold back a giggle.

After a long stretch of staring at him, though, not one word coming to her mind, he lifted his eyebrows in question. "Soph? Something I should see?"

Right.

She gave herself a small shake and pointed to two men now lifting covered crates out of the back of the van. "This particular bride had a special request," she said.

"Okay. Um." He frowned doubtfully. "Weddings aren't exactly my area of expertise. What does special mean?"

"*Meow.*" The small sound came from at her feet, and Sophie jerked her gaze down to find Snowball sitting between them.

In a fluid movement, Sophie leaned down to scoop her up and cuddle her close. "You should not be out here." She sent a pointed look at Daniel, who glanced over his shoulder at the front door, which was still closed.

"I don't know how you get out, young lady," Sophie said to the cat. "But today you need to at least stay out of the front yard."

The men set down one of the crates and opened it, and a majestic, long-necked bird with snowy white feathers and a distinct black marking across its face waddled out.

A bark of laughter burst from the man at her side. "Swans." He turned his head, including her in the laughter. "No way."

"That's what I said when I read it in the details." She grinned. "I thought you'd get a kick out of it."

A tiny little growl came from the cat in her hands, and Sophie glanced down to find Snowball glaring at the offending birds, her ears pinned back.

"Stop that," Sophie warned her. "They are supposed to be here for a few hours, then they'll be taken away."

Daniel reached out and ran a hand over Snowball's fur, and, surprisingly, the cat settled.

"Are there seven?" he asked.

She shook her head. "Sadly, just two. But still . . . swans."
She waved a hand encompassing the pair now toddling
among the chairs.

He didn't say anything, and she peeped over to find him
watching her, almost searching her face.

"What?" she asked. Did she have spinach in her teeth
from the breakfast quiche or something? Snowball gave a
squeak of protest at being held so tightly, and Sophie loosened her grip.

"I don't know," Daniel said, still searching her face. "You
seem . . . different?"

Different from when she'd arrived, he meant. "I'm not annoyed at you," she pointed out.

He huffed a laugh. "That's not it. I think . . . are you
happy, maybe?"

Happy? "I wasn't unhappy before," she pointed out.

The look he shot her told her what she already knew.
There *was* a difference, though he kept the words to himself.

A gesture she appreciated. He really was trying to be less
of what she'd called him—an interfering know-it-all. Only,
Tilly was right. That was just how he showed he cared.

"In a few days, I'll have another surprise," she said. Cow-
ardly to redirect, but maybe she was a coward.

"There's no way you have maids a-milking."

Sophie hugged that secret to herself and gave nothing
away as they both turned back into the house. "I have to be
available for the wedding all afternoon," she said instead.
"Can you handle Giselle?"

"All on my own?" The exaggerated horror on his face
could have won the man acting awards. He was handsome
enough to earn them on the "it" factor alone, in her opinion.
That hadn't changed since they first met.

"The full committee will be with her, so hopefully that will tone her down a bit," she offered. "Let me know when they arrive. If I can break away, I will."

"Will do."

They paused in the foyer, knowing they needed to go separate directions. She opened her mouth to wish him a good day, but he cocked his head. "Exactly *how* good looking were those brothers?"

Laughter bubbled up from within a place that had turned bright inside her. All lit up. She pursed her lips, pretending to seriously consider his question. "They were *very* good looking," she said, keeping a straight face.

"Very," he muttered. His eyes took on a dangerous glint, and her heart tripped over itself in response. "Maybe I should kiss you again."

She managed to tamp down on the urge to hop right into his arms and instead held Snowball up between them like a kitty shield. "I am a professional, and you're at my place of business."

He dropped his amused gaze to Snowball, then back up to her. "So that's a no?"

Another shake of her head and she turned away, tossing a casual "Have a good day" over her shoulder.

"A kiss would have been more fun," he called back.

"That's a mighty fine idea, young man," Mr. Muir's voice sounded from over her head. "I say kiss a pretty girl every day if you can manage it."

"Excellent advice," Daniel agreed as she slipped into her office, taking the cat with her, cheeks on fire.

She should be irritated a guest had overheard them, because this *was* her work, but she just couldn't find it in her.

I don't bother to set up watch at Sophie's office window because Sophie said that the swans would be contained in small pens at the front, and the window looks out the back.

Jumping up onto the brocade-covered chair, I deliberately sharpen my claws on the material.

"No, no, no," Sophie croons, and she picks me up and puts me back on the floor.

She clearly has not gotten the message. So I jump back up and do it again. *Pop. Pop. Pop.* Sophie needs to understand that bringing even more birds onto *my* property is unacceptable. This is my domain, my kingdom, and my land to protect. Birds are off-limits.

After the partridge incident, she should know that.

I find myself back on the floor. "Bad kitty," Sophie scolds.

No, I'm not. I ignore her.

"Do I need to lock you up in my room?" Sophie asks next.

I shoot her a glare and hop back up on the chair. This time I turn a few circles and settle down. Then I stare Sophie right in the eyes, lower my head to rest on the tops of my front paws, and give a very loud, very irritated huff.

Sophie chuckles, but at least she says, "Don't worry. The swans will be gone in a few hours."

I intend to spend that time thinking of a way to get even with Sophie for letting those monstrosities near my home.

Daniel glanced around the fancy restaurant and held in a long-suffering sigh with difficulty. He definitely should have kissed Sophie instead of letting her run away to her office this morning. Mr. Muir was right. Not about pretty girls, but about kissing Sophie every day. That sounded like a fantastic idea.

Maybe the rest of his day would have gone better if he had.

Because sitting across from Giselle Becker in one of the nicer restaurants in town—white tablecloth, fancy dishes, and flowers and candlelight between them—was the capstone of what he would label a *Day*. Capital D. Emphasized with italics and a growly voice.

On a day when the crew had an opportunity to make a ton of headway thanks to better weather, some poor soul driving down the road into town had skidded on an icy patch and taken out the transformer that happened to provide electricity to the entire Weber Haus property. That had required getting his own generator up and running, which was fine, but also caused problems with the Christmas Market setup. In typical fashion of the last few weeks, of course, that had happened right when the committee had come by to inspect the progress before the Market kicked off.

Giselle had been in rare form. Sophie had to put her on the phone with the power company directly and let them handle her.

Otherwise, the final check of all the booths and decorations and the temporary dance floor for performances, the sound system checks, all had gone fine. Sophie had returned to the wedding coordination, and the *very* good-looking brothers, while Daniel had ended up . . . here.

"When will your dad arrive?" he asked, checking back toward the entrance.

Her smile when he turned to face her was this side of smug. "Oh, he's probably caught up with work. He should be here any second."

"I have an early morning tomorrow," he reminded her.

"You're such a hard worker, Daniel. Which is exactly why we want you for this job." She patted his hand, which rested on the white tablecloth, and he drew back, taking a swig of his water so he didn't offend her as he avoided her touch. He hadn't missed the "we" part of that statement, either.

Giselle's smile turned into a pretty little pucker of lush lips. "I'll order for him so that we don't have to wait too long."

"Sounds good."

They ordered and sent the waiter off for the food. Giselle sat back, eyeing him from under lowered lashes, toying with the stem of her wineglass. "Why didn't we ever date in school, do you think?"

He had a hard time not choking on his drink and thought fast. How to put this in a non-offensive way? After all, her father was possibly the source of his next big job. "I didn't date a lot," he said slowly.

"That's too bad." Her smile certainly made her beautiful.

She was lovely regardless, on the outside, with wide green eyes and blond hair that was close to the color of honey, styled in such a way that only highlighted her features. Rosebud mouth, perfect skin, and a figure that he'd guess most women envied and most men drooled over.

Only he found the fact that she knew how to use that smile to get what she wanted unnerving rather than appealing. It might have worked if he hadn't seen the condescending side of her—the part that dismissed anyone beneath her attention as unworthy of anything else good in life as well. The part she'd shown him in high school and shown to Sophie since the first day they'd met.

"I think we could have had fun together," she said next.

Not likely. "Well . . . even then I was into woodworking and construction. Do you have an interest in those topics?"

The tap of a nail against the stem of her glass might've been a warning, like a rattlesnake tail, or merely a sign of her thinking about it. He honestly wasn't sure which. "Not in school, probably, but I help Dad with that side of his business now. I have been told I have quite the eye, you know. If you get this project, we'll be working closely together."

Not an idea that thrilled him, but he could deal with it. "I assume you already have an architect on board? Often they prefer to use their own contractors for all the stages."

"They'll work with whom we ask them to." She waved off his concern.

"Hi, darling." A scratchy voice that sounded like a man

who'd never taken the cigar out of his mouth sounded from behind him, and Daniel turned to find George Becker moving around the side of the table to give his daughter a kiss on the cheek. "You started without me? I thought I was early."

Daniel stood and gripped the man's hand firmly, and, after practicing with Sophie lately, kept his mouth shut about the timing, because he and Giselle had been there almost forty-five minutes. Either Giselle's father had a rocky concept of time, or she'd given him the wrong one. Regardless, bringing it up would be a dumb move.

"I ordered for you," daughter assured father, who didn't seem too surprised as they all took their seats.

George turned to face Daniel. "My daughter tells me you run a fantastic construction crew."

"I'm a construction engineer, and, yes, my crew is solid."

"You're on the upgrades and expansions for Weber Haus, she says."

"Yes."

"I've seen your work. Excellent quality. Too bad about all this weather lately."

"We do what we can to work around it and keep momentum." Better to hold back that he'd be a full two months late on the project, and only if he made the latest deadlines.

"So, you wanted to speak with me about working on our country club project?" George asked next.

Daniel had to pause before flicking a glance at Giselle, who blinked back in wide-eyed innocence. "Giselle mentioned the project and it sounded like a terrific opportunity."

"It is."

Most awkward dinner conversation on record. "When are you looking to get started on construction, sir?"

"February or March depending on the usual pre-work hurdles."

"That timing would be great for my team. We wrap up our current project by New Year's and have a short one in Janu-

ary which should be done by the end of the month." *If* the
Brockman Group decided to go with him. They were still
waiting on the Weber Haus project. He kept that bit to himself. "Would you be interested in a tour of the site to get a
better idea of how we work?"

"No need."

Okay. What was the point of this meeting then? Because
Giselle's dad was acting completely uninterested. Daniel's
first instinct was to say that out loud, but something stayed
his tongue. A small voice in the back of his head was asking,
What would Sophie do in a situation like this?

Daniel set his mouth in what he hoped was an imitation of
her guest smile and scoured his brain for the best thing he
could say. Something helpful. Something . . . "What do you
need from me to help you make a decision?"

George Becker cocked his head, expression turning sharper,
more assessing. Daniel had no idea if that was a good sign
or not.

"I'll arrange for the architect to visit the site and talk
to you."

That was the end of it, apparently. Dinner arrived and they
ate their way through it, chatting of nothing in particular, focused mostly on the holidays. All while Giselle beamed at
him . . . as though she was personally responsible for his success in life and he was hers to be proud of.

Outside, bundled against the cold, saying their goodbyes,
she slipped her arm through his. "Daniel will take me home,
Dad, since it's not on your way."

He did his darndest not to double take. They hadn't arrived together, so where was this coming from? How had she
gotten here in the first place?

After saying goodbye to George Becker, who now had
Daniel's number and promised to be in touch with a date and
time for the architect, they turned to walk to his truck, where
he'd parked it down the street. "I hope you don't mind," she

said. "I came earlier with a friend of mine to shop and assumed I could get a ride home with one of you. Only Dad lives at the other end of town from me."

"No problem." He was tempted to ask Sophie to step up the fake PDA tomorrow. He definitely wouldn't mind having her lips pressed to his again, but that idea didn't sit right with him anymore. Like it made light of the real sparks flying between them and also implied that he couldn't handle Giselle on his own.

He situated Giselle in the truck, then went around to his side and started it up. "Which way?"

They made it to her house, probably in record time, and he'd never been so glad for four-wheel drive in his life, the packed snow crunching under his tires as they rolled along carefully. He pulled up outside her door and put the truck in park, then waited.

"Walk me to my door?" she asked. Again, with the beautiful and deliberately beguiling smile.

His mother had always taught him to be a gentleman. Teeth gritted, he got out, helped her down, and walked her up the small, shoveled path, waiting with impatience while she spent an inordinate amount of time fiddling with the locks.

Then she turned to him with that sweet, canned smile. "I think Dad liked you."

"As long as he likes my work, that's what matters."

She must've been the worst body language reader in history, because he stood back enough that he was down one step on her sidewalk, hands tucked in his back pockets, body turned slightly away.

And yet, Giselle still had the nerve to go up on tiptoe and kiss him. A lingering kiss that he held still under.

Even then, the expression she offered him as she stepped away was all siren. "Maybe next time we can have dinner without Dad."

It was incredibly tempting to bring Sophie's name up, but he decided to be vague yet firm. "I'm sorry, Giselle, but I'm seeing someone else, and I don't think she'd appreciate my being out with another woman in what might be construed as a date, even if it was just business."

There. Not entirely a lie. If he had his druthers, he'd be seeing Sophie more often than he was, and as a date. Dinner with her over a romantic candlelit table didn't sound like a root canal. It sounded like . . . Christmas.

The best kind of Christmas. Like the time when he woke up as a kid to find the overnight snowfall had transformed the world into a winter wonderland. Then to find a brand-new, top-of-the-line road bike waiting for him under the tree—that had been a pretty darn good day. A simple dinner with the woman managing Weber Haus would easily top it.

Damn. He was falling hard for Sophie Heidt.

This must be how it felt inside a snow globe when someone shook it up. Ignoring Giselle's wide-eyed stare, he tossed a vague good night in the direction of the woman he wished were Sophie right now and wandered back to his truck in a haze.

Then drove home to the woman he was pretty sure was going to break his heart.

Chapter 14

❧

Something was sitting on her chest. Not a heavy something, but not just the blankets, either. Sophie dragged herself out of the clinging arms of a vivid dream—one involving fairy lights and kissing—and opened her eyes to find two blue kitty eyes staring directly into hers, visible thanks to the glow of the clock on her bedside table. Sophie practically went cross-eyed trying to focus.

"Morning, Snowball," she murmured in a drowsy, sleep-hoarse voice.

Immediately, the kitten revved her engines and her purr vibrated through Sophie's sternum. With a chuckle Sophie ran a hand down the cat's back, and Snowball sort of squinted her eyes, her expression turning blissful and her purr hitting a whole new gear.

"The Christmas Market starts today, Snowball," Sophie said. The bright and cheery sounds of seasonal music already drifted over from the shops.

The purring continued.

"I need you to stay in the house. There are going to be way too many people around and I would worry about you. Can you do that for me? Please?"

Snowball's purr cut off and she got to her feet, still standing on Sophie's chest, then stretched, her butt in the air as she leaned back on her front paws, mouth spreading wide in a tiny kitty yawn showing her pointy, still-white teeth. Then she jumped to the floor and padded silently to the door, suddenly more visible in the shadowed room because Sophie's phone alarm went off, the screen lighting up.

As though it knew the cat needed a spotlight to follow.

Snowball looked pointedly at the door, then at Sophie with all the expectancy of a diva at the top of her career. Even her soft meow overflowed with attitude.

Sophie eyed her suspiciously. "That was not an agreement, little cat. I mean it. Stay inside and out of trouble."

Snowball sat and lifted a leg to bathe it daintily.

Even though logically she knew cats didn't speak human, Sophie still gave a frustrated *grrr*. The last thing she needed to worry about today was the cat. "I have to get dressed first," she said as she flipped back her comforter and dropped her feet to the freezing floor. The thin woven rug in her room did little to dispel the chill.

Shivering, she ran into her bathroom and a nice, hot shower. Twenty minutes later, wet hair hanging down her back and towel wrapped around her body, she stood in front of her closet debating what to wear.

Which, of course, was when a knock sounded at her door.

She cast an annoyed glance at the clock. Who the heck was at her door at this time of the morning?

Unless an emergency had cropped up.

Uncomfortably aware of her state of dress, or lack thereof, she only cracked the door, keeping her body hidden behind it, to find Daniel standing on the other side.

"Can I help you?" she asked.

He opened his mouth only to pause, a decided twinkle lighting his eyes in the dim light of the hallway. "You're only wearing a towel right now, aren't you?"

"A gentleman wouldn't ask," she said primly, even as her cheeks flamed with heat that had nothing to do with the fact that she preferred to turn herself into a lobster when she showered.

Why she was suddenly shy about this, she had no idea. She exposed far more skin in the summers when she wore a swimsuit. But something about standing here with Daniel, as though they were the only two people awake in the world right now, her skin still damp and flushed from her shower, felt . . . like she was asking for trouble.

"Maybe I'm not a gentleman." He winked.

Images from her dream swirled together with entirely real memories of what it felt like when his lips had been on hers, and Sophie had the sudden urge to do something out of character. Like drag him into her room.

To cover the urge, she stayed firmly entrenched behind the door and rolled her eyes. "Did you need me?"

Lips twitching, he still followed her lead and nodded. "I heard you moving around and wanted to catch you before we both got caught up in our day."

He paused. Long enough that she raised her eyebrows. "Yes?"

A grin suddenly lit him up. "I like that word when you say it."

What? Yes?

Another wave of that unaccustomed heat flushed through her again. "Why did you want to catch me?"

"Right. I was going to suggest that we go to the Christmas Market together over lunch?"

Like a date?

"After tag teaming it and everything . . ." he tacked on.

Oh. She shouldn't feel disappointed about his reasons or the fact that this wasn't a date. *Then what's this pit in the center of your chest?* a small voice piped up. She was getting in deeper by the day.

She wrote her alter ego voice off as nonsensical and ignored it. "I was planning to go at lunch, so that works for me. You want to meet me there?"

Daniel shook his head. "I'll swing by here and pick you up."

That definitely sounded like a date. Now she was one of those people who lived off wishful thinking. "Okay."

He opened his mouth as if he was going to speak; then his gaze dropped to hers and he closed his mouth slowly before giving his head a shake. She got the distinct impression he was arguing with himself. "I'll see you then," he said, almost abruptly, and turned on his heel, walking away with the softest clomps she was sure he could manage.

Slowly, Sophie closed her door, thinking through the encounter.

Only to look down and then around the room with a quick sweep of her gaze. Snowball had slipped out. She flung the door back open and hurried down the hall, whisper-hissing the cat's name.

She hit the top of the stairs at the same time that Daniel came back up them, the cat clutched in one hand, feet dangling, and Snowball's face the epitome of tantrummy toddler.

"She followed me—"

He lifted his gaze from the cat and went completely still. The sparks that fizzed just below the surface anytime they were in the same room ignited in his eyes, pulling an answering buzz from her body, her heart picking up to march double time, and Sophie found herself holding her breath.

Daniel shook his head once, twice. Again, seeming to argue with himself.

"My name is going to be cemented on the naughty list at this rate," he murmured, then stepped into her, his free hand going around her waist, drawing her up against him while he held Snowball to the side with the other. "But even I'm not made of stone, Soph."

On that confusing statement, he dropped his head and

kissed her. Hard. As if he wasn't quite in control. Against her back, his hand trembled and a sense of wonder poured through her like warm cider in her belly at that small sign that she was right. He wasn't in control and she'd done that to him. Made him feel that.

A small sound escaped her throat, a little telling whimper, and she wrapped her arms around his neck, going up on tip-toe, and offering him more.

Daniel didn't need any more encouragement, grunting against her lips before turning the kiss into something extra-ordinary. Softer and yet more complete. Sweeter and yet hot. Lovely and exciting all at once, sending such a swirl of sensa-tion and emotion through her that all she could do was hang on for the ride, losing herself in his touch.

"That's what I like to see," Mr. Muir's craggy voice sounded directly behind her.

With a yelp, Sophie jumped back, her hand flying to her towel as her gaze shot to Daniel's, no doubt reflecting her panic that a guest was seeing her in this state.

In the next heartbeat, he placed himself bodily between her and Mr. Muir, hiding her from view. "I'm sorry if we woke you."

Sophie grabbed the back of Daniel's shirt and buried her face in his back, trying not to groan audibly as embarrass-ment swamped her in an avalanche. Every inch of her body was probably bright red with mortification.

"I told you. Pretty girls *should* be kissed, and often," Mr. Muir declared, laughter lingering in his usually grumpy voice and seeming to be in no hurry to go back into his room.

Sophie found her backbone somewhere in her melting-with-mortification body and cleared her throat, poking her head around Daniel's shoulder. "Well, I should finish getting ready for the day," she said to the old man, who smirked at her with evident glee. "Daniel was bringing Snowball back for me."

"Is that what you young folks call canoodling these days?"
Mr. Muir teased, creased face wrinkling like a Shar Pei with
his grin. "Odd word choice, but okay."

"Come on," Daniel murmured, and they shuffled past Mr.
Muir's door together, Sophie doing her best to keep Daniel
between them, moving so that she was at his side and then in
front of him. At her open door, once she was inside, she
turned and held out her hand for the cat. Only she couldn't
quite look him in the eye.

Instead of handing her Snowball, though, he reached out
and, fingers under her chin, tipped her head up so that she
looked at him. "You should definitely be kissed," he murmured, the warmth in his eyes stealing every molecule of air
around her before he placed a quick but potent kiss on her
lips. "And often."

On that declaration, he handed over the cat, then closed
the door for Sophie with a soft *click* that sounded as though it
could've been a cannon boom the way it echoed through her.

"Good for you, young man," she could hear Mr. Muir
saying on the other side.

Daniel's deep voice didn't respond as Sophie dropped her
forehead to the door, eyes squeezed shut. "Well," she said to
Snowball, still not opening her eyes. "That's one way to start
the day."

"*Meow,*" Snowball piped up, sounding as though she were
happily agreeing.

At that, Sophie did open her eyes to lift the little cat up to go
nose-to-nose and glare at her. "*You* needn't sound so proud of
yourself, you know. That was a highly unprofessional situation
for me to be in. What if Mr. Muir tells Miss Tilly about it?"

Mortification wouldn't be her only problem. Her job might
very well be on the line.

Snowball lifted her front paws and put them on Sophie's
cheeks. Then meowed again softly, as though to say, "Trust
me. Everything will be fine."

Sophie sighed, the tension magically draining from her, and smiled. "I hope you're right."

Daniel whistled to himself as he stowed his hard hat under the desk, getting ready to head over and collect Sophie for the Market.

"You've been in an awfully good mood today, boss," Levi said as he did the same.

"I have?" Daniel asked.

He might be walking on clouds after that kiss in the hallway this morning, but he prided himself on his work ethic. He'd gotten straight down to business on the site.

"You've been whistling all day."

Huh. Now that Levi mentioned it . . . Daniel gave himself a mental head smack. One amazing kiss and he was turning into Snow White and whistling while he worked.

"Well . . ." he hedged. "Can you blame me? It's sunny, still cold enough that the snow isn't melting and turning this place into a mud pit, and we're getting a lot done on the outside trim." He shrugged. "I'd say that's worth being in a good mood for."

"Yeah, sure." The doubt rampant in his friend's voice said enough.

"What?" Daniel asked. Then regretted asking because that was the same as admitting he was making up reasons to be so happy.

"You're smitten," Levi said.

Daniel grimaced. Yup. He'd never hear the end of this now.

Levi's rare toothy grin was on full display. "Don't deny it, man. It's nice to see you so happy."

No use trying to lie his way out of what would no doubt become months of teasing. "You're not wrong . . . but I'm not so sure about her."

Levi snorted as if that was a stupid thing to say. "You

don't see how she looks at you when you're not paying attention. I'd say that if she doesn't realize it yet, it's because she's so busy with everything else going on around you both."

"She just came out of a relationship that burned her childhood dream to the ground, and now she's rebuilding. I'm not sure she's ready to let herself be anything more than attracted. And I have no intention of being a rebound."

The kisses, especially this morning, told him that she was, at the very least, attracted. Only attracted didn't mean smitten.

"Then give her time, but don't back down."

Daniel lightly punched Levi in the shoulder. "When did you get so smart about women? Last time I checked, the most recent date you've been on was in the Dark Ages."

Levi smirked. "A bit too close for comfort, am I?"

Yes. Daniel just shook his head. "I'll be back after lunch."

"Got a hot date?" Levi called after him. Also too close for comfort, because Daniel regarded this as a date but deliberately hadn't put it that way to Sophie so he wouldn't scare her off.

Unfortunately, Giselle chose that moment to round the building, making a beeline straight for him.

"Dang," Daniel muttered under his breath, as he closed the gate to the temporary chain link fence he'd had erected around the site after the vandalism incident behind him.

"There's trouble," he could hear Levi muttering under his breath behind him.

Giselle beamed, thankfully far enough away to have missed that little byplay. "There you are!" she trilled. "I've been searching for you all morning. Have you seen the Christmas Market yet?"

"Not yet," he said with reluctance. "Is there anything wrong?"

"Of course not, silly." She made it to him and linked her arm through his. "I thought we could walk through together. After all, we worked so hard to make it a success."

When had Giselle and he become a "we"?

"Actually, I was about to go get Sophie so she could see it, too."

The mention of Sophie did nothing to stop the juggernaut that was Giselle with a plan. "Well, we can make our way through the Market on our way to the house to get her," she said with a reasonable smile that didn't fool him in the slightest.

"I promised her that we'd see it together," he said, gently disconnecting Giselle's hand from his arm.

She gave a twitching shoulder shake, then caught his expression and seemed to rethink her pout, instead transforming back to reasonable in a blink. "I totally understand. She played a part in the success, too. Let's go behind the shops, then, to pick her up."

A part? Sophie'd done more than that.

Unheeding of the way he stiffened, Giselle linked her arm back through his and proceeded to drag him in the direction of the house. And he couldn't do a thing about it without being incredibly rude to the daughter of the man who was currently Daniel's best bet for another big project to put on his résumé.

The second they walked in the door to Sophie's office, he knew he wasn't just stuck between a rock and a hard place, but more like a granite boulder and dynamite.

Sophie was sitting behind her desk, with the window to her left, blinds wide open, showing the exact path he and Giselle had taken, arm in arm and probably looking more than a little cozy together. She was clacking away on her keyboard and raised her head with a pleasant enough smile. One that didn't touch her unusual eyes, which were a dark, swirling mercury.

"Giselle asked to join us," he said by way of explanation since the woman in question was standing right there. "You ready?"

"Actually . . ." Sophie waffled. "I had something come up and I'm waiting for a phone call."

Yup. Regardless of why, she was trying to back out of going to the Christmas Market with him.

"They're calling your cell phone, I assume?" he asked.

A long pause, no doubt trying to find a reason to stay behind. "Yes," she finally said with slow reluctance.

"Then you can always step away if they call while we're out."

"It'll be too loud," she pointed out. "This is a meeting with the hotel chain that Weber Haus partners with."

"I'm sure they'll understand if you explain that you're inspecting the Christmas Market being held on the grounds. Thrilled probably."

"If Sophie can't come," Giselle piped up, "we shouldn't push her. Her job is quite important."

The flash in Sophie's eyes could have been gratefulness, but Daniel suspected it was more a cynical sort of laughter. Because Giselle's attitude had been nothing but condescending from the second the two women had met.

"Well, in that case," Daniel said, "I'll go back to the job site and work until you're ready, Soph. I can always take my lunch break a little late."

Sophie grimaced. True, she covered it quickly, but he caught the expression all the same. "I couldn't ask you to do that," she hedged. "I'm not sure when—"

"Or I could just hang out in here until you're ready." To prove his point, he plopped his behind in the nearest chair, an antique bit of nothing that groaned a protest under his weight.

He glanced around in wide-eyed innocence, ignoring Giselle's impatient frown. "Do you have any magazines?" he asked. "Or I guess I could catch up on my social media."

He proceeded to pull his phone out of his pocket and make a big show of swiping away and humming to himself in mock commentary.

"Oh, good grief," Sophie muttered under her breath.

He swallowed back a grin.

"But, Daniel, I have to leave in an hour," Giselle wheedled.

He couldn't pass up that opportunity. "Then you should definitely go on without us." Hopping to his feet, he ushered her out of the office quickly, so she didn't have time to object.

"But . . . I was hoping you and I—"

"We'll try to catch up with you quickly. Maybe Sophie can call and get an estimated time or arrange a better day for her meeting."

Giselle shuffled her feet, but he had her down the hall and into the kitchen before she could offer more than that token protest. She turned on the small stairs leading away from the back door, slipping a bit on an icy patch in heels that weren't exactly practical for the weather. Luckily, she managed to stay upright, glaring at him like that slip was his fault.

"Have fun," he said with a wave.

Sulking was not a good look on that pretty face. "You'll at least text me when you're on your way?"

"Of course. See you later." He shut the door before she could come up with a better way to get him out of the house without Sophie.

Tempting to dust his hands, but he didn't. He had a different woman to tackle now. Back in Sophie's office, she raised her head as he entered, then raised her eyebrows when he plopped back into the chair, phone at the ready.

"Don't mind me," he said. Then continued scrolling through his social media.

"It might be a while," she warned.

He didn't lift his gaze from his phone. "The guys can get back to work without me. I'll walkie-talkie over if I have to."

"I'm sure Giselle would much rather—"

He dropped the phone in his lap. "Frankly, I don't care what Giselle would rather."

Which only earned him a skeptical little frown.

He sighed. "She ambushed me as I was leaving the construction site to come over here. I couldn't very well be rude. I could really use that job her father has starting up."

"And the kiss you shared with her last night on her front step?" Sophie asked. "Was that about not being rude?"

"How on earth . . ." He paused, then shook his head. Small towns. Even with their newest addition, word apparently traveled fast. "She kissed me; I didn't kiss her back."

"Like you didn't kiss *me* back."

Daniel jumped to his feet and, hands planted on her desk, leaned closer. "That's different and you know it."

Sophie's jaw tightened on a look that was pure stubborn. "Do I? We're not dating. We've only just become friends, of a sort. You don't owe me anything, Daniel. So, if you need to schmooze a different woman—"

Suddenly he wasn't playing anymore. "*That's* what you thought I was doing with you? Buttering you up so you'd work with me and stop being a pain in my—"

He cut himself off with a snap of his teeth because he knew his own righteous anger had driven him too far.

The flash of hurt in her eyes told him so a heartbeat before she jumped to her own feet. "I have work to do. Please leave."

I swing my head back and forth, looking first at Sophie, glaring at her now-empty doorway, then at Daniel's back as he stomps away and out of the house.

That big, dumb oaf.

How could he hurt Sophie's feelings like that? I'm tempted to go all banshee kitty on him again and attack his legs, but . . . even I could tell he didn't mean it.

Sophie obviously didn't catch it, but I could see the regret that flashed over his features the second he cut off those words. Besides, I also caught his own hurt in the way his fists curled in on themselves when she accused him of flirting with her to get what he needed.

If I'm going to fix this for them, I'd better move fast.

I sprint from her office, ignoring her call. Then down the hall, into the kitchen, and . . . Yes! The door is still open as Daniel is leaving.

I haul kitty butt right out the door, ignoring his shout, too. I have a plan now. One that involves getting both of them to chase me. Maybe it'll put them on the same side again. Going just fast enough for Daniel to keep up as he runs after me, I head for the one place I know neither of them wants me to be.

His construction site.

As if those fences could ever keep me out.

Chapter 15

Damn that cat.

Hurt-driven anger spiked his blood and increased his pace as he chased Snowball over the uneven ground, his still-untied boots that he'd been putting on when she'd shot outside crunching in the snow. Except his thoughts weren't entirely on the cat, but on Sophie. How could she believe anything so vile about him—playing on women's sympathies or flirting with them to get what he wanted.

What had he ever done to make her believe such a thing?

Still, he kept going after Snowball because he knew Sophie would be worried sick about her, especially with the added bustle of the Christmas Market on top of everything else. He had to admit he would worry, too. With another shout, he ran after the streak of white fur, though a tad hard to track her across snow, since she blended in so well.

Snowball avoided going through the shops, instead going around the back of what had once been the barn, then behind the carriage house. He rounded the corner of those buildings to see her making a beeline for the site.

Dawning horror had him risking slipping himself as he tried to get to her fast. Given the saws, power tools, nails, and other construction paraphernalia they were currently using, the place was dangerous for such a tiny creature.

Picturing Sophie standing over bloodied pieces of dead cat, he put on a burst of speed as she climbed up and over the fence and he followed. He was so focused on catching her he didn't stop to put on his hard hat. He burst into the downstairs of the building, looked around, and spied a set of snowy pawprints leading out the door to the back side, followed by a flash of white tail as she disappeared outside, to where all the worst things for her were currently set up in a kitty death trap.

Daniel didn't pause or check as he followed, because all his men were on a lunch break. Not that he was really thinking it through, focused only on getting the cat. At full speed, he burst outside only to have Henry, a plank of wood hefted across one shoulder, be standing there and happen to swing around at the exact same time.

Daniel, almost in slow motion, watched the wood coming at his head even as he could do nothing to arrest his momentum. He heard the painful loud *crack* of contact as much as he felt the reverberation through his entire body. A second before all consciousness deserted him, a brief sensation of falling backward registered, followed by another loud *crack* and a starburst of pain splintering through the back of his head.

Then darkness dragged him under.

Consciousness returned a few times, sort of like swimming in rough seas and getting his head above water briefly before a wave would crest over him and he'd be back out. Mostly, in those vaguely lucid instances, he was aware of impressions . . . sounds.

The men gathering around him and someone yelling to call an ambulance. He tried to open his eyes at that. Daniel hated hospitals. No hospital. He'd be fine in a second, he wanted to tell them.

But someone had stuffed his mouth with cotton wool and

his eyes weren't listening to his brain, which was telling them to open. They remained glued stubbornly shut, as though weighted down by cement bags.

Then silent darkness again.

Then Sophie's voice. Uh-oh. Sophie didn't like blood. She'd told him so. "Daniel? Can you hear me? Squeeze my hand if you can hear me."

Squeeze her hand? Was she holding his hand? He couldn't feel anything.

Darkness. Silence.

"What kind of shoddy business are you running here, Sophie Heidt." This was Giselle's screech. Then red and blue lights flashing close by, creating a dance of colors across his lids.

Darkness. Silence.

A vague awareness that he was no longer lying on hard, cold ground, but moving, inside a vehicle maybe. Hopefully not a hearse. Something was over his mouth, another something squeezing his arm.

Darkness again. Silence again.

The next time he came to was . . . easier. Less fuzzy, less heavy. Though he still couldn't make his eyelids function. What was working fine were his ears. He could hear the kind of silence that wasn't total silence. Soft beeping off to his left and the low murmur of voices, but not right there with him.

He concentrated hard and, with a flicker of dim lighting, managed to force one eye to crack open. Only the second even that low concentration of light hit, he groaned and squeezed them shut again. That triggered all the rest of the pain in his body to go on red alert. Blood thundered into his head, every burst of his heart pumping pounded into his cranium with a whoosh of sound followed by an electric shock of agony.

"Ow." He was dimly aware that the word came from him.

A gasp, from someone else, managed to pierce the thundering whooshes of blood, and then he could feel a small, cool hand slipped into his.

"Daniel?" a soft voice whispered.

Sophie.

He cracked open one eye again, barely, to find her face hovering close by. Her lips wobbled, the expression tremulous, but that could also be his fuzzy vision.

"You're in the hospital," she said.

That explained the beeping. "Don't like hospitals," he managed to mutter.

"I know. You have a concussion. The doctors are worried about swelling of your brain because you won't stay awake. Let me get a nurse."

He managed to tighten his hand around hers. "Don't go."

Was that his voice? He hardly recognized the weak sound of it, a threadbare whisper, though even that much sent the pounding in his brain to ultrasonic levels.

"I won't," she said. "I just have to push this button."

A new beeping joined the sounds in the room.

Memories struck then, with all the subtlety of a sledgehammer joining the thumping pain in his head. Front and back.

"Snowball?" he asked.

He focused on the way her lips softened and tipped up. "Safe and sound at home."

"Good."

He relaxed, closing his eyes.

"Daniel, who has the authority to make medical decisions for you?"

He wanted to frown over that question, mull it over, because something about it seemed wrong. Ominous.

"Should I try to get in touch with your parents?"

"No." He must've shouted the word because his brain splintered into a thousand pieces. The pain so overwhelming that it drowned out everything else. Everything except not wanting to worry his parents, who'd already gone through the agony of losing a child. No way was he making them worry in a hospital again.

"Okay." He was vaguely aware of her comforting voice. "I won't call them. Yet."

He would have smiled at the Sophie-ism if he weren't in so much pain. Now who was bossy?

At some point he knew a nurse had come into the room, poking and prodding, lifting his eyelids to shine a light in them. But he didn't care. He needed to sleep more so he could stop hurting so much.

And Sophie was here.

Daniel's world became centered on the pain in his head—sometimes pummeling like a jackhammer to his skull, other times dull like a toothache, but always there. That and the barely functioning moments between deeper sleep that they wouldn't let him stay in for long, waking him up with deliberate shakes and calling his name. Mutterings about a concussion, but these only made him irritated every time.

More voices drifted through his head on and off for he wasn't sure how long. He was aware when the nurses would come in to check him. Aware that Sophie had left, though he wasn't sure where or for how long. Then she was back, her face hovering in fuzzy focus anytime he opened his eyes.

At some point he would have sworn that Peter was in his room, saying something blearily like, "You had to go and copy me, didn't you?"

Daniel would have smiled, but expressions moved his facial skin, and that made his head hurt worse.

Giselle was there, too, he thought, her voice sounding nearby and at her most annoyed. "I have every right to be concerned about him," she was saying.

"He's not even awake, Giselle. I'll call you when he's lucid." This from Sophie.

Daniel tried to shake his head. He wasn't particularly interested that Giselle was visiting him in his hospital room.

Then quiet again. Had Sophie left, too?

He cracked an eye, wincing with the pain from the light, then winced again at how wincing made it worse.

Sophie leaned over him, and he would have frowned if he weren't trying so hard not to move his face. She looked . . . very un-Sophie-like. Haggard would be the best way to describe it—face pinched and drawn and pale, and her eyes dull. No makeup. Hair all over the place. And so damn beautiful.

"Giselle was just here wanting to check on you," she said, speaking softly. "You want me to get her back?"

"No," he croaked in a voice that still didn't sound like his own.

A cool hand slipped into his. "I can't stay much longer." She gave him a crooked, teary smile. Or was his vision playing tricks on him? "You sure know how to give a girl a good scare, Daniel Aarons."

He managed a weak grin. "All part of my plan."

"You have a plan?" Her chuckle was soft enough that it didn't send the shards through his brain. "Do share."

Only he was drifting away again, unable to keep his eyes open much longer. "It involves kissing," he said. "Lots and lots of kissing."

"Sounds nefarious. Who are you kissing exactly?"

"You . . ." He concentrated and tried again. "You can kiss me if you want."

A snort reached his ears, the sound so Sophie that he gave a mental chuckle. Then a whisper of a touch feathered across his dry lips. "Charmer," she whispered.

"Yup," was all he managed before drifting back to sleep.

I'm curled up on Sophie's bed when she gets home from the hospital. The door opens and she comes in . . . shoulders slumped, asleep on her feet. Though, at least tonight she's smiling a little, as though enjoying a happy secret.

That doesn't make me feel any better.

I messed up. All I wanted was for both Daniel and Sophie to chase me so that they'd spend time together. Maybe even laugh and fix their fight. Instead, Daniel got hurt. Really bad. I lift my paw and lick at it. Again. I stepped in the blood coming from his head when he stopped moving in that frightening way and I ran over to check on him. I can't seem to get this paw clean enough now, even though it's been days.

I hurt Daniel.

Sophie didn't yell or anything, though I've never seen anyone look more worried than she had right at that moment when she caught up to both of us.

She had skidded through the doorway and gone so white, she could have competed with my fur. Then she dropped beside him on her knees and sort of took over, snapping instructions at Daniel's men, one of whom she had pick me up and hold me. Even though I wanted to stay by Daniel, I didn't object.

The fact that Daniel wouldn't wake up and he had to be put into an ambulance might have scared me the most. The siren was so loud, and all the lights, and he drove away in it, Sophie watching him go before she took me back to the house and left me with Mrs. Bailey before leaving to follow.

All. My. Fault.

Lukas, and Emily, and Miss Tilly all came home while Daniel's been in the hospital, but I've been sleeping in Sophie's room even so. She needs me right now.

She's not been sleeping very well.

Sophie had never been so tempted to shove another human being out a second-story window in her life, picturing Giselle's shocked face if she did.

Daniel was awake and finally clear-eyed and sitting up

talking. Thank the heavens. Taking a two-by-four to the head before hitting concrete with the back of his head on the way down had been a darned good attempt to leave the world. It had involved way more blood than she ever wanted to see pouring from a body again in her life, soaking the ground and the top of his shirt. Fighting her own woozy reaction to that had taken a back seat to taking care of Daniel.

The relief when the hospital called had sideswiped her in a rush of emotions she wasn't remotely ready to unpack, so she'd focused on getting there, glad they'd contacted her.

It had practically taken an act of government to get the hospital to do that much . . . calling her with an update. Because she wasn't a blood relation or his next of kin—both of whom were unreachable on their cruise. Not to mention Daniel had forbidden her to contact his parents, the demand slurred at her every time he woke up.

She'd eventually managed to convince the hospital staff that, as his boss, and because the accident happened on Weber Haus property, she needed to be kept in the loop. Really, though, the night nurse, Sheila, probably felt bad for her, given that Sophie hadn't hidden her emotions all that well when it came to a certain unconscious man.

Finally, they'd determined that on Daniel's insurance he had Peter listed as his emergency contact—who was hardly out of danger himself. Peter's hospital had let him go on his parents' recognizance. Either that, or he was checking himself out of the place, he'd informed Sophie when he'd shown up in Daniel's room.

She liked Peter already.

But neither of them had managed to keep Giselle out. And the nurses, who were well aware of Giselle's father's standing in the community, didn't dare bar her entry.

Which was why Sophie had arrived this morning and walked into the room to be greeted with the sight of Giselle practically draped across Daniel's chest, her wobbling voice describing how upset she'd been all this time and how *other people* had been keeping her away when she'd only wanted to sit quietly at his side.

Sophie couldn't tell from Daniel's expression what he thought of all that until he said, "That's really sweet, but I've already told you, Giselle, I'm seeing someone."

Sophie must have made a sound, because he jerked his gaze up suddenly, and all the air sucked right out of the room.

Sparks.

Good thing they'd taken the oxygen tubes out of his nose, or the whole room would've gone up in flames with the way her skin was tingling alone.

I'm in love with him.

How that was even possible after such a short period of time, and such a rocky start, she had no idea. Maybe she was reacting to the trauma of seeing all that blood and his ashen face as he lay, unresponsive, on the ground. Or this was a rebound from Malcom, except this didn't feel like a rebound. In fact, it didn't feel anything like what she'd had with her ex. This was different.

More.

Except she was still planning to go off and pursue her dreams after her year here. Love wasn't supposed to be part of the situation. Maybe she'd get over this in a day or two and they could return to . . . whatever normal looked like for them.

She tried not to think about kisses. Quick, hard, urgent ones, or long, slow, and soft.

The bigger problem was, this discovery tied her tongue up in a knotted bow, words suddenly a blithering mess of incoherence in her head.

Daniel gave her a quick, confused frown and tipped his head. "Soph?"

Giselle jerked upright, though she remained sitting on the bed, hands still clinging to him. She directed an impatient glare over her shoulder at Sophie. "You were *supposed* to call me when he was awake," she accused.

"I only just got here," Sophie pointed out.

The other woman's shoulders twitched like a live wire. "Well . . . It's a good thing I'm friends with hospital staff who thought to give me a call."

Friends? Sophie kept an eye roll to herself. The woman had no doubt threatened their jobs if she wasn't notified.

"That is fortunate," was all Sophie said. Then she turned to Daniel. "What's the word?"

"No permanent damage. If I can keep food down today and manage the pain, I can go home tomorrow."

Tomorrow. So soon? "But not back to work, of course."

The look he shot her could have melted the North Pole. He really had been hiding a gorgeous face under that beard. The staff had shaved it off to fit his oxygen mask better. As she'd suspected, chiseled jaw with an unexpected cleft in the chin and lips she could only think of as kissable. "Worried about me?" he teased, voice lower, gruffer.

She crossed her arms and raised her eyebrows, determinedly unimpressed on the outside.

He gave in. "Not back to work for a week or so."

"Oh no," Giselle said. "We can't have that. You should take off much longer. Your health—"

"I'll listen to my doctors." Daniel cut her off, still staring at Sophie.

Sophie was still struggling with the completely ridiculous and close to overwhelming urge to shove Giselle off his bed and out the window. Either that or run out of the room so she could think in privacy.

She was already researching the best places to start her dreams over and had a short list. Practically had a vision board made in her head. This place and this time were not when she should be thinking about romantic relationships, or kisses, or anything that might break her heart all over again.

"Hopefully it doesn't cause problems for your crew," Giselle was saying as she only half listened. "The way Jannik Koch tried to step in and take over for you was over the line. Daddy was not impressed when he heard about that."

Sophie winced as Daniel did a double take. "What's this about?" he asked.

"Miss Tilly took care of it," Sophie assured him. "Levi has everything well in hand. You just worry about getting better."

She could see the gears turning. The little he'd told her about Jannik had made her suspect the other man played dirty in business. But the way Jannik had tried to step in the second Daniel was in the hospital had been just plain ugly.

At least George Becker seemed to have acknowledged that as well. Small-town rumor mills could be useful sometimes, it seemed.

"I can see you're being well cared for." She took a backward step toward the door.

Daniel's frown deepened.

"Don't feel you need to go on my account," Giselle simpered.

"I'm way behind on a few things at the inn," Sophie replied. "And I'll check on the Christmas Market while I'm there."

"Oh." Giselle waved a careless hand. "The rest of the committee has it well in hand. I've been assured it's going even better than expected."

"I still haven't seen it," Daniel said. Still frowning as he watched Sophie.

She hadn't, either—a little busy being at the hospital these last few days—but she didn't want him feeling guilty about that. "So . . . Peter is back. He's still technically on forced rest at home," she said. "Do you need someone to come pick you up and take you—"

"I'll handle that," Giselle insisted.

Sophie had been about to run. One foot half out the door already. But something rose up inside her and balked.

She was pretty darn sure that Giselle didn't mean anything to Daniel. He'd just said so a moment ago and had said as much that day he'd got clunked in the head, only she'd been too jealous to listen. But now . . . now the thought of letting anyone else take care of him, or hold his hand, or . . .

Holy smokes, I've got it worse than I thought.

"Actually." Sophie stepped inside before she could overthink herself out of it and crossed to his bed. "I was sort of hoping to do the honors."

Taking his hand and offering him a smile wasn't entirely about warning Giselle off. This was owning up to the fact that she had real feelings for him. Maybe . . . maybe setting down roots in Braunfels wasn't a bad idea. Dreams changed every day, and she'd found herself loving it here more and more. At the very least, she had a year or two to figure it out, to see where this attraction between them went.

Like that uncharacteristically snap decision had set off a chain reaction, everything inside her loosened up, setting free a sort of fizzing happiness to zing through her, champagne bubbles all bottled up.

Giselle frowningly glanced between them, and Sophie almost expected a snide comment or some kind of fit, but to her shock, the other woman stood up. "So Sophie is the woman you're seeing?" she asked, not angry, more slightly wounded.

Daniel offered her a gentle smile. "I guess you thought I was playing hard to get."

Giselle's red lips twitched. "Something like that." Then she did that pouting thing that Sophie was really starting to turn envious of. No woman had a right to look that beautiful while pouting. "Don't mess this up," she told Sophie with a return to her usual arrogance. "He's one of the good ones."

On that note, the blonde left the room, closing the door behind her, and Sophie stared after her in shock. Giselle had been surprisingly gracious, in her way, about that. Maybe she'd misjudged her.

Every moment of working to get the Market ready crowded into her brain and she shook her head. Maybe not.

A sharp tug on her hand tumbled her to sit on the bed beside Daniel, and she turned surprised eyes to find him watching her with a look that stole her breath.

"What?" Now that they were alone, she honestly had no idea how to act. Hotel Sophie seemed too cold in this situation, but she'd never been in love before. Malcom had been about loneliness more than anything, she realized now. It didn't come close to comparing.

Daniel cocked his head, grinning. "I really want to kiss you right now."

For getting rid of Giselle? Or because he truly wanted to kiss her? The questions must've shown on her face, because he chuckled. "I—"

The door opened to admit the nurse. "Visitors' hours are up, I'm afraid," she said in a kindly voice as she bustled over to check Daniel's IV and all the beeping gadgets he was hooked up to.

Sophie had no idea if she regretted not getting to know what Daniel was going to say, or if she was relieved to get a bit of a thinking break. She got to her feet, only he still held her hand, so she squeezed his in a friendly way. "Call me with the time you'll be released, and I'll be here."

"Not even a peck on the cheek for a man who's in the hospital?" he teased.

The nurse chuckled as Sophie shook her head at him in exasperation. "Flirt," she said.

"With you? Always."

Then Sophie surprised the heck out of herself as she leaned forward, hands on his chest, and offered him a quick kiss. Or she meant it to be quick, but he kissed her back, sort of taking over. He raised a hand and cupped the back of her head gently as he kissed her and kissed her. The sweetest, most heart-stopping kisses. Ones she never wanted to end.

Except a cleared throat from the nurse had him stopping, both of them breathing hard as he let go, staring into her eyes. "Now that was a terrific goodbye."

Laughter punched from her. The man should come with a warning label. Cheeks flaming, she backed away. "I'll see you tomorrow."

"Looking forward to it." His words floated out his door as she hurried away.

Chapter 16

Leaving the hospital was unexpectedly strange. After the odd, calm loneliness of lying in a hospital bed most of the day, he felt as though he'd been there for ages. He hadn't been able to read or watch TV because both activities hurt his head, so mostly he'd slept a lot. There had been constant interruptions from the nurses coming to check him regularly and daily visitors, but he'd never left the room and the world had shrunk down to it. Now, coming out into the gray mist of morning was akin to returning to the real world after being forced to cut all ties with it.

At least today was overcast, and not in that "the silver clouds are almost shinier than the sun" kind of way, but in a nicely drab way that didn't hurt his eyes or his head. He was already trying to wean off the medications they'd given him for the pain, never having liked them much.

But what was stranger was Sophie.

She sat in the driver's seat, practically white knuckling the steering wheel, staring straight ahead, and saying nothing. After the way she'd staked a claim in front of Giselle, and then that parting kiss, he'd hoped . . . Only she was being weird.

"Snowball steal your tongue?" he teased.

She flicked him a glance. "She'll be happy to see you. I think she's missed you."

Which was a non-answer if he'd ever heard one. "Did picking me up take you away from a lot of work?" he asked.

Maybe she was worried about her checklist and her schedules.

"I have a few days off," she informed him. "Miss Tilly insisted, even though they weren't exactly relaxing while they were away."

"You earned a break," he said.

He was tempted to reach over and peel the fingers of one hand from the steering wheel so he could give that hand a squeeze. But he suspected, as tightly wound as she was acting, that doing so would end up with them in a ditch and him back in the hospital. No way was he going back there. Not ever again if he could help it.

"You seem . . ." What was the right word that wouldn't offend her?

Sophie sighed. "I don't do well with time to myself," she said ruefully. "I never know quite what to do and usually end up working anyway."

Daniel smiled at that. "I have to leave the work site at the end of the day, but I still go home to get stuff done on other projects."

A small thing to have in common, being workaholics, but he liked that about her. Maybe because other girlfriends had complained about his tendencies that way, but he suspected she never would.

She's not your girlfriend, a smart-aleck voice piped up. *Yet.* But he had hopes.

He ignored himself. "How's the Market going?" he asked next. Because she was still being super quiet. Like warning bells quiet. Had that show for Giselle been just that? Her way of helping him get the other woman to back off?

Sophie huffed a laugh, her hands easing up on the wheel. "I still haven't been out there. The fates seemed to conspire against me." She perked up. "Maybe that's what I'll do today. I still need a few more Christmas presents for my family."

Daniel opened his mouth, but she pulled up to the front of the house, tires crunching on thicker snow, more of which had clearly fallen while he'd been holed up in hospital hell.

"We could have parked and walked," he said. "I'm not that much of an invalid."

"Ah. A tough guy, huh?" She smirked, and he didn't quite trust the Cheshire-ness of the expression.

The second he walked in the door, he knew why. "Welcome home," a host of friends whisper-shouted in deference to his traumatized noggin.

Daniel laughed, then winced, though he managed not to put a hand to his head. "I wasn't expecting this kind of homecoming."

He glanced over his shoulder at Sophie, who'd snuck in behind him. "I'm terrible at secrets," she said.

"*That's* why you weren't talking all the way here?" He managed to keep his laugh to a soft chuckle, not nearly as painful.

He turned back to his friends. Tilly, Emily, and Lukas were there. So was his crew. All of them grinning widely. Pete stood near the back, hands shoved in his pockets, looking gnarly with half his face green and yellow with healing bruises. Not that Daniel came off much better with his double black eyes and stitches in the back of his shaved head. They'd shaved off his beard, too. The rest of Peter and Emily's family had turned out. And . . .

He tried not to scowl.

"Mom? Dad?" He approached them, accepting hugs. "You're *supposed* to be on your cruise."

"Not when you are in the hospital," his mother said. She leaned back after hugging him, hands grasping at his arms and tears in her eyes as she inspected his face. "You look terrible."

"But I'll heal," he assured her.

A spike of guilt pierced his heart at the worry lingering in her expression, like a concern hangover. She'd already lost one son. It's why he hadn't wanted them called, to put her through that when she was so far away and couldn't do anything.

"Who called you?" he asked.

His dad squeezed his shoulder, then tipped his chin at someone behind Daniel. "Sophie called us yesterday and we got on a flight this morning."

He turned his head to look at her, remembering very clearly asking her not to contact them. Multiple times. She'd gone against his express wishes. He wrestled with the sudden urge to strangle her and to forgive her all at the same time.

His feelings about that must've shown in his face, because she held up both hands. "*After* the hospital assured me you were in the clear, so there was nothing to really worry them with."

Daniel grunted, still not super happy about it, and Sophie leaned closer to whisper. "I know, but I wasn't going to hold Tilly off any longer. She wanted to call them the first night and has been quite upset with me for refusing."

"Uh-huh."

Her lips pursed, in an adorably annoyed way that reminded him of Snowball in a snit all of a sudden. Only she didn't get to be annoyed with him.

"Your parents should be given the choice to be here for you." She was still whispering.

"That's not what I wanted," he whispered back.

Her lips twisted. "I know. I'm sorry. But yell at me later, okay?"

As if he would do that.

"The cruise wasn't very good anyway." His mother, watching them and no doubt getting the gist of the conversation, waved a careless hand. Then immediately contradicted herself. "We'll join back up with them in Greece."

At extra expense to them. Pile on more guilt. He gave Sophie a pointed stare and she grimaced, silver eyes begging for understanding, suddenly all contrite.

He turned to his father. "When did you get home?"

"This morning," he was informed. "We almost didn't make it in time to be here to welcome you home."

Sophie elbowed him in the side and hitched her chin at his parents, and he had a good idea what she was getting at. "Well, whatever way it happened, I'm glad you're here," he said.

And watched his mother blow out a silent breath, her shoulders relaxing a bit.

The hugs and handshakes for the rest of the gathered group came next. Henry was practically incoherent in his relief. "Really glad I didn't kill you, boss."

"It would have been my own fault," Daniel assured the man.

He hadn't thought about how the incident might shake up his employee, too. So stupid to run around the site without the proper protection. He'd probably still have a black eye, but no concussion or hospital stay if he'd been wearing his hard hat.

All because of a cat and the woman he'd fallen for.

"Good news," Levi said as he gingerly slapped Daniel on the back. "While you've been out, the weather has held, and we're mostly caught up."

Shock hit about the same time as realization, and he bent a look on his foreman. "How hard did you have to work the crew to pull that off?"

"Worth it for you, boss."

Tears stung the back of his eyes and he blinked them back. Maybe a knock in the head had turned him soppy. "Thanks."

"Besides." Levi grinned. "We wanted to put Jannik Koch's nose out of joint after that stunt he pulled, trying to get Miss Tilly to hire his crew to finish things out while you were in the hospital."

"Like I would ever do that," Tilly muttered, along with a few dire imprecations about Jannik.

"I appreciate that," Daniel said. He also made a mental note to pull a larger bonus for all the men from his own paycheck. Coming in on time meant more business. He'd be fine.

When he got to Pete, he paused. "You look terrible, man."

Pete snorted. "This is what you'll look like in a few weeks."

He wasn't wrong, and Daniel grinned. "Am I crazy, or were you in my hospital room taunting me with trying to copy you?"

Pete's usually unsmiling lips crooked up on one side. A grin for his dour-faced friend. He'd once joked that Peter should play the Grinch in the school play because all they'd have to do was paint him green and otherwise he had the part nailed.

"I have no idea what you're talking about," Pete said. "You must've been delusional. Seeing things and stuff."

"Uh-huh." Daniel shook his head. "Good to see you up. You gave everyone a bad scare."

"Says the man with twenty stitches in his head."

"I wasn't in a coma."

"I'll tell you later how concerned the doctors were with the amount you were sleeping," Pete assured him dryly.

A tiny sensation, like a breeze against his ankles, had him glancing down to find Snowball sitting at his feet. She was pawing lightly at his jeans, as though trying to gently capture his attention. The closest he'd seen the cat come to begging. Even her bright blue eyes in her tiny face could almost be called . . . contrite.

She meowed at him, the sound soft.

Bending over, slowly and carefully, which was *not* second nature, he scooped her up and held her in the air so that they were face-to-face. "I'm not mad at you, Snowball. I know you didn't mean for anyone to get hurt. But no more running around construction sites. Okay?"

She meowed again. Absolutely an agreement. The darn cat really did speak human, and no one was going to convince him otherwise.

With a nod, he tucked her into his chest and ran his other hand over her back. A gesture of forgiveness. For the first time ever with him, her motor of a purr started up, vibrating against him like a toy plane trying to take off, except she snuggled into his chest.

"It's a Christmas miracle," Emily stage-whispered. "Get a camera. Quick. No one else will believe it."

Which set everyone off laughing, and Daniel and Pete both wincing.

"I thought she hated you," Miss Tilly said, taking the tiny cat from his hands.

"Hate is strong language," he said.

"She attacked you the first time we met," Sophie's dry voice piped up from across the room. "It's how you got her out of the tree."

Which only made everyone laugh again.

"We've made up," he said. Though he still had no idea how that had happened. Except he was pretty sure it started when he asked for her help with Sophie.

He glanced over the heads of his family and friends to find her standing a little way back. Starlight-colored eyes sparked at him, even with a barrier of people between them, and suddenly all he wanted was to wrap his arms around her and sit for a while. Just be.

"We'd better get you up to bed," his mother said. "I talked to your doctors and they gave me all your instructions.

You're supposed to rest all day today and as much as you need tomorrow."

Daniel had no way to swim against the tide of well-meaning people who ushered him upstairs and into his bed, where they left him lying in dim lighting and already bored silly before his mom, the last out the door, closed him in with a *snick* that sounded like his doom.

A tiny meow sounded a split second before Snowball jumped up on the bed with him, so small the bed didn't even jiggle with her presence. She carefully padded up to him and stood there and stared in his face for a long moment.

"It's just you and me, Snow."

Which was apparently the right thing to say, because she happily curled up against his side and set to quietly snoring.

Daniel petted her absently.

Everyone had come up with him . . . he noticed . . . except for Sophie.

It's dark outside when Daniel suddenly gets up from the bed, which rolls me over as his weight dips the mattress and my legs go flying in the air before I'm fully awake. I blink once I stop moving. I yawn and stretch while keeping a bleary eye on what he's doing. He goes to the window and looks out. I don't need to join him to know what he'll see. The bright lights from the Christmas Market. They close down later on tonight, but the lights stay on all the time. *All* the time. Makes it hard for a cat to catch some zzz's.

Daniel sort of smiles to himself before he's moving around with more purpose. He sits on the edge of the bed, dipping it so that I roll his way again, and puts on his shoes.

I'm up now. Humans put on shoes only when they're going outside.

Sure enough, he grabs a thick jacket and his wallet and cell phone. "Stay here, Snowball," he says.

Then leaves me in the room, closing the door behind him.

Only, I am sure all the other humans told him that he should be resting today. I'd better follow him, to make sure nothing bad happens.

Sophie's cell phone pinged, and she was more than happy to stop rereading the same paragraph a hundred times and getting no further along despite the effort. She'd been wanting to read this book for ages, and it wasn't remotely holding her interest.

She picked up her phone and her heart, determined to ignore her head where Daniel was concerned, did a little flip of happiness at the sight of his name on the screen.

Opening the texting app, she buttoned her lips around a smile at the words. **I'm bored.**

She typed back. **Doctor's orders.**

The doctor ordered me to be bored? Came the immediate answer. **Seems kind of mean.**

You're supposed to rest.

I've rested enough. Break me out of this joint.

She bit her lip, staring at the words lighting up her screen. So tempting.

The dots showed up and she waited for his next text, which came through a second later. **We can stay close by. Visit the Christmas Market at night with all the lights. If I start to feel bad, we come right back.**

So tempting. Like Santa would disapprove, but Mrs. Claus might give her a nudge. That kind of tempting.

"Sophie Heidt," she told herself. "He's just home from the hospital. One of you should have a little common sense."

Two seconds later, she sent a text back. **Meet me in the kitchen in five.**

She'd never gotten ready so fast in her life. Not that she had to do much, only needing to swap out comfy yoga pants for jeans, put on boots, and grab her jacket and earmuffs. She almost wondered if she'd bump into him on the way down, but Daniel was waiting for her in the kitchen also wearing similar warm, casual clothes . . . and a grin that made her want to bubble over with laughter.

Being around him lightened her up. Maybe this feeling was what made reindeer fly.

"I like you in jeans," he commented, his gaze running over her in the nicest possible way.

"My day off."

"You're allowed to have them every once in a while," came the dry reply.

She ignored him and put on the thick jacket she'd brought with her and the earmuffs.

"I like it."

He reached up to pull a beanie over his head but stopped and grimaced. "Um . . ." He glanced her way.

"Catching on the stitches?"

"Yeah."

"Sit down." She waved at a kitchen chair. Once his head was more on her level, she gently and carefully fitted the beanie over it. Even with patchy bald spots, he still had lovely hair. Thick and straight. Soft against her fingertips.

She swallowed. "Okay?"

"Yup." He stood and caught her by the hand. "Let's go."

Sophie tried not to get flustered at the fact that he didn't let go of that hand as they walked around the side of the barn, past their pear tree, and onto the main thoroughfare of the shops, now packed with stalls for local, and some not so local, vendors to sell their wares.

"You did a wonderful job with the decorations," she said. "It looks very . . ."

"Christmassy," he supplied. Then shrugged. "We didn't choose them, just hung them."

"Now you decide to be modest?"

"What? I'm always modest." He winked.

Sophie's stomach, like a puppet on a string, did a little flip, even as she marveled at the difference a few weeks made. How had she gone from wanting to stick her pen in his eyeball every time he was around to being deliriously happy to be holding his hand and smiling at him?

To distract herself, she looked away, focusing on the shops. Except the atmosphere around the Christmas Market only added to a settling, yet exhilarating, sense of . . . contentment.

The tents they'd brought in had white sides with pointed red tops, matching the surrounding buildings perfectly, and the lights had been strung across the thoroughfare in such a way that everything was lit up and glowing.

The thick scent of mulled wine filled the air, along with the sound of festive music and the twirling of the small carousel Giselle had insisted on bringing in. She'd been right about that one. Children laughed and called for their parents as they whirled on by. A glittering wonderland.

The vendors themselves had so many different lovely things to consider. Handmade gifts including wood carvings, tree decorations, and soaps. Different foods with a particular emphasis on regional delicacies.

"Sophie! Daniel!" a voice called out.

She looked around to find Clara standing with a man who Sophie guessed was her husband, Jason, along with Emily, Lukas, and Miss Tilly.

Daniel leaned closer, warm breath brushing her cheek. "Let's say hello, but then go off on our own."

Sophie turned her head and got tangled up in his gaze, which was an appealing combination of intensely compelling and adorably hopeful.

There was nothing she could do about the way her heart warmed, sending a glow right through her. "All right," she murmured.

His slow smile was about the best thing she'd ever seen.

She probably wouldn't have looked away if the others hadn't caught up to them. A round of warm hugs only added to the sense that this moment was one of the most perfect of her life. Kind people, Christmas spirit, and . . . Daniel.

"Aren't you supposed to be in bed?" Miss Tilly wagged her finger at Daniel.

"Don't tell Pete," he begged, expression comically horrified.

Emily sniggered. "We'll give you one hour, then you'd better be back in bed."

"Two hours," he shot back.

"Want to make it thirty minutes?"

Daniel shifted his gaze to Lukas behind her in a clear appeal for backup, but Lukas held up his hands, clearly not willing to go against anything Emily said in this matter.

Daniel huffed. "All right. An hour."

Clara squeezed Sophie's arm, pulling her attention away. "Did you ever find a gift for your older sister?" she asked, referring to their impromptu shopping day.

"Not yet."

"Well, four shops down, there's a precious collection of glass animals. All hand blown. Didn't you say she does something with animals?"

"She's a veterinarian." Sophie smiled. "I can't believe you remembered. Thanks! I'll definitely check it out."

Daniel's hand crept into hers; though awkward through their thick gloves, her heart still took off.

"Oh, Daniel," Miss Tilly piped up. "I know it's bad timing, but I was thinking about those covered walkways we were talking about, now that construction is on track to finish on time."

Everything inside her froze solid like the carved ice sculptures she knew were around here somewhere. This couldn't be happening to her. *Not again.*

Sophie would've jerked her hand right out of his if he hadn't held on tight. Ignoring Tilly's shocked blink, he spun to Sophie so they faced each other.

"She brought it up. I swear. I didn't mention it at all."

Sophie paused at tugging on her hand to eye him with a swirling mixture of hurt and hope.

"He's telling the truth," Tilly said from his other side. "Though I'm not sure why it would be a problem."

Still holding tight to Sophie, Daniel faced the older woman. "Sophie had suggested covered walkways and I told her no. I don't want her thinking I went behind her back with the idea."

Sophie relaxed the rest of the way, enough that she sensed the tension leak from the man still holding her hand.

"Oh, I see." Tilly was now glancing between them. "Well, I decided I want them."

"Told you it was a good idea," Sophie murmured beside him, deliberately teasing to show him she'd stopped worrying.

He squeezed her hand in response, and she smiled secretly to herself.

"We'll add them after the new wing is done, though, rather than try to do both," Tilly continued. "Is that something you can fit in quickly?"

Daniel nodded. "I might have to send a half crew, so it could take longer, depending on another project, but sure."

He turned to her. "Ready to go?"

She nodded and Daniel backed away, tugging Sophie along with him, addressing the others as he did. "If I'm going to get the most out of my hour, we'd better get moving."

The rest of the little group didn't seem to think it strange that they left, simply waving them away with happy grins. "Make sure to drop by my bakery for treats," Emily called after them. "We're doing free samples of my apple streusel tonight."

Daniel waved a hand as they strolled away.

"I was all set to be mad at you," Sophie said. He turned

his head only to tangle her up in dancing hazel eyes that reflected not a small amount of relief. "Good thing you explained quickly," she added.

Daniel grinned. "I knew *exactly* what you were thinking."

"I should've known you wouldn't do that."

"Especially when I didn't want to do the darn covers
anyway."

She stopped and plopped her free hand on her hip. "What
do you have against covered walkways anyway?"

Daniel reached out and tucked a stray tendril of hair behind her ear, the move so natural she almost leaned into his
touch. "If I added one more thing to the new wing, I'd miss
the deadline, which I'm already tight on anyway."

"Which affects the guests," she filled in. No wonder he'd
been so adamant.

"That, and I have several new business deals tied to how
well I bring this one in. On time, and under budget."

Sophie's head snapped back at that. "I wish you would've
told me that."

He brought her hand up to his lips and placed a kiss on the
back. Not the same through her glove, but still enough to
make her cheeks glow a little warmer. "That was before we
figured out our communication issues," he said.

"I'm glad we figured that out." She gave him a wide-eyed
mock shake of her head.

Daniel laughed. "Come on. Let's look around."

They did stop to check out the glass menagerie of animals
that Clara suggested. Sophie found a gorgeous iridescent blue
butterfly, and Daniel teased her about not knowing vets
worked on butterflies, too. Which she ignored, because she
knew Mila would love it. Afterward, Daniel stopped and
bought them a bag of roasted chestnuts to share and hot
ciders to wash them down with.

They made their way slowly through the series of shops.
Mostly slow because it seemed as though practically every

vendor knew Daniel. Knew him and had heard about the accident, or, if they hadn't, still had to comment on his poor bruised face.

He did look pretty awful. If kisses had magical powers to heal, she'd be kissing every inch of his face right now. Unfortunately, she was pretty sure she'd make him hurt worse if she tried that.

With every single person who stopped him, Daniel made a point of introducing her and drawing her into the conversation. Suddenly Sophie remembered what she'd missed most after moving to the city—the caring. Yes, small-town life could be claustrophobic with everyone in your business, but the caring that came with that . . . She'd missed that.

Plus, Braunfels wasn't entirely like her hometown, which was much, much smaller. Maybe not as claustrophobic. Either way, she found as they went along that her well-used guest smile, which was sincere only up to a point, turned warmer and more authentic with each new person.

Music started up, coming across the loudspeaker, and the petite older woman whom they were talking to—who sold beautifully knitted items of various sorts—shooed them out of her tent. "The Sankeegee Troupe is dancing," she said. "You don't want to miss that. Go have fun."

Obediently, Sophie's hand once more in Daniel's like that was a natural place to be, they hurried around the gazebo to the other end of the shops, where the dance floor had been set up. Right in time to catch the start.

With the crowds pushing in, Daniel moved to stand behind her, his chest up against her back.

He leaned down to whisper in her ear again. "Ladies dancing and lords a-leaping. It totally counts."

Suddenly she wasn't paying that much attention to the dancers because she was surrounded by him. Sophie frowned as the realization sank deep that she didn't want to just look back on this. She wanted more moments like this one.

With Daniel.

"Too bad we skipped a step," he murmured next.

Meaning the maids a-milking, and Sophie grinned.

"Actually, we didn't miss it," she murmured back. "*You* did, but we can fix that."

"What does that mean?"

"You'll see." She quickly pulled out her phone and pulled up a short video, then handed it over her shoulder to Daniel.

A burst of a laugh shook him against her back, and Sophie didn't bother to hold in her own chuckle.

"No. Way," he said. "You milked a cow?"

"A demonstration as part of the Market," she tossed over her shoulder. "I told you I grew up on a dairy farm . . . and you thought I was a city girl."

"Could've fooled me in those prissy boots and a jacket that wouldn't hold out a sneeze let alone a winter wind."

"I didn't have time to shop," she excused. "Anyway. Not eight maids, but close enough to count. Don't you think?"

"Yup, it counts. Is that . . ." He paused and she had a pretty good idea what caught his attention. "Is Snowball sitting at your feet?"

"She was my helper." After all, the little cat had been part of all the other Twelve Days shenanigans. "Too bad she's missing this."

"Actually, I'm pretty sure I spotted her up on top of the barn a minute ago."

That got her to turn and face him with wide eyes, the press of the crowd keeping her up against his chest. "Why didn't you say so?"

"Because she'll be fine. Besides she's Tilly and Emily and Lukas's worry now."

He handed her phone back, still chuckling, then wrapped his arms around her and propped his chin on the top of her head. She closed her eyes and let herself enjoy. Soaked him in.

His warmth, and the feeling that she didn't want to be anywhere else in the world.

"This is nice," he murmured.

Sophie snuggled into him, forgetting all the reasons why she shouldn't, knowing full well she was lit up like the entire Christmas Market. Might as well slap fairy lights on her and call her in love.

"Now all we need are pipers and drummers and we've got a complete set."

"I have no idea where you think we'll come up with either," she said into his chest.

The ring of her cell phone, buzzing from the pocket of her coat, had her making a face, because it cut right through their perfect moment.

With a muttered, "Sorry," she fished it out, then blinked at the number. One she had unprogrammed from her phone when she'd left but still had memorized after ten years of seeing it daily. Why was the Crown Liberty hotel calling her?

She glanced up at Daniel. "I should take this."

Already walking away, she put the phone to her ear. "Just a moment, please. Let me get somewhere less noisy."

She made her way through the crowds and stalls to go around the side of the carriage house, which suddenly turned both quieter and darker as the building blocked out the Market and revelers.

"This is Sophie Heidt," she said.

"Sophie, this is Felix Sommerholder."

She sucked in what she hoped wasn't an audible breath at that. Malcom's father—owner and CEO of the hotel chain that her dream hotel was part of—was calling her? Why?

She summoned her most professional voice. "Yes, sir. What can I do for you?"

Chapter 17

Sophie stood in front of her closet, hands on her hips, trying to decide what clothes to bring for her interview. Not that standing there staring while she mentally debated going at all was getting anything done. For the second time in five minutes, she reached for the same conservative black suit, only to hesitate. Again.

She'd only be gone for a few days—the rest of the ones Miss Tilly had given her off already as a thank-you for everything she'd done while they'd been gone, along with an extra day Sophie had requested this morning at breakfast. She hadn't told Miss Tilly why, which felt a bit underhanded. Guilt oozed through her, sitting heavy in her stomach, like eating a dozen jelly donuts in one shot.

Pulled in a million directions by her heart and her head and her options, not to mention an underlying urge to thumb her nose at Malcom, she had no idea how this trip was going to turn out. *But . . .* this was her lifelong dream being dangled in front of her.

She had to at least go and listen to their offer.

Under the layer of guilt and the bubble of pressure taking up residence in her lungs was a layer of her own personal vindication.

Turned out her ex was not such a hotshot when he had to

handle all the spinning plates of hotel management on his own without her there to guide him and to sweep up the broken pieces when he dropped the plates. Apparently, he'd decided he'd rather go the executive route than manage the hotel directly. She'd had no problem interpreting that as his father was disappointed—after only a month, that might be a record—and moved his role to something less impactful.

One of her questions would definitely be what kind of interaction she'd have to have with her useless-except-for-his-perfect-teeth ex. If she had to report to or deal with him in any way . . .

She paused, hands hovering over the black suit again as that oozy feeling got worse. Not guilt, though. More . . . reluctance. Because Weber Haus and Braunfels were starting to feel like home. Because . . . Daniel.

Unexpected. A complication she hadn't anticipated.

She couldn't think about all that. Not until she'd made up her own mind. Sophie gave herself a shake and grabbed a white suit. Fancier than she usually went, it had been an impulse buy. One she'd never dared to wear but looked killer on her. The boost to her confidence would help. Carefully slipping it into a hanging case with a few other items, she zipped it up.

She'd go, listen to what they had to say about the position, then make a decision.

That simple.

With a last glance around the room, she scooped up the deep leather bag she used for her laptop, as well as her purse, and carried everything out of her room and down the stairs. She halfway expected to bump into Daniel on the way. This was about the time he started to stir, usually in the kitchen for coffee and one of Mrs. Bailey's breakfast pastries fresh out of the oven before heading out to the site.

Only he was still resting today, so he didn't have to be up.

She'd sort of hoped to tell him about this in person. With a sigh, she let herself out the kitchen door and trudged through the fresh snow that had fallen overnight to where she and other inn employees parked their cars, loaded up as quickly as possible, laid her purse and bag on the floor in the back seat.

She paused once she was in the driver's seat, then fished out her phone and composed a quick text to Daniel. **Got a few more days off. In the city. Check with Tilly for anything you need.**

She stared at the words, her thumb hovering over the Send button. Should she tell him why she was in the city? This was almost worse than leaving no word at all.

Slowly she deleted the text and put her phone down. She'd think about it and send him a message once she got there.

She might've watched the lights of Weber Haus fading in her rearview mirror, doing her best to tamp down the sensation of wrongness at driving away. A few hours later she navigated narrow streets, traffic, and rude pedestrians to pull into the circular drive for hotel guests where she stopped in front of the valet stand.

"Miss Heidt." James, one of the valets, grinned as soon as he recognized her. "What are you doing here?"

"Dropping in for a visit," she said as she handed him her keys and a tip.

Then she opened the back door to get her purse and gasped. Because two blue eyes in a white fluffy face stared at her from where Snowball was curled up on the back seat, blinking sleepily.

"Snowball." The word burst from her and made the little cat jump.

Shaking her head, and grateful she wasn't wearing black, Sophie scooped her up with alacrity. If she jumped out of the car and ran off, she'd never find her in the city and Miss Tilly would be beside herself.

So would Sophie.

"You little sneak. How on earth did you get in my car?" she demanded.

Not that she had time to discuss it. She needed to get the rest of her things from the car and check in. All while toting a fluffy white cat.

Maybe the staff wouldn't notice.

"What's with the cat?" James asked.

"A stowaway," she said, and smiled at his confused blink.

"Errr . . ." Now he was looking her over like he worried her leaving the Crown Liberty might have derailed more than her career. "I'll have Curt bring your luggage up to your room."

Holding on to Snowball, who at least was staying still, she collected her computer bag and her purse and headed inside.

"You're lucky pets are allowed at this hotel," she muttered at the cat. For a hefty pet fee, too. She'd make sure to pay for that herself. The hotel was covering the cost of her stay for her interview.

She didn't even want to think about the image bringing a cat to an interview would portray. Almost as bad as bringing her mother to an interview, which a recent college graduate had done not too long before Sophie had left the hotel. She'd ended that interview as soon as the situation was clear.

Terrific.

Smiling and saying hello to staff she'd worked with happily for years, she had to stop multiple times. Only as she moved along, Sophie couldn't shake the sensation that she didn't belong here anymore. And not because she was carrying Snowball.

Yes, she'd enjoyed working here. Loved it. She would have said that she loved everyone, well . . . most everyone she worked with and had many lovely friends. Only it struck her that while she was on friendly terms with the people who worked here, she wasn't friends with any of them. Not really. She hadn't had a phone call or a visit from any one of them or the urge to check on them on social media. Malcom had been the only one she'd spent any kind of time with outside of work hours, now that she thought about it.

Her life before Weber Haus somehow now struck her as . . . hollow.

This is your dream. You've worked for over a decade to get here, she reminded herself, shaking off the thoughts.

Between catching up with folks and the big deal they made over Snowball's adorableness, along with a few questioning glances that seared into her back as she walked away, Sophie managed to get checked in and up to her room, where she finally let Snowball go.

She eyed the cat with a narrowed gaze, lips twisted in frustration. "What am I supposed to do with you now?"

Snowball cocked her head as if that was a silly thing to ask, then proceeded to wander the room, cautiously poking her head into spaces and sniffing.

At the very least she should call the inn and inform Miss Tilly so they didn't worry. Then, if Snowball had to stay here, she'd need to get a litterbox and food and water and bowls and . . . what a mess.

She had no idea why, but when she went to dial Weber Haus, she brought up Daniel's number instead.

"I know, I know, I know," he said by way of answering the phone.

Sophie's eyebrows shot up and she paused, mouth wide open. What did he know?

Ha! I knew sneaking into Sophie's computer bag would work.

After all, I snuck into Emily's oversize purse lots of times. In fact, that's how we met Lukas the first time. The plan was human proof.

Last night, when she was out with Daniel at the Christmas Market, I followed her when she went into the dark places by herself. She was on the phone and talking about hotels and a job.

"I can be there tomorrow for an interview," she'd said. "Thank you so much, Mr. Sommerholder."

An interview? Tilly has had to interview a lot of people this year as Weber Haus needed more staff. Including Sophie.

I know what that means. It means she's going to leave us and go to a new job.

Only she can't!

Doesn't she know she's supposed to stay at Weber Haus and make it her forever home, and find her forever family, the same way I've found mine with Tilly and Emily and Lukas? Only Sophie's supposed to be with Daniel and make the town home and help Miss Tilly run the inn.

It's so obvious to me. Why are humans so darn blind when it comes to their lives?

So, I decided last night to sleep in Sophie's room and not let her out of my sight. That way I'd make sure I went with her to this interview. If I'm lucky, Daniel will have to follow and bring her back. Even if that doesn't happen, I need to see for myself what might be better than Weber Haus.

I'll admit, the hotel is pretty in a super fancy way. I do love shiny things, and there were lots of them everywhere. Sparkling chandeliers hanging from the ceiling and glittering in the marble floors. Sophie is obviously well liked by the people who work here, the city is noisy and big and a little scary, and the hotel itself is a little . . . impersonal. Despite the shiny things. I can't see what she might find more appealing here.

With a little huff, I hop onto the bed, which has a fluffy white duvet. The lovely soft kind I can sink into. I curl up to watch Sophie as she talks with Daniel.

"Um . . . what do you know, Daniel?" Sophie's voice was completely confused.

Which was why he slowed his brisk walk from the site—where he hadn't been working, just checking on progress, which was still right on track, thanks to his men—back to the house. The soft sounds of Christmas music and revelry coming from the Christmas Market reached him even on the back side of the barn between buildings. He ignored the noise as he tried to hear Sophie over it. "Didn't you call because of the pipes?"

He grinned, waiting for a comment about their pipers piping. Which had been the first words out of his mouth five minutes ago when Tilly called his phone sounding urgent about water coming from the attic. He'd confused the heck out of her, which had wasted a minute. Sure, the reference was a stretch, and busted pipes were nothing to laugh at, but this was his and Sophie's thing.

"Pipes?" she asked, voice utterly bewildered.

How did she not already know? "Sleeping in this morning, huh?" he teased.

"Daniel . . . what pipes?"

He recognized that tone. His girl was getting frustrated. "Apparently one of the pipes in the house burst. Water everywhere coming down the attic stairs already. You should go find Tilly right away. I'm on my way over—"

"I can't. I'm not there."

Not here? "Where are you?"

"At the Crown Liberty."

He pulled up short and actually pulled the phone away to stare at it with a frown before putting it back to his ear. "Your old hotel?"

"Yes." Her voice had gone toneless.

"Why are you there?" If she was getting back together with her ex . . . After last night when they'd held hands and laughed and talked and the way she'd kissed him back when he'd taken her home . . .

She might have sighed, hard to tell over the connection

and when he couldn't see her face. She was so good at the polite voice for guest things on the phone. "It's a long story, but the reason I'm calling is because Snowball is with me."

He shook his head. "Wait. I'm confused. You went to your old hotel, hours away, and . . . took Snowball with you? Does Tilly know?"

"I didn't take her, she stowed away," Sophie said slowly and succinctly. "I didn't call Tilly because I didn't want to worry her, and if she's dealing with busted pipes . . ."

Despite still wondering what the heck she was doing at the hotel—the dread trying to eat a hole in his stomach already telling him that none of her reasons were ones he wanted to hear—he caught the gist of the problem.

"When do you come back?" Maybe Miss Tilly wouldn't notice until then.

"Tomorrow night, maybe the next day."

Three days in the city at her old hotel. Daniel clenched his jaw hard enough to set off a tic of muscle in his cheek. "You're there to get your job back, I take it?"

Or worse, the boyfriend called and wanted to reunite? Maybe the guy wasn't such an idiot after all. Daniel kept that bit to himself.

"The CEO called and wanted me to come in for a . . . chat."

A chat to bring her back to the hotel then. Daniel closed his eyes. Because three things hit him all at once.

He loved Sophie Heidt to distraction.

He didn't want her to go back to that fancy old hotel. He wanted her here. With him.

But this was her dream. A childhood dream, and if anyone knew about those, he did.

She'd told him how long she'd been working for that specific job for that specific hotel. Of course, she couldn't pass this opportunity up.

"Does Tilly know where you are?" And why?

"Not yet. I wanted—"

"I understand." She wanted to get her ducks in a row with one job before leaving the other. Completely understandable.

Even if he hated it. Even if he desperately wanted her to stay here. With him. Forever.

He'd known she would break his heart. He should have been more careful with it. The ache growing in his chest, making it hard to breathe, wasn't going to go away anytime soon. That he knew for certain.

"So . . . you called your friend Daniel, who has the day off and is probably bored anyway, to drive hours to where you are and bring Snowball home. Is that it?"

A long pause followed his question. Long enough that he opened his mouth to ask it again, not sure she'd heard.

"I wouldn't have worded it that way," she said, voice gone soft.

"No," he said. "I don't guess you would." He grimaced, knowing full well she couldn't see his face. He was being a jerk. This was her shot and he shouldn't make her feel bad for going after it. He took a deep, silent breath and let it go. "Let me get the house set with the plumber, then I'll come out to you."

"Actually, you're right. You're supposed to be recuperating. I'll keep her here—"

"No, Tilly shouldn't have anything else to worry about today." He left hanging the fact that she'd have to worry about getting yet another hotel manager after Sophie left, because no doubt she was going to be offered the job.

"I could meet you halfway," she offered.

"When is your interview?"

"In three hours."

He shook his head. "That doesn't work. It'll take me at least an hour to help Tilly before I can get on the road. You'd barely get back in time. What if you hit traffic?"

"Should you even be driving? I should call Emily maybe—"

"I saw the doctor today. I'm cleared to go back to work in a week and cleared to drive. I can bring Pete, if you're worried."

"So, the two men with brain injuries are going to watch out for each other?"

"I needed something to keep me entertained today anyway. It'll be fine."

Silence. That long silence that told him she was thinking again. "I'm sorry, Daniel."

"No problem. Seriously. I'll call when I'm close."

"Thanks."

He couldn't think of anything else to say about it, so he hung up.

"Young man?" a now-familiar crotchety old voice called out.

Daniel swiveled his head, searching around for where Mr. Muir might be, but didn't see him anywhere.

"Look up," came the next shout.

He did, to find the older man leaning way too far out of his second-story window, wearing a thin white undershirt and jeans pulled up to his ribs. How he hadn't fallen out yet was a miracle. "Mr. Muir?"

"After you fix the pipes, come chat with me before you go talk to that young lady."

Daniel blinked. "You overheard?"

"Enough to have a good idea."

"I'm in a bit of a hurry," he said. He didn't have time for whatever latest stunt the gentleman had decided to pull.

"Not so much that a good dose of common sense isn't helpful."

Right. Common sense from the man with two turtledoves and a too-big Christmas tree in his guest room at a Victorian inn. "I'll try."

Which was how, after calling Pete—because Sophie was right that he probably shouldn't be attempting such a long drive on his own—then helping Tilly turn off the water to the house and clean up the mess, he found himself knocking on Mr. Muir's door.

The pit in his stomach had only gotten heavier and grown spikes as he'd been with Tilly, knowing what he knew and what she didn't.

The door opened and he was beckoned inside to find the turtledoves' cage covered. "It's nap time," Mr. Muir explained.

Okay then. "This will need to be quick, I'm afraid," Daniel said, only to get waved at as though he was the one slowing things down.

"Despite young people's biases, old people do have the ability to be quick and to add value, you know."

"I'm sure—"

"Don't make my mistakes," Mr. Muir cut him off to say.

Daniel paused, eyeing him closer. "What mistakes would those be?"

"Do you want to know why I came here?"

Which sounded like a non sequitur. Daniel still asked. "Why?"

"Chasing the memory of a sweetheart." Mr. Muir plopped down on the part of his bed not blocked by Christmas tree branches and gave Daniel a serious look. "When I was about your age, I visited this town and fell deeply in love with a woman here. We spent a glorious summer together, but in the fall, I left her behind to pursue a bigger job far away. Back then we didn't have things like virtual phone calls with our faces, and long-distance phone calls were expensive. We lost touch, and that was that."

"I'm sorry to hear that."

Mr. Muir nodded and shrugged at the same time. "It's a common story, and I eventually married, quite happily, though I often thought of this woman. My wife was a good person, and I loved her. I'll always miss her. But . . . my heart belonged to someone else, even through a long and wonderful marriage."

Daniel tried to picture it but couldn't wrap his head around a happy marriage if you loved someone else that much.

"Old, silly regrets," Mr. Muir said. "I came back here chasing dead dreams like a fool."

Had he learned that the woman was no longer alive? Or not in town? Daniel wanted to ask for more details but didn't want to be nosy. "Why are you telling me this?"

Mr. Muir straightened, thick white brows practically meeting over his eyes. "Because you don't run across that kind of connection every day."

Okay?

"The same kind I see when you and Sophie look at each other."

Daniel startled. He hadn't even realized that Mr. Muir had been around enough to notice. Then again, he'd had no idea the man was eavesdropping on his phone call, either.

"If you love her," Mr. Muir said, "then don't make my mistakes, son. Figure it out. Whatever it takes."

On that pronouncement, the older man got up and went to his door, opening it wide. "Now go rescue that blasted cat."

Daniel, head spinning from the gist of that conversation, was out the door and all the way to his car before even realizing it. Though, even with that advice, he still had no idea what he was going to do.

So he got in the car and headed over to Pete's.

It took him about five minutes to explain the situation to his friend, who hadn't even asked when Daniel had called to ask him to drive to the hotel with him.

Then Pete sat in silence as they drove along for five solid minutes. "Are you in love with her?"

The question made Daniel grip the steering wheel harder. He flicked his friend a glance, then blew out a long breath. "Head over work boots."

"What are you going to do?"

His shrug felt ridiculously stiff. "Nothing I can do. I'm not going to get in the way of a dream she's had since she was a kid. I can't say I like the way she's sneaking around Miss Tilly's back, but I get it. I'm sure she'll give the proper notice and do everything right there."

"Have you thought about going with her?"

He had. Every second of sopping up water in the attic. Part of him wanted to say he'd drop everything to follow her . . . and if his was the only life impacted by that decision, he would. Except his crew depended on him for their livelihoods. Had left other jobs because of loyalty to him.

He said as much to Pete.

"I don't even know if she'd want me to. It hasn't even been a month yet. We've shared some laughs, some kisses, but that's about it."

Only that didn't feel like it. What they'd shared was . . . more. A connection. They'd become partners in a sense. He liked the guy he became around her and hoped maybe she liked who she was around him, too.

He caught Pete's grimace in his periphery. "I'm the last person to give you advice," his friend said. "I can't stick a relationship like a gymnast with a broken foot can't stick a landing."

Daniel glanced over at his friend, who stared out the front windshield. "I've never heard you talk like that."

Or that bitter tone.

Pete crossed his arms. "Today we focus on your problems. Mine . . . that's for another day."

After almost two decades of friendship, Daniel knew when not to push. "I have enough to keep us going for a while, probably."

Pete's mouth quirked in the nearest thing he got to a smile. "I was just thinking that."

Two hours later, Sophie answered on the first ring. "Are you close?" she asked, sounding anxious.

"I'm pulling up to the hotel now."

"I'll come down. I'm meeting the people interviewing me in the foyer and we're going to happy hour and an early dinner."

"Then don't come down," he cautioned. "What will they think if you run into them while holding a fluffy white cat?"

The pause of silence had him picturing her biting her lip. "Good point."

"I'll come up and get her."

"But—"

"I have Pete with me. He can wait in the car, so no need to park it."

Another pause. He wasn't sure why this time. "Okay. I'm in room 412."

Hanging up, he pulled to the side away from the valets. "Be right back," he told Pete.

"Take your time." Pete reclined his seat back and closed his eyes.

"It's not like that. She has an interview soon."

Pete didn't bother to open his eyes. "Yup."

Daniel shook his head and walked indoors, telling the valet he'd be back in a minute on his way by. The elevators in this hotel moved at the speed of sloth—maybe uber rich people like to be leisurely?—but finally dinged and the doors silently opened on the fourth floor. At Sophie's door, he knocked and barely waited two seconds before she pulled it wide open, Snowball clutched in one hand.

"*Meow,*" the little cat said, visibly brightening with an expression along the lines of, "Yay! Daniel's here!"

A nice change from full-attack kitty if she wasn't the cause of so much angst.

Besides, Daniel hardly noticed her as he took one look at

Sophie—gorgeous in a sleek white pantsuit and killer black high heels, her golden hair pinned up, and her expression as vulnerable as she'd ever allowed him to see, her feelings raw and mashed all together. She blindsided him.

With a grunt of reaction, he stepped into her, took her face in his hands, and claimed her lips, swallowing her gasp, then groaning when she melted into him. Somehow, she managed to keep the cat out of their way, or maybe she dropped Snowball. As often as they kissed while holding her, they were getting good at it.

He didn't care.

All he cared about was the softness of her lips against his, the hitch in her breathing at the way she clung to him. The real world of tough decisions tried to intrude, so he kept kissing her and kissing her. Maybe if he did that long enough, the decisions would go away.

Only he knew that wasn't going to happen. He also knew that kissing her this way wasn't going to make her choices any easier. Because when it came down to it, this *was* her choice, and hers alone. Chasing her dream. He shouldn't get in the way of that. Shouldn't make it harder on her.

Slowing his kisses, softening them until he was sipping at her lips, he pulled back with a grunt and put his forehead to hers, eyes closed. "Sorry. I just . . ." Just what? What could he tell her that would help? He sighed. "I was bowled over by you in full Sophie hotel manager mode."

A sound between a laugh and a groan slipped from her and he lifted his head, opening his eyes. Ready—even though he really wasn't—to walk away.

"Daniel, I—"

He kissed her quickly to stop her from saying more. "This is your dream, right?"

She nodded slowly, wide eyes on his, darker today, like a sliver of moonlight, no doubt from stress of an interview and the added worry of the cat.

"Then you should go for what you want." He swallowed. "What will make you happy in the end." Even if that wasn't him, though it hurt like hell to even think that.

Sophie opened her mouth, then closed it again.

He got the picture. "You go knock them dead, Sophie Heidt."

Trying not to see the way she blinked, or how her silvery eyes clouded with confusion, he simply scooped up Snowball and turned away, tossing a "good luck" over his shoulder as he walked out of her room.

The best he could do. The hardest damn thing he'd ever had to do—walking away from her. Giving her the space she deserved to figure everything out for herself.

Chapter 18

Sophie made her way downstairs after Daniel left, her head and heart in a fine muddle. Because he'd kissed her as though she was the most precious thing in the world, and more than part of her heart was hoping he'd ask her to stay with Weber Haus. Only he didn't do that. Instead, he'd told her to chase her dream and be happy. Then he'd walked away.

Like it was no big deal.

As she rounded the corner into the foyer, a tall, unmistakable man rose from one of the deep-seated wingback chairs, unmistakable to her because he was essentially the older version of Malcom. Just as handsome with his sharply angled face, his hair still naturally dark, merely graying at the temples, which gave him a distinguished air, bright blue eyes, and the same perfect-toothed smile. Their dentist must make a mint keeping all those teeth in top form.

Hiding the snarky thought behind her best polite guest expression, she made her way to him, holding her hand out, which he shook. "This meeting is long overdue," he said.

She raised her eyebrows in slight question, not sure why he chose to open with that remark.

"You have been a rising star in the Crown Liberty, our flagship hotel, for some time now. I usually make it my business to nurture the careers of folks like you."

"That's nice of you to say." Keeping her professional expression in place this time was a bit of a struggle. Because promoting his son over a rising star wasn't exactly nurturing careers. At least, not necessarily the right ones. The ones who had put the time in and truly earned it.

"The rest of the board will meet us at the restaurant," he said. "Shall we?"

With a hand at her back, though discreetly not actually touching, he escorted her outside and into the back of a waiting black chauffeur-driven car. Not a limo. Felix Sommerholder was too subtle for that, unlike his bright yellow Porsche–driving son. In minutes she was ushered back onto the street outside a restaurant whose name she recognized. Brazilian with one of the hottest chefs on the rise and, of course, exclusive. She was suddenly extremely glad for the power outfit she'd chosen—stylish, especially with the heels, and making the most of her figure, while still maintaining that professional edge.

As soon as they walked in, Felix raised a hand at someone Sophie couldn't see over the maître d's head. They followed the lanky, tuxedoed man through the restaurant to a more private corner next to the windows with a lovely view of the city bustling by outside. Only the second the maître d' stepped aside, the signal from Sophie's brain to her feet stopped functioning and she practically left skid marks on the subtle paisley carpet in her abrupt halt.

Because Malcom—his face a comical, if she was in a generous mood, combination of hopeful and contrite—was getting to his feet from the table where several other board members were also rising.

The right thing to do in this more than awkward situation, the professional thing, would be to shake his hand and pretend he wasn't an oozing, slinking slug of a human being. This was her chance to showcase those diplomatic skills that would make her a terrific hotel manager for the Crown Liberty.

Instead, she was more of a mind to douse the slug with salt and watch him melt.

She turned to Felix, who by some miracle hadn't plowed through her when she'd stopped so abruptly, and managed that polite smile for him. "I'm sorry, but if this job involves working within a hundred miles of your son, I'm not interested. I thank you for your interest and apologize for taking your time."

"Wait a moment, please." Felix's voice was the only thing that kept her from walking away.

She raised her eyebrows in cool question. What on earth could he possibly say to make this any better?

"After the last month of . . . shall we say misunderstandings . . . Malcom confessed that all the excellent plans and ideas he'd presented as his own actually came from you."

Sophie stared at the older version of her ex, wondering what to say. Had his son truly fessed up? Or did Felix, who was no dummy, figure it out on his own and drag the truth from his lying progeny? Given the dangerous glint in the blue eyes staring back at her, she had a decent idea the latter had been the case.

"I see," was all she said.

"He is here to publicly apologize to you. Then, if you wish, he does not have to join us for drinks and dinner. He won't be involved with your new position in any remote way, I assure you."

That, if she were honest, was a gazillion times better than she'd expected this to go. Even so, she hesitated. Only she'd come all this way to hear them out at least. "All right."

Gathering herself, she turned back to Malcom, whose face, she was more than happy to see, had turned the shade of a lobster boiling away in the pot of hot water he'd made for himself. Underlying her quiet flash of retribution, a small hint of pity lingered. This had to be tough for him. She eyed the man she'd dated for a long time, thought she was in love with, and felt . . . nothing. Nothing beyond that vague sadness that, to impress his rather impressive father, he'd betrayed the one person who would have helped and supported him, had he only asked.

As she stepped up to him, Malcom tried a smile, which died as she didn't return it, then glanced over her shoulder, probably at Felix, before pulling his shoulders back and facing her directly. "I apologize, Sophie, for taking advantage of you and our relationship. There is no excuse for my behavior. I hope you can forgive me, and that my poor judgment won't affect your decision when it comes to returning to the Crown Liberty."

A very nicely put apology.

She was tempted to ask who had written it for him to memorize but didn't. He was almost visibly squirming already, having to do this in front of his father, the board, and restaurant onlookers sitting near enough to eavesdrop. Also, now that she could see beyond her own hurt and anger, memories bubbled up. Things he'd said, comments about the instances where his father hadn't been there, hadn't praised, had put more pressure on his son than what was needed.

She softened enough to offer him a hand to shake. "Thank you for that apology," she said. "I understand why you did. The pressure to live up to your name and your family legacy must be tremendous." She shot Felix Sommerholder a significant look, though his expression turned perplexed, so he clearly wasn't ready to realize or acknowledge his own fault in this mess, before turning back to her ex. "No hard feelings. But don't ever do it again. To anyone."

He'd never get the chance to do it to her again.

"Really? That's big of you, Sophie." Malcom grinned suddenly, that little-boy-lost expression she'd always found so endearing in full force, and for just a blip of a second, she remembered why she'd been attracted in the first place.

Only as she gazed at him now, mostly without the lens of hatred coloring him in muck, she still felt nothing. No attraction. No need to be with him. No tug that she used to experience around him. No urge to spend a little more time with him.

All gone.

Clearing her throat, she turned to the rest of the table and greeted them in turn before they all took their seats. She allowed Malcom to stay, not even minding, much, that she ended up sitting right beside him with his father on her other side.

They kept the comments to vague pleasantries as they perused the menu and ordered. Then, as soon as the waiter left, Felix kicked off the interview, and Sophie settled in to impress.

Sophie still hasn't come home, and it's been ages. From Miss Tilly's bedroom window, I've been watching down the drive for her to arrive so that I can run and bring Daniel back here. Only she still hasn't come home.

Please come home.

I thought when he showed up at the hotel and kissed her that my plan had worked. But then he took me and walked away. Left her there.

What was he thinking?

Nothing good, because he's been in a horrible mood ever since. I even heard him snap at his big, neckless friend. When he wasn't snapping, he was brooding.

Come home, Sophie. Please don't break his heart.

Waiting sucked.

The pounding of the hammers and buzz of the saw around Daniel hardly registered as he worked with his men on finishing up the inside trim for the extended wing of Weber Haus. Almost done. His crew had finished the outside in record time while he was in the hospital, teasing him that they didn't need him around after all. The landscapers had started today. Not that they could do too much beyond cleaning up and prepping the beds. They'd put in plants in the spring when the ground wasn't so solid. Meanwhile, in the next week he and the crew would finish out the interior trim. Decorators were slated to get started on the upper floor as soon as they were done, working in conjunction while they finished the lower floor.

Hopefully all in time for New Year's. His part would be done at least. The rest depended on the other contractors getting their pieces done in time. Tight, but doable. At least the decorators were less weather dependent.

Not that his head was focused on any of that right this second. Heart and soul had dragged the rest of him along on a ride of obsessing over a certain silver-eyed hotel manager.

And how he was still waiting for any news. She'd been radio silent. Not even a text.

Patience was not exactly his middle name. He read the endings of books first and looked up movie plots online before deciding what to watch. As a child he'd always tracked down where Christmas presents were hidden and figured most of them out long before Christmas morning.

But, out of every moment in his life, waiting for Sophie to come home and share what happened . . . share her decision . . . was by far the hardest.

Like Sisyphus, trying to roll that boulder up the hill every day only to have it roll back down and have to start back over. Not that she'd been gone days. It had only been twenty-four hours since he'd seen her at the hotel, but the longer it took her to return, he considered that to be a sign she was being romanced. Wined and dined and encouraged to stay and pursue that dream of hers.

He had no doubts. She was amazing. They'd be lucky to have her.

If he were in her shoes . . . if someone did that for him and his business, which was his own dream . . . would he snap it up if it meant leaving Sophie behind?

Daniel paused mid-hammer swing, realization smacking him so hard between the eyes, a flash of his earlier headaches from his concussion spiked for a second.

No. He wouldn't. But that's what he was doing by making his business the reason to stay behind if she decided to pursue hers.

She couldn't change the hotel she'd focused her dreams on, but his dream . . . yeah, he'd disappoint the crew who wouldn't want to move with him, all being local guys with families in the area, but he could sell the business to Levi and they'd keep going. Then he could follow Sophie anywhere. Was this that kind of love?

Yes. No doubt in his mind, yes.

"Forget waiting." He stepped down the ladder away from the crown molding he'd been installing. "Levi—"

"About dang time, boss."

He blinked at his foreman. "What?"

"For the last day, you've been moping around here like a kid who got coal in his stocking Christmas morning. As useless as a lump of coal in the twenty-first century, if you ask me."

Daniel glanced at the white molding and conceded that he'd completed very little of the trim in the time he'd been working today. "Me or the coal?"

"Both. Whatever you need to work out," Levi said. "Go do it. For all our sakes."

Right.

Daniel was out of the building and halfway to the house before he realized he was still wearing his hard hat. This morning when he'd gotten to work, he'd found that the guys had attached a sign to it that read, "Wear me, Daniel."

The fact that he'd barely chuckled at the joke should have

been his first clue that he needed to be somewhere else, with someone else, today.

He snatched the hat off his head but didn't bother to go back. He needed to change clothes and get in the truck and go. Maybe a text to her wouldn't go amiss, to make sure she wasn't on her way back. No need to pass each other on the road without realizing it.

Which would be just his kind of luck.

Pausing at the back door to the house to take off his boots took forever. The kitchen was empty, but he didn't bother to wonder where Mrs. Bailey was. Breakfast was over and lunchtime wasn't for a while yet. Daniel ran up the back stairs to his room, shucked work-dusted jeans and shirt before showering, then dressed in a clean pair of jeans but paired with a button-down shirt and his nicer pair of boots. If he was going to do this, he'd do it right, making sure Sophie knew she wouldn't only be getting a work-rough construction man.

He intended to head down the back stairs again, but Snowball flashed down the hallway in a streak of white and practically tumbled over herself as she stopped at his feet.

Her meow was sharp and urgent before she ran a few feet away toward the front set of stairs.

"I have to go," he told her. "My car's out back."

Daniel might have sworn she rolled her kitty eyes. She meowed again, sharper, even more urgent, and ran a few more steps. Shaking his head, mostly at himself for his own flights of fancy where Snowball was concerned, he followed.

Then stopped at the top of the main staircase as several voices drifted his way. Tilly, but also Emily and Lukas and . . . Sophie.

He glanced at Snowball, who proceeded to run down the stairs.

"Thank you for taking time from your shops." Sophie's voice floated up the stairs he was now making his way down.

"I felt that I owed you an explanation of what's been happening."

"Sounds ominous." This from Tilly.

"I was offered a promotion at the Crown Liberty, the hotel where I used to work." Sophie didn't beat around the bush, and he would have chuckled at that if he wasn't focused so hard on what she was saying.

"I went there to be interviewed, as well as to interview them," she continued. "I'm sorry I didn't tell you my intentions when I left."

"You went on your own time, Sophie." Tilly again. Only why wasn't she asking why Sophie needed to interview so soon after taking the job at Weber Haus?

"That's kind of you to understand. You see, the job I was interviewing for is the one I've wanted since I decided to go into the hospitality business as a girl. I picked that hotel, and I was so sure. Which I'm sharing so you understand why I had to go, if you know what I mean."

"If anyone understands chasing a dream, it's us," Emily said, and Lukas agreed.

Daniel stood shamelessly out of sight in the foyer, outside the small sitting room where he'd kissed Sophie, where she was now speaking with the Webers. He smiled at Emily's comment. There was a reason he was friends with these kind people. Emily's dream of opening her own bakery had only come true the last six months or so as the shops had opened on the property. And Lukas had almost lost Emily because he'd been too busy globetrotting as a sought-after photographer, also a dream.

"Again," Sophie said, "Your graciousness is appreciated. I hope you also understand when I say that I—"

"Don't say it." The words burst from him as he quickly rounded the corner.

Sophie, casual again in jeans and a golden sweater that

made her eyes turn that starlight color again, spun around, staring at him. "What?" she asked.

He hadn't expected to do this in front of an audience, but he didn't care. "Don't decide anything," he said. "Not yet."

She didn't pull her gaze away from him as the air between them turned thick with words unsaid and feelings unexpressed. Only he couldn't tell from her expression how she felt about . . . any of it. "Why not?" she asked.

Daniel swallowed. "Because you don't have all the information yet."

Sophie blinked, then cocked her head. Please let that be a smile. "What am I missing?"

"Me."

She took a sharp, shuddering breath that might as well have been a punch aimed at his gut, and he was across the room in two strides, arms around her. "Somewhere between partridges and pipes and a white fluffy escape artist devil cat, I fell in love with you, Sophie Heidt."

A laugh burst from her, but the way her eyes lit up made his heart sing. "You did?"

He nodded. "I'm saying I love you. I'm saying I fell hard and fast for you. Snowball didn't even need to get me whacked in the head for it to happen. I was already there. I want us to be together," he said, the words tumbling over themselves. "So, if you're making a decision, know that wherever you go, I'll go, too."

Sophie lifted a hand to his cheek. "You'd do that? Start over with your business in a new place for me?"

Daniel's chest ached with the pain of having to let go, heavy inside him, and yet at the same time he knew Mr. Muir had been right. He'd traded dreams. Sophie was his now.

"I would."

She shook her head, and his already aching heart dropped to the bottom of his feet. Then she put her forehead to his. "I love you so much," she whispered.

His heart took off like a Santa flying around the world in his sleigh. "You do?"

She nodded. "So, it's a good thing for you that I also fell in love with Weber Haus, and Braunfels, and the crew, and—"

She squeaked as he lifted her straight up, squeezing her hard and burying his face in her neck. "You're staying?" he asked into her hair. Not daring to believe it.

"I'm staying."

He lifted his head, and her smile lit up the entire room even better than the Christmas tree in the corner. "I told them no, even though I wasn't positive I'd have a job to return to if you'd warned Tilly."

Daniel shook his head. "That was your secret to tell."

"Thank you." He knew without her saying that she was thanking him for not telling, but also for letting her make this decision on her own. Mostly.

Daniel cocked his head. "You really love me, huh?" He grinned and she side-eyed him, waiting for a punchline. "What did it? The muscles, right?"

Sophie's laugh was pure heaven, her grin wide and reflecting his own. "I think it was the take-charge attitude. I just couldn't resist."

"Huh. Well, I couldn't resist the way you frowned at me all the time."

At her snort of laughter, he dropped a quick kiss on her lips.

"Best Christmas present ever," he murmured.

And kissed her again, lingering over the touch this time, ignoring the sounds of Tilly and Emily and Lukas sneaking out of the room, taking a protesting Snowball with them.

Epilogue

I sure am in high demand today. Not that that's anything new. But today is turning out extra special.

It's Christmas morning and things couldn't be lovelier. Just this once, because the holidays are usually the best time for business, Tilly insisted that her family all be together to celebrate so many blessings—health, the completion of the additions to the property, the success of the Christmas Market, and, of course, Christmas morning.

Emily's entire family is downstairs, including all her brothers and her parents, and Lukas and Tilly, of course. They finished eating breakfast in the dining room and are cleaning up from that before moving into the formal living room at the front of the house to open presents. That's the best part for me. All that paper to pounce on and shred.

I unsheathe my claws and sharpen them on the runner in the upstairs hall in anticipation.

"Come here, you." A hand scoops me up before I even see Daniel is in the hall with me.

He's acting funny. Sort of sneaking around, checking over his shoulder until he gets into the room he was using during construction. Once the door is closed, he plops me down on the bed.

"I have a job for you, Snowball. Something for Sophie. You game?"

I sit down and cock my head, eyeing whatever it is he's holding up. *"Meow."*

He understands that I've agreed, because he kneels down in front of me and starts to tie something to my collar.

For Sophie?

That's funny, because Lukas has already explained to me that, at the end of present opening, he's going to do the same thing for Emily. Only he's going to tie a ring to my collar. Human men clearly have a lack of imagination from time to time. Not that I object.

"You're the one who knows us both best," Daniel says as he finishes what he's doing and leans back to study the effect. Not that he needs to bother. I'm adorable. "So, I'd like you to be part of this."

I preen, making sure to lick at my fur so that I look my best for whatever he has planned. Because he's right. I *did* bring him and Sophie together. In fact, I'm fairly positive that without me, they'd still be arguing all the time.

I was so scared when Sophie called all the Webers into that sitting room a few weeks ago, after she came home from the hotel interview thing. I just knew she was going to make the wrong decision, and that's why I went and got Daniel. Good thing he was already in the house and I'd heard him come in. Even in socks with no shoes, the man walks with the weight of the elephants I saw once in Lukas's photos.

But they figured it all out.

That's two couples who've found their happy families because of me. I'm like the happily ever after Christmas fairy.

"This is what we're going to do," he whispers.

The small tread of kitty feet sounded a heartbeat before Snowball showed up in the kitchen, where Sophie was helping to put away the breakfast things they'd just enjoyed. The small cat leapt up on the kitchen table beside her and meowed.

"No, no," Sophie said automatically, and put her back on the floor. Then turned back to Emily and Tilly, to whom she'd been telling the good news. "I'm so excited that George Becker hired Daniel for the new country club. He couldn't have given him a better Christmas gift."

"I'm pretty sure you're his favorite gift this year," Emily teased with a wink. "But this is probably a close second."

"George called last night?" Tilly asked through Sophie's happy chuckle.

Sophie nodded and opened her mouth to tell the story, only to have the cat jump back up, with a louder, more annoyed meow and paw at her. That's when she spotted the small roll of paper tied to her collar.

"What's this?" she asked.

Slipping it out, she unrolled it and chuckled. A message from Daniel? When had he done this? He was supposed to be having Christmas with his parents this morning. They had plans to get together later today. At least, that's what they'd agreed as of last night.

But the note read, *Come over to my house. I can't wait to share Christmas with you any longer.*

Her smile might have lit up the entire town, and she knew it.

"Um . . ." She lifted her head to find Emily and Tilly and Emily's mother all beaming at her. "Is that from Daniel?" Tilly asked.

Sophie nodded.

"Then get going," Emily shooed her out of the door with a flap of a dishtowel. Sophie barely had time to grab her jacket on the way out. Then had to turn right back around and hand Snowball, who'd snuck out with her, to a chuckling Emily.

It had hardly been any time at all, and she was more in love with Daniel than she had been the day she'd made the terrifying choice to follow a new dream, even if she didn't know where it might lead.

As she pulled up to his house, Daniel was standing on the small front porch, sort of breathing hard, which was odd. Had he been at the house and then driven back fast to beat her here? Not that it mattered. He was grinning and bouncing on his toes as though he couldn't wait a second longer, putting her in mind of what he must have looked like as a small boy on Christmas morning. He walked down the shoveled path as she got out of her car, and dropped a quick kiss on her lips.

She went up on tiptoes for more, but he shook his head. "We're going to miss it if we don't hurry."

"Miss what?"

Only he refused to answer as he hustled her inside, got her out of her jacket, handed her a steaming mug of hot chocolate, and snuggled them both down on the couch. Then he grabbed the remote and pointed it at the TV.

She frowned. They were going to watch TV? If he put on sports, she might stage a minor rebellion and dump the hot chocolate on his head.

"Miss what?" she asked again, with way more suspicion.

"This." The screen clicked on and a second later, sound came through the speakers.

Sophie gasped, then laughed in delight at the image of drummers in a parade, dressed up in red coats with brass buttons and white hats with red plumes of feathers atop them, rat-tat-tatting away at their drums as they marched along.

Twelve drummers drumming, to be exact.

"Merry Christmas, love," Daniel whispered as he nuzzled her ear.

"Best Twelve Days of Christmas ever," Sophie whispered back, and felt his smile against her cheek.